Let Love Happen

By Maxine Ferris

Cover Art By Betsy Morphew

Kids At Heart Publishing LLC
PO Box 492
Milton, IN 47357
765-478-5873
www.kidsatheartpublishing.com

First published by Kids At Heart Publishing LLC 3/17/2017
ISBN # 978-1-946171-00-9
Library of Congress Control Number: 2017937086

Printed in the United States of America
Milton, Indiana

This book printed on acid-free paper.

To order more copies of this book go to
www.kidsatheartpublishing.com

*The books at Kids At Heart Publishing feature turn the page technology. No batteries or
charging required.*

Dedication

This book is dedicated to Spartan Professors, who true to the university's Land Grant Mission share useful research-based knowledge worldwide and to Montessori Directors and Directresses, who with caring and skills, unleash the curiosity, creativity and love of learning in thousands of children annually.

ACKNOWLEDGEMENTS

As is often the case, many friends and family members encouraged me to take on this first time project — writing a romantic novel. A number of P.E.O. Chapter BB sisters read parts of the preliminary draft and expressed interest in reading more; their comments motivated me to continue working on the book. Several professional friends — Betsy Aho, Ellen Hoste, Rose Ann Swartz and Patricia Orlowitz — read specific chapters and offered pertinent suggestions to clarify and validate ideas expressed. My husband, Jake Ferris, insisted that the copy be proofed and proofed again even after I was certain that errors had been corrected.

Information concerning Jatropha, Mozambique and the Indian Reservation was gained through extensive on-line research in the public domain and discussions with professionals familiar with these subject areas. Publisher, Shelley Davis, was a most helpful partner in managing the many details involved in the book's publication.

However, very special appreciation is due to my long-time dear friend, Katha Heinze, who once again responded to my call to not only be the book's editor but also serve as its "critic in residence." Her candid comments, suggested nuances and background as a professional communicator, elementary principal and grandmother added to the richness and reality of the text.

Credit should be given for the song used on page 291, "Go Now In Peace" to Don Besig for the music and to Don Besig and Nancy Price for the words.

CHAPTER ONE

Ian Mahoney collapsed his tall lanky frame in the lounge chair that the movers had placed in the four seasons room and gazed out into the darkness that blotted out anything on the adjacent Indian Hills Golf Course. The trip from College Station, Texas had been more arduous than he'd expected -- more potty breaks and stops so the nearly four-year-old twins could stretch their legs and run around. Thank goodness he had filled the portable cooler with enough bottles of water, juice boxes, fruit, cheese and veggies to keep Michael and Mia content. The DVDs and recordings of their favorite books had also been a big help in entertaining them during the long drive.

Fortunately, the movers had arrived previously and positioned the furniture more-or-less as his rough floor plan had directed. Getting the twins "down for the night" had been relatively easy since the little souls -- like their dad -- were exhausted from the long drive. But Ian was not quite ready to call it a day and pondered the wisdom of this move to the community he had enjoyed as a child. Although his relationship with God had become somewhat strained the past two years, he closed his eyes and thanked the Lord for their safe arrival. He also expressed hope that life, in what he remembered as a caring supportive community, would bring peace and resolution to the sad ending of his marriage, when his wife was killed in a car accident.

Life since Laurie's death had been quite a challenge for the young father who, while a brilliant scientist, was ill prepared to handle the multi-tasking that being a single parent required. Eventually, with the help of a series of church friends, home helpers and volunteer babysitters, at least his work life was back on track. Enrolling the twins in a Montessori Preschool had been a Godsend for them, as well.

Life with Laurie, his soul mate, had been almost too good to be true. A talented journalist and excellent home-maker, Laurie had opted to be a stay-at-home mom after the twins were born. Although the family income was not all that great, the young couple was content to live modestly and enjoy the blessing that came from having a pair of beautiful healthy children. Then without warning, one December evening Laurie's life was snuffed out by a drunken driver when she was on her way home from the Christmas pageant rehearsal at church. Ian was still very angry at the young man who had run a red light and crushed Laurie's little Toyota… and life as they knew it.

A Plant, Soil and Microbial Sciences Assistant Professor, he had recently received a sizable grant from the U.S. Department of Energy to pursue plant breeding research. The plant, Jatropha, was thought by some to be the "miracle" crop destined to produce the best plant stock for biodiesel fuel. This plant might prove to be not only a financially-viable export for developing countries around the world, but it might also provide a more sustainable fuel source for America's trucks, buses and trains.

News of this grant made Ian a highly sought-after candidate for other universities interested in renewable fuels. It didn't take long for them to start calling. Excellent offers arrived from both the University of Nebraska and Iowa State University. Department members were cordial;

university facilities were first-rate; and there were pleasant neighborhoods where housing was available. But visits to both Lincoln and Ames didn't feel quite right. Then "out of the blue" came an invitation to interview for a tenure stream position as Associate Professor at Michigan State University. What a surprise!

Ian had spent the first eight years of his life in Michigan when his father, Big Mike Mahoney, had been a professor in the university's Department of Horticulture. The family had live in nearby Okemos, and young Ian had started his school life at the Ojibwa Montessori School.

Ian's subsequent visit to East Lansing and his interviews went well, and although the salary was lower than what he had previously rejected, he knew that the benefit package and school's environment would more than compensate for the difference. He accepted the offer eagerly and began to prepare for the move back to Michigan. This time he would follow his heart rather than his head, which cautioned that making such a move could be risky.

The Department of Plant, Soil and Microbial Sciences, as it is now called, is housed in a relatively new building adjacent to a large reconfigured university garden, unique children's garden and expanded arboretum. When Ian's family had lived in Michigan, the university gardens had been located in the center of campus, an area that was now a lovely green space.

Ian's father had always teased that his preference was to live in Okemos, east of campus, so he never had to drive to and from work with the sun in his eyes. At that time, Okemos was a charming village with many Indian-named subdivisions with well-kept tree-lined yards. Ian's drive through the community in 2015 revealed that the core of the village hadn't changed that much. The village square was much the same, however, there are now numerous new neighborhoods with beautiful but pricey homes, as well as condo and apartment developments.

Finding, serendipitously, that the house where his family had lived was on the market and within his price range was, indeed, a pleasant surprise. "It will be like coming home," Ian thought, "a home where Michael and Mia can thrive and grow into happy well-adjusted youngsters." Moreover, it was closer to the campus than some of the newer neighborhoods.

"And now," Ian thought, "I'm finally home." And so he was…settling into his new (old) home, relaxing in his living room, contemplating the last few crazy months and wondering what the future would hold.

As he sat there he thought about the old neighborhood and what a great place it was to grow up. Although he assumed that his former neighbors had moved, Ian hoped that those living on Ottawa Drive would be just as friendly as those he remembered. He had noticed some basketball hoops and backyard play equipment, so he assumed that there would be playmates for his twins and perhaps even a handy babysitter or two. He was looking forward to getting acquainted and hopefully developing some meaningful friendships.

But enough "wool-gathering," as his mother would say. Time for him to get some shuteye. Tomorrow would be soon enough to begin meeting challenges and getting to work. "Please, God," he prayed, "grant me the serenity to accept the things I cannot change, the courage to change the things I can, and the wisdom to know the difference."

CHAPTER TWO

Peggy Gerber, popular Montessori Directress at the Ojibway Montessori School, pushed a strand of her long taffy colored hair from her face and headed for the second-hand red Chevy Volt that was her pride and joy. Releasing the sun roof to capture the breeze that was offering a bit of relief from the hot humid August day, she set off for her apartment. It was good to be back in Okemos after spending most of the summer with her family on their farm in the Saginaw Valley.

Today had been quite busy -- but fun busy -- as she worked to ready the school's greenhouse for its fall plantings and programs under the leadership of a part time grad student, Zach. Having just completed her first course in a Master Gardener Program, Peggy's repayment for the course was to provide management of the small greenhouse, built several years previously by funds raised by the school's Parent and Guardian Association.

As she drove the short distance to her apartment, she reflected on the chain of events that had brought her to this point in her life, a life she thoroughly enjoyed. Growing up on a farm, Peg was accustomed to working in the garden. As a 4-H member, she had entered home-grown vegetables and clothing she had designed in the county fair. Attending Michigan State University was a given for her and her three brothers. But finances were tight. A small 4-H Scholarship helped, but thanks to a suggestion from her academic adviser, she was able to get a part-time position at the Ojibwa Montessori Pre-School to help with expenses, as well. The position was perfect, since her major was Early Childhood Education.

Peggy loved working with the young children at Ojibwa and knew it enhanced her resume. The only thing missing she felt was that she had been unable to fund a Study Abroad experience -- something that many of her classmates had added to their collegiate resumes. However, thanks to her loyalty and hard work over the four years, the Trustees of the Montessori School had offered to finance her Montessori certification. Their sponsorship had enabled her to study in Bergamo, Italy at the program's training center. Perfect! What a wonderful time that had been -- experiencing a new culture and becoming grounded in the principles that made Montessori such a unique creative experience for young minds.

Now she was about to begin her fifth year as a teacher at the school. Peggy's career path could not have been better. She loved being part of this excellent school, known for it's excellent teaching staff and beautiful facility. It was located on a wooded lot that included some wet-lands and a play area for each classroom. Coming to work each day was a joy for Peggy.

She had found a small church where she served as the co-leader of the youth group. Last year she also became a regular volunteer at the nearby Nokomis Cultural Learning Center where she taught Indian crafts and could learn about the history of her community. She felt at home in Okemos and hoped she would never have to leave!

The only cloud on her horizon was the growing complex relationship with Donn Bahler, a close friend of her older brother J.R.. Donn and J.R. had grown up together and had been team-mates on their high school basketball team. They had remained friends since then even though Donn had gone to the University of Michigan instead of State. Being an only child, Donn had gravitated to the Gerber household and for years had regarded Peggy as the tag along little sister.

In the last couple of years, however, that had changed; and he had been pursuing a more personal relationship with Peggy, who had blossomed into a very attractive, poised, fun-loving, young woman. Donn was smart, determined and highly-motivated.

He was rapidly advancing in the hospitality industry following his graduate work at Cornell University. He had become the manager of a hotel and conference center in Traverse City. He was convinced that he was on his way to even more prestigious assignments and felt Peggy, with her warm, out-going personality and excellent people skills would be a definite asset for him as a wife.

Donn's family was quite wealthy and had high expectations for him. He had been over-indulged as a child, and it was no doubt that up-bringing that led him to believe that he was entitled to preferential treatment. While he was a talented basketball player in high school, he was offended that he was not elected team captain and that he was expected to be a role player not the point guard. J.R., who was easy-going and loved by all, respected Donn's ability and did his best to encourage him to contribute his special skills for the good of the team.

It was true, Donn Bahler had a number of talents on and off the basketball floor and was a hard worker, but his ego and drive to please his father were a bit much for others to tolerate at times. The Gerber family was more laid-back; so he felt quite at home with them and seemed to enjoy the less-demanding pace and general acceptance they all felt, which was quite different from the situation at his home.

Peggy had a close relationship with her three brothers. She looked up to J.R., who was several years her senior. They shared a love of the outdoors and often took camping trips together. J.R. was getting along well in his job as a Farm Management Consultant.

Sam was only a year younger than Peggy, and they were often competitors. He sometimes complained that he was always being compared with her at school since she was much more studious and well-behaved. He, on the other hand, was quite the jokester. In time, he had come into his own, however, and recently had even passed the bar and begun to practice law.

Jake was the baby of the family or the "caboose," according to their dad. He had a kind heart, and as a child he was constantly bringing home wounded birds or befriending stray dogs and cats. His plan was to become the family's veterinarian. All four sibling loved animals – especially horses.

While Peggy had no trouble including Donn in family activities, along with friends of all of the brothers, she had always regarded him as just that – her brother's friend. Now that they were adults, Peggy was happy for Donn and his professional success and at first found his attention rather nice, since she rarely had time to date in college. But as he became more serious about them as a couple, she had to admit her doubts about him. He was too career-driven to get involved in the community, something her family had always valued. And he never went to church; nor did he seem to have a spiritual compass, which was important to her.

But probably the biggest negative was his lack of respect for what he called her "calling." He could not believe she would choose to spend her life teaching "runny- nosed" little kids. Her sense was that life with Donn would mean becoming a stay-at-home wife and "arm candy" to impress those vital to her husband's professional advancement. Peggy's mother had certainly been a great role model as a supportive wife and mother, but she had also had her own career as a popular Home Economics teacher. "Ah,well," Peggy mused, "Decisions about marriage are still way in the future. For now, I'm happy to have things just as they are!"

CHAPTER THREE

After a good night's sleep everybody in the household was up early. Breakfast of cheerios, milk, juice and some great peaches picked up the evening before was over rather quickly, and the twins were sent to get dressed for the day's trip to the grocery store. As Ian was putting the last dishes in the dishwasher, there was a knock at the back door. There stood a cute, pony-tailed teenager carrying a foil wrapped plate.

"Hi," said the visitor. "Welcome to the neighborhood! I'm Libby your next door neighbor. Before Mom went to work we made you some brownies we thought you might like."

"Come right in, Libby. Many thanks for the brownies. I know we'll love them. Can you stay a few minutes?"

"Sure. I'm ready for a little rest. I've been walking the neighbor's dog, a big black Lab named Midnight. I'm pooped."

"How about a drink of milk, water or juice?"

"Water would be fine; thanks."

"It is certainly nice of you to walk the dog."

"Well, I'm not old enough for a regular job, so I am doing a lot of odd jobs this summer to earn some money."

"That's a great idea. Getting ready to shop at the mall for school clothes, I'll bet."

"No, not really. I am trying to make enough to go with our church youth group to an Indian reservation out west next spring. We spent a couple of days at a soup kitchen in Detroit this spring. It was an awesome eye-opener!"

"What a great experience for you and other kids. You mentioned that your mother was at work. Does she work on campus?"

"No, actually she is the pastor of our church and had an early meeting this morning with one of the committees." Her official name is Rev. Rebecca Lane, but most everybody calls her Pastor Becky."

"My name is Ian Mahoney, and I will begin work at the university after Labor Day. My almost four year old twins are Michael and Mia."

"What do I call you? I suppose you are both a Dr. and a Professor."

"Well, Libby, most of my students called me Doc."

"Doc it is then."

"Tell me, Libby, what kind of odd jobs are you doing this summer?"

"You name it, and I am your girl. I can walk pets, mow the lawn, weed, clean, baby sit if it is not too late, run errands, wash cars, help older people who need assistance and just about anything a strong able-bodied girl can do."

"Wow! That's some resume for a person your age! I am impressed. Your folks must be very proud of you."

"I think that sometimes Dad would like to trade me in for a girl who is more quiet and reserved."

"I'm not so sure about that," chuckled Ian, "so tell me about your Dad."

"Oh, Pop is the American History teacher at the high school. He is writing a book about Chief Okemos. He's been gone the past couple of weeks helping my grandparents down-size and move into a retirement center in Ohio. He'll be back this week-end. When he's at home in the summer, he helps the widows in the neighborhood as their on-call-handy-man."

"Well, I'll really look forward to getting to know him, then. I'm not very handy around the house, so it'll be great to have an adviser next door."

"I have an older brother, too. His name is Bob, and he's spending the summer up in the UP as a lifeguard and counselor at a Boy Scout Camp. He'll be a junior at MSU in the fall. He wants to work internationally when he finishes his degree."

"We look forward to getting to know your whole family, Libby."

"I've told you about us, now how about you?   Do you have a wife?"

"Not any more, I'm afraid. Laurie, the twins' mother, was killed in an automobile accident nearly two years ago. She was a journalist. We lived in Texas. My parents are retired and live in South Carolina. I have no brothers and sisters."

"Gosh, I'm so sorry! Please forgive me!   There I go again. Mom is always reminding me to think before I barge in asking questions."

"That's all right. You had no way of knowing and were bound to be curious after all my questions about your family."

"Mom said that she had heard that you once lived in this very house overlooking the golf course."

"That's right. We lived here until I was about eight. Then, when my Dad became a Department Head, we moved to the state of Washington where I went to high school and began college. My Mother will be pleased that a former owner turned most of the patio into the four season room. She always complained about having such a long narrow living room. The addition makes it much nicer. But that is about the only change that's been made, I think."

"This is a nice neighborhood, Doc. People are very friendly, and there's lots of kids. So how old did you say the twins are?"

"Nearly four, but sometimes they seem quite a bit older – maybe because they've had to grow up without a mother in the house."

"Will you have a nanny?"

"Not exactly. They'll be attending the Ojibwa Montessori School after Labor Day. But I need to hire a part-time housekeeper and locate some reliable babysitters to call when I need them."

"You can check my references. I like to babysit and have certificates from both the Red Cross and MSU courses on babysitting."

"That's good to know. Thank you, Libby. I imagine you and the twins will get to know each other rather quickly."

"Do the twins look alike? My brother and I don't."

"Mike is tall and has red hair. He looks a lot like me. Mia, on the other hand, is quite petite and takes after her mother with dark hair and eyes. Although she is small she sometimes seems like the older of the two and once in a while even acts like a little mother. She's a very caring little girl and quite outgoing. Mike is the quieter twin."

"I can't wait to meet them. They sound like a lot of fun. You said they'll be attending the Montessori School?"

"Yes, the Montessori School on Mt. Hope where I went as a child."

"If they're attending the Montessori School, they must be pretty sharp. I sometimes sit for a couple of kids down the street who went there. Brother, do they ask a lot of questions!"

"Montessori does tend to make kids curious, and since children learn at such different rates you never know what to expect. Mike asks a lot of "why" questions. Mia is the book-worm and can pretend to read a book after hearing it read only a few times. They both like to color and build things."

"Mom knows lots of people and a lot about the community, too. She can probably help, if you have any questions."

"You're a mind-reader, Libby. I'm sure I'll count on her help."

"Thanks for the water and conversation Doc, I had better get going. I promised to pick off the dead petunias for Mrs. Smith while they are gone, and time is a wasting."

"Libby, I wonder if you and your mother might be free to come over for some watermelon after dinner tonight. There are a number of questions I'd like to ask her. The sooner they're answered, the easier my life will be."

"I think that would work. When she checks in with me this noon, I'll find out for sure and let you know if we can't come."

Just then the twins came bounding in the door. When they saw a visitor, they stopped short, bumping into each other.

"Hi, you must be Michael and Mia," laughed Libby. "I'm Libby from next door."

Michael smiled shyly, but Mia ran up with a big grin and shouted a cheerful, "Hi, Libby, I'm Mia … and this is Michael, my brother!"

Libby laughed again and said, "I am so happy to finally meet you, Mia and Michael. Welcome to our neighborhood. I know we are going to be great friends!"

"What a warm welcome," thought Ian as he and the twins got in the car and prepared for their shopping trip. "Having that family next door certainly seems like a blessing for us all."

CHAPTER FOUR

As the threesome headed out of the driveway, Ian told the children, "The grocery store where we always shopped is quite near here. My Dad never minded shopping there, since unlike some stores, they never changed where things were shelved; so he could take Mom's list and quickly go from aisle to aisle to get everything on the list. Watch for a big sign with a lady pushing a shopping cart. That will be Schmidt's Store."

But as they turned the corner, no such sign appeared. "Oops! My mistake. The grocery store is no longer here. See, the sign now reads 'Playmakers' That's a shoe store."

"Where else can we get food, Daddy?" asked Michael. "I hope we can find some corn on the cob. I'm hungry for roasting ears!"

"Me too," added Mia.

"We'll go to Meijer. It is just down the road across from the mall. They have food, but just about anything else you could want, too."

"It looks like a busy place. See all the cars in the parking lot!" Mia noticed.

"Shopping here will take longer than I thought, so you'll just have to be patient as we get all the things we need," Dad said.

"We'll be good helpers, Daddy," promised Michael.

"Let's get the cleaning supplies and laundry soap before we get the food."

After practically filling the cart with non-food items, they moved to the grocery aisles.

"They have lots of different healthy stuff. How many ears of corn do we want?" asked Michael.

"Oh, a half dozen, I guess."

"That would be six -- one, two, three, four, five, six," counted Michael as he put them in the cart.

"Here are those little tomatoes we like," said Mia. "But look, they have some that are yellow too. Let's get both kinds."

"Michigan has lots of different vegetables, so we won't go hungry," Dad laughed.

"This is a funny looking thing. See the big leaves. What's it called? Can you eat it raw?" Mia said pointing to the display of leafy vegetables.

"That's a bunch of kohlrabi, Mia. I used to grow them in my garden in the back of the house," Dad recalled. "They're sort of like a sweet radish, and yes, you can eat them either raw or cooked."

After adding carrots, celery, lettuce and several other vegetables to the cart, the three moved on to the fruit section.

"Daddy, why does it say 'R-E-D' by those peaches? Peaches aren't red."

"You are a good little reader, Mia. It means that this kind of peach is called 'Red Haven.' They were actually developed in Papa Mike's department at Michigan State."

"Don't forget the watermelon for tonight," Michael reminded them.

"Right, and here are some Howell melons," Dad pointed out. "They're another fruit that's grown around here. We probably need to get some apples and bananas, too."

Then it was on to the dairy department to pick up some cheese, milk, yogurt and ice cream as well as some turkey hot dogs, sliced ham, shrimp and chicken to grill. Bread they picked up on the way to the checkout counter.

"Daddy, look at those cool green shirts!" the twins called out in unison.

"Those are Michigan State t-shirts. See the big green 'S' and Sparty, the school's mascot? I had some t-shirts just like them when I was your age."

"Can we get one? Please! Please! Please!" cried the twins.

Luck was with them. One was available for each of them in the right size – including one for Dad -- so three more items were added to the brimming cart as they made their way to the checkout.

"Thanks for being such good helpers, you guys. You two are the greatest! I think we have time for a quick trip around town. Would you like to do that? I'll show you where I went to school and some fun places we can visit when we have a little time."

"Okay, Daddy, yes! We'd love to do that!" agreed the twins.

It was a short distance to the township hall and the adjacent historical village as well as the small cultural Indian museum -- places they would want to visit when time permitted. Then it was a quick drive to see Central School, where Ian had attended elementary school before leaving for the west coast.

"It looks just the same," he commented.

"I think it looks old. Did Papa go to school there too?" asked Mia.

"No, he and Mimi grew up in another state. Tomorrow we'll see your school, which is much newer and has lots of trees around it," their father told them.

Then it was home to unload their purchases, have lunch and continue putting the house in order.

"No naps, Daddy, please?" begged the twins. But shortly after they put away their books and toys, each found a bed too tempting to resist and stretched out for a short nap. Ian smiled when he looked in on them, grateful for their amazing cooperation and flexible natures.

As he continued to unpack and put things away, Ian reflected on the fact that so much had happened in the past two and a half years. Nothing was more vivid than the memory of his mother's surprise visit in College Station. One afternoon, six months after Laurie's death, without notice, red-haired Katie Mahoney barged into his office on campus. While she had never hesitated to state her opinion, she seldom offered advice. This time she was very direct and commanding.

"Mark Ian Mahoney, just look at yourself. How long has it been since you had a haircut?" she asked pointedly. "Just look at you! You look as if you've slept in your clothes!"

"Mother, I've been way too busy and tired to worry about my appearance," sighed Ian.

"That may be, but things have to change!" she announced.

"I know, but losing Laurie hurts so much!" he said quietly. "I still can't imagine life without her! And I know the kids miss her terribly. I just don't know how to fill that void."

"We all feel her loss, son," Kate said soothingly, patting Ian on the shoulder. "Grieving is natural, and we all must go through the process. But Laurie's mom and I -- and the men too -- have decided that we can't allow things to continue as they are."

"You, Dad, Hal and Helen have decided what?" Ian asked surprised and a little put off.

"After Helen's visit last week, she called us and was quite disturbed with things at the house and with the children." Kate said.

"I know the house isn't that neat, Mom," Ian admitted, "but

the kids are healthy. You know our church friends have been helping me take care of them. Others have brought in meals. Having our usual babysitters and a couple of new ones has helped me be able to work both at home and here on campus. We're managing."

"Son, we know you're trying," she persisted, "but this patchwork of help and dependence on friends can't go on indefinitely."

"I know that!" Ian responded indignantly.

"Yes, but it has already gone on too long. Hal, Helen, Dad and I decided that all of us needed to come to Texas and talk with you face to face. We thought that together we could help you come up with a plan to improve things. You know that the four of us have never interfered or tried to tell you and Laurie how to run your lives, but this is different. You need our input now."

Those were hard words for Ian to hear. He knew that things weren't great, but he was doing his best. It's just that he was exhausted and constantly worried about the kids. When he did have a moment to himself...Ian just sat around thinking about how wonderful things had been before the accident. He knew things had to change...but it was all so overwhelming, he just hadn't known where to start. As difficult as it was to admit... he knew that he did need their help.

Sitting back in his chair, and emitting a big sigh, Ian said, "Okay, Mom, I'm listening. What do you guys think I should do?"

"Well, since I got here two days ago, we've been exploring ways to get you over the hump. We know your cash flow has to be tight right now, with funeral expenses and added child care costs. We're all willing to help in that department too."

"I'm all ears." Ian's interest was peaked.

"Helen's been looking into part-time, household help that is affordable and reliable. My assignment has been to look into a daycare or preschool for Michael and Mia."

"Wow" Ian said, surprised and truly touched. "You guys have been BUSY...I hardly know what to say!"

Kate went on, encouraged that her son was not offended. "Helen found a highly-recommended home care agency that helps families with a variety of services – including cleaning, cooking and child care. I have their contact number so if you're interested, you'll need to call and discuss exactly what services you want and the hours you need. They'll try to have the same people be your helpers, but that may not always be possible. That's the only draw-back we can see in hiring them. You'll have to decide if it'll work for you. Helen did talk with a number of their clients and checked all their references, so we know that they're reliable."

"That sounds great, actually," Ian said. "I know I need to hire someone to help me, but it all just seemed so overwhelming. I really do appreciate the suggestion, and I'll look into it right away. What did you find out about daycare or preschool for the twins?"

"Well, there's a small, private Montessori preschool only a few blocks from your office," she said excitedly. "They also have daycare available at the same location."

"Is it like the Ojibwa Montessori School I went to?" he asked.

"Yes, it's a certified Montessori program," Kate went on. She was a huge advocate of the Montessori concept and knew a lot about it. "It's not like those that I've sometimes called 'Montessori-light' programs. You know the ones that use the Montessori name without having a credentialed staff."

"Mom," Ian laughed. "You always were a 'Montessori snob!' Are the twins really old enough for a Montessori program?"

Having attended Montessori himself, Ian was actually an advocate, too. He just hadn't thought about it for his own kids yet."

"Actually, this particular school has a toddler program that would be perfect for the kids. Here's the address and phone number. I checked it out earlier today and liked what I saw. They even have room for our two, since they have ongoing enrollment. Why not stop by and see what you think. But do get your hair cut first and put on some halfway presentable clothes," she admonished.

Ian rolled his eyes, but laughed good-naturedly, "Well, you guys certainly HAVE been busy…and your suggestions would surely make things better than what they are now. But both home help and the Montessori program will be pretty expensive…and frankly, I can't really afford it right now."

"We know that finances are tight, so the four of us have agreed that you need our help. So, we've started a small fund to help you get things under control."

"But Mom…although I'm truly touched and overwhelmed, I really couldn't accept…." he began.

"No buts!" she interrupted. "The four of us insist! Think of it this way. All four of us have been worrying ourselves sick about you and the kids. We want to know that the three of you are healthy, happy and moving on with your lives. So, really, this is an investment in our own peace of mind, as well as your well-being!"

"By the way, I went shopping this morning and put some basics in your pantry and refrigerator," she added. I also bought the twins a few new outfits that actually fit!"

"Mom…you're really too much! Mia, Michael and I appreciate you for keeping us from looking like we dress from the rag bag….and for the food donation, too." Ian said with heartfelt thanks. "And Mom, I get it. You're right about everything else, too. It is time for the three of us to start planning for not only today, but for tomorrow and the day after that, as well. How can I ever thank you, Dad and the Calhouns?"

"Ian, you and the twins mean the world to the Calhouns and to us." She said as she looked quickly away to hide the tears that were threatening to over-spill her eyes. "Helping you out like this is our gift of love to both you and Laurie."

That visit was almost two years ago. Smiling at the memory and thinking of how he had come to realize the parents' not-so-gentle push was just what he had needed at the time. He thought about how far he had come since those early days. Ian was overcome with love and appreciation for the difference the Calhouns and his parents had made in his life. After a quick prayer of thanks, a feeling of well-being came over him, and he drifted into a relaxing nap of his own on the couch.

CHAPTER FIVE

Before dinner, Ian focused on arranging furniture, unpacking the kitchen items and finding places for their clothing. There was so much to do for one person! When they had moved into their townhouse after the wedding, it was Laurie who took the lead in organizing and combining their households. Whatever she decided was fine with him. Now he not only had to make the decisions; but worse still, he had to remember where he put things since his memory about such matters was sketchy, at best.

He wondered what the pastor would be like. The only female minister he knew was a short, round-faced, white-haired lady who resembled what his children thought was Mrs. Santa Claus. She was much-loved because of her devotion to the older congregants, and she was a faithful visitor to hospitals and nursing homes. She had been most helpful to him and the family at the time of Laurie's death. Her prayers with them had been most appreciated, but she had not been able to help him resolve his anger toward a God who could allow such a tragedy to occur.

Getting to know the pastor's husband, the history teacher, was something he looked forward to doing, as well. He had always enjoyed getting to know men who had different interests...and he was delighted to have a handyman next door who could help him when he got stuck with home maintenance repairs and projects. His talents were practically non-existent when it came to fixing things around the house.

Before he knew it, the time had come to prepare dinner and get ready for the arrival of the visitors. He hoped it would be a fun evening and that he'd get some answers to his most pressing questions.

"That corn-on-the-cob was great, Daddy!" said Michael.

"Yeah," echoed Mia, "and so was the shrimp!"

"You are good little eaters," their Dad responded. "Libby and her mother should be here any minute."

He had barely gotten the words out of his mouth when there was knock at the door, and Libby sang out, "Hello! We're here!"

"Please answer the door, Michael, and bring our guests into the kitchen," Ian requested.

"Welcome to the neighborhood! I'm Rebecca Lane, Becky, to friends and neighbors," Becky said cheerfully as she swept into the kitchen.

"Thanks, I'm so glad to meet you, Becky. I wasn't quite sure how to address a female pastor," Ian admitted. "Just call me Ian."

"Nor was I sure what to call you." Becky responded. "Some at the university prefer to be called Doctor or Professor."

"Not me. Anytime I hear one of those terms used in reference to me I look around thinking they are talking to my Dad. I told Libby it was okay for her to just call me Doc, which is what my students used to call me at A & M."

As slices of juicy red watermelon were passed around and consumed, the group exchanged pleasantries about their day's activities. Mia took the opportunity to tell the visitors that she was the older twin, to which Michael responded, "Ten minutes doesn't count!"

After they were finished eating, Libby asked if she might

take the twins for a walk around the neighborhood, perhaps to meet some of the other children who lived on the block.

"Great idea, Lib," said her mom. "That will give Ian and me an opportunity to discuss some of his questions about the area."

"Let's move to the living room, where it's more comfortable," suggested Mahoney as the children hustled out the door.

"Before we begin on the questions," Becky said with a warm, earnest look. "Let me tell you how very sorry I am that you lost your wife in such a tragic way."

Ian took a moment before responding, "Thank you, Becky. We had a great life together. I have to admit, I've been quite lost without her. I was always sort of a loner, a bookworm or as some say, 'a real nerd,' but Laurie was just the opposite -- an outgoing people person, who brought me out of my shell. She was a wonderful wife, mother and friend. We met at the University when she interviewed me as a new faculty member. She worked for University Relations there.

We had special chemistry right from the start…and married about a year later. After the twins arrived, Laurie decided to stay at home with them. She became very involved at our church and volunteered in the children's ward at the hospital, also. I miss her more than I can say." Ian's eyes misted over as he shared such deeply held personal feelings. He was surprised that he could talk about Laurie with this near-stranger. He was rarely able to open up to others about his painful memories, but somehow Becky made him feel… safe.

"Grieving is never easy…regardless of the circumstances, and none of us handles it in quite the same way," offered his neighbor. "It has been said that no real peace can come until one forgives the person or persons who caused our pain."

"I'm afraid I'm not anywhere near that place yet. I'm still so angry at the drunken driver who cut Laurie's beautiful life so short…and, frankly, even at God for allowing it to happen! I guess I hope that someday I will be able to reach a place of forgiveness…but I'm just not ready."

"Well, at least you have forgiveness as a goal," Becky offered. "That's a good start. I know that sometimes it's hard to understand God's ways. I'm often asked why a loving God lets bad things happen to good people. But maybe it's because he has a plan. Perhaps because in the end…difficult—even impossible burdens--make us stronger and open new paths to happiness that only he can see right now."

"I'll bet you are a great pastor, Becky," murmured Ian. "Perhaps one of these days we can discuss the whole grieving/healing process. It's hard for me to talk to people about Laurie and my mixed-up feelings about God…but somehow…here I am talking to you!"

"That's a promise, Neighbor…whenever you are ready," she said and she patted him on the knee. "Now, what are your questions about our little village?"

"At the moment I have only two," he began. "First, how do I find a good pediatrician for the twins? They are pretty healthy, but with children their age -- about 3 1/2 -- accidents and emergencies can happen unexpectedly. I don't want to be caught unprepared…and they'll be due for their annual checkups soon."

"That's a very good question, Ian." After thinking for a moment, Becky said, "For starters, you should know that the Family Practice Clinic on campus has some excellent physicians, but you might prefer something closer, say…in the downtown of the village. We use the campus doctors, but the wait time can be pretty long sometimes."

"Yes, I think something in town would be my preference

right now. I don't want to have to rely on a walk-in clinic except for emergencies."

"Actually, there is a small two-person clinic near the four corners that has an excellent reputation," Becky suggested. "One of the doctors is a bright, personable young Chinese woman who has a great rapport with children. Her partner, a semi-retired grandfather, is a member of my church. He is a very caring fellow and a highly-respected physician. He and his wife moved here to be near their son and his family. They also volunteer one day a week at a free clinic in downtown Lansing. That gives you an idea of what kind of person he is."

Ian brightened, "That sounds like just what I've been hoping to find. If you can give me the details, I'll contact them first thing next week."

"Great!" Becky said. "I'll send the info over with Libby in the morning."

"Many thanks. Now for the second, harder question. How do I go about finding reliable, part-time help?" He paused, then continued, "In Texas, I ended up using people from a home help agency. While they were responsible and personable for the most part, it wasn't always the same woman who showed up. That was hard on the kids, who were already missing the consistency and reliability of their mom."

Becky nodded, "That must have been difficult for the children to understand. Please help me understand what exactly you want this person to do. Are you looking for a cook, cleaning person, nanny, taxi driver or maybe someone to do the laundry?"

"Well, probably a bit of all of them." Ian admitted. "The twins will be in Montessori School for much of the day, and since I am not teaching, I have a flexible schedule. I plan to drop them off at school each morning, but having a safe driver pick them up at the end of the day and care for them until I get home is a must. And it certainly would be nice to have a home-cooked meal ready to pop in the oven or microwave, so I can spend time with the kids after work."

"How about shopping, cleaning and doing the laundry?" Becky asked.

"I imagine that most cooks would prefer to do their own shopping," he said. "I plan to do most of the cleaning and yard work, but I could sure use help with the laundry. I've been thinking that four or five hours, five days a week should do it -- at least for now. Of course more time will be needed if the kids are sick or have time off from school."

"I think I get the picture," Becky offered. "Probably if she came around noon or one and stayed until you got home – maybe 5:00 or 6:00? Would that be about right?"

"Exactly!" Ian nodded.

"Do you have any age or other restrictions?"

"No, not really," he said. "Perhaps a middle-aged woman with the energy to play with the twins and keep them on the right track -- a sort-of surrogate grandmother. My parents have retired to a Dell Webb Retirement Community outside of Hilton Head; and Laurie's parents still live on their small ranch in Texas. Having positive experiences with an older person here in Michigan would be great."

"I think I've got it and may know just such a person," Becky said brightly. "Let me think about it, talk it over with God this evening and give the gal I'm thinking of a call in the morning. I'm sure we can find just the person your family needs."

"I really appreciate your help, Becky!" Ian turned as they both heard laughter from outside the front door. "Look who's back! How was the walk?" Ian asked jumping to his feet.

"Oh, Daddy, we met some kids who are just our age!" exclaimed Mia."

"…and we don't have to cross any streets to get to their houses!" added Michael.

"That's a relief," Ian sighed loudly. "Thank you so much, Libby. I really owe you."

"No, it was my pleasure," Libby laughed. "You have great kids, Doc! It was fun taking them around the neighborhood. Did Mom remind you about the Labor Day picnic?"

"No, she didn't," Ian replied, "but I seem to remember getting a flyer in the mailbox about some such event."

"Every year we close off the street," Becky explained. "We pull out some tables and grills and have an end-of-summer neighborhood celebration. It will be a great way for you to meet your neighbors."

"What a fantastic idea," Ian said. "What do I need to bring?"

"People bring their own meat to grill, some paper plates, a chair or two and a dish to pass," Becky said.

"Daddy, that's so funny," piped up Mia. "Why would we want to bring a dish to pass? Is it to take up a collection like at church?"

"No, honey," chuckled her dad. "It means that each family will bring a dish of something to share with others. We can bring a big salad."

"That would be fine," said Becky.

"Dad always tells a story about Chief Okemos," Libby added, "and Bob will bring his guitar and lead us in some camp songs, AND we'll end the picnic by making s'mores before the grills die out."

"What are s'mores?'" asked Michael. "Is it something to eat?"

"Oh my, yes," was Libby's reply, "but let's keep them a surprise until Monday night."

The visitors departed, ending the evening with hand-shakes for the adults and hugs for the kids.

"I can't wait to tell my parents about our neighbors," thought Ian. "I wonder if there are any families still in Indian Hills who lived here when I was a child. It'll be fun having Mom and Dad visit and reconnect, if there are still folks around that they knew back then. Becky is certain to be a great resource for us all!"

Becky and Libby were equally pleased with the visit.

"Isn't he nice, Mom?" bubbled Libby. "I hope you can get who I think is on your mind to become his housekeeper. Those twins are a lot of fun -- curious too. You should have seen them shake hands with people we met. They are very polite for such little guys."

"I, too, look forward to getting to know them better," her mom replied. "I've heard a lot of nice things about his parents from several people who knew them when they lived here. I suspect the professor is a very conscientious daddy; otherwise those motherless tots would be less mature and not so cheerful. I think your dad will enjoy getting acquainted, too. I know that Ian has a load on his shoulders – and caring for his children is foremost in his mind. But being the leader of a big international research project is demanding, too. Blessings on him. I know we'll do all we can to support the three of them!"

"Righto, Mom," chirped Libby. "Bob and I will do our part, you can count on that!"

CHAPTER SIX

The twins bounced out of bed when their father called them, eager to have breakfast and go visit their new school.

"I want to wear my new Spartan shirt," said Mia.

"Me, too!" added her twin.

"That'll be fine," their dad laughed, "now hurry and finish your cereal and juice. We don't want to be late."

The drive to the Ojibwa Montessori School was brief. Only a few cars were in the parking lot on this August morning, but the friendly School Administrator, Grace Foster, was at the reception desk waiting to greet them.

"Hello," she said. "You must be the Mahoney family. I've been eager to meet you."

"Yes, I'm Ian Mahoney and these are my kids, Michael and Mia," Ian said. "I've been excited to meet you, too, and to see the school. You know, I went here as a child. The school seems so much bigger than when I was in preschool here."

Grace laughed, "Well, it probably looks bigger….because YOU'RE a lot bigger! But, actually, we've completed several expansions over the years; and now we even have a full-sized gym and a greenhouse. I'll bet you'd like to start by taking a tour."

"Absolutely! Everything looks ship shape and ready for classes to start." Ian remarked as he turned to the kids, "Are you ready to see your new school, Guys?"

"Yes!!!" the kids replied in unison.

"We've given everything a fresh coat of paint, and most of the staff was here this past week getting their classrooms ready for the kids. This is always such an exciting time for all of us, and we're ready for you and all our students to arrive on Tuesday," said Grace.

"I understand that you have a diverse and experienced staff," Ian noted.

"That's true," Grace replied. "The lead directresses are all fully certified and have been with us for several years. The aides are sometimes MSU students majoring in early childhood education or retired teachers, and often one or two of the directresses have international roots."

"I seem to recall having one or two teachers who wore long native attire from their home country when I was a student here," Ian said.

Grace thought for a minute, "Actually, I believe in the early years, we had several staff members from Sri Lanka. Outfitting them for our winter weather took some doing, I understand."

"My parents often said they were glad there was an international dimension to the program," Ian recalled as they moved into a classroom.

"Yes, that's an important part of who we are," Grace replied.

"Wow! Look at all this fun stuff!!" exclaimed Mia.

"Can we try it out, Dad?" asked Michael.

"Hey, slow down there, Partner," Ian suggested. "You'll get to try everything next week, let's just take a look today."

Grace chuckled, "It's okay, Michael. I don't blame you for wanting to get started. Why don't you and Mia try out those chairs and check out the hamster cage over there, while your dad and I finish chatting." She indicated the table by the window, and the kids rushed over to take a look.

"As you can see, most of the toddler and primary classrooms are about the same size and have age-appropriate furniture. Each has access to its own outdoor play area, and each has its own bathroom. Every classroom also has a full set of Montessori equipment -- even a set of bells. And, as you can also see, some have homes for live animals such as a hamster or a bird cage. We do serve lunch, also."

"I'm glad the twins can be part of your extended-day program, Grace. From my totally-unbiased perspective," he laughed, "they are ready for it and will gain a lot from being part of the smaller afternoon group."

She nodded. "We added before and after school day care a couple of years ago. It's important since in many of our families both parents work outside the home. It's just one way we have evolved to meet the changing needs of our families."

"Come on, kids…let's go see the gym!" coaxed Grace.

"Don't forget to push your chairs in," Ian reminded them. "We're off to see the rest of the school!" They headed down the corridor and came to the double doors open to a spacious well-lit gymnasium.

"Hey, you guys, come see the nice big gym!" Ian urged. "I imagine it gets plenty of use during the winter and when it is too cold for outside play."

"Yes, that's true," Grace said as Mia and Michael raced across the shiny floor. "We also provide structured health/fitness/recreation classes and use the space for various parent gatherings and special events. We have such things as movie nights, chili and pancake suppers, special classes and our popular international night buffet. Maybe if we added a middle school or had more children in the elementary program, it would be used to field a basketball team -- which some parents would love. We're always looking for ways to enhance our program."

"The facility is certainly impressive," Ian admitted. "That's probably part of the reason the school has such an excellent reputation. When I started in the program, we met in a church basement and the shelves had to be closed and stored each weekend. You've come a long way since then!"

"Yes, both the facility and the quality of the staff are well respected, but we've had a long history of trying to get it right....since 1968, you know. With parent support, we continue to improve. We recently completed a strategic plan for the next five to ten years – so we're looking to the future, as well."

"Well, I'm a believer." Ian said. "The twins actually attended Montessori toddler classes in Texas and loved it, so I'm a big advocate of the program."

"Well, you will fit in well with our other parents...most of whom are totally committed to the Montessori approach, in general, and Ojibwa, in particular." Turning to the twins, Grace said, "How about we move to the library and take a little break?"

Heading around the corner, Mike and Mia chattered like magpies. They were so excited about their new school. They just couldn't wait until Tuesday.

"Mia, Mike, I've laid out some books you might like to look at," Grace offered as they entered the surprisingly well-stocked library, "or, if you'd rather, feel free to do some drawing at one of the easels. There are markers in the trays. Your dad and I will sit over here and fill out some paperwork."

The twins rushed over and immediately busied themselves. Mia chose to look at the books, and Mike began drawing a picture of horses.

"I think you already faxed me most of the required

information about the twins, their allergies and special needs. Have you found a doctor yet?" she asked. "And how about contacts, if we need to reach someone in your absence?"

"I'll be lining up a doctor by Tuesday," Ian said, "and with the assistance of my neighbor, Pastor Rebecca Lane, will hopefully have a part-time housekeeper/nanny by early next week, too."

"That's wonderful," she said as she handed him a folder. "Here's a packet of information that includes the school calendar, information about our Parent Guardian Organization and general school policies and procedures. We also have a website you will want to check out for current school and classroom information."

"These materials will certainly be helpful." Ian said. "This is a much larger school than the one the kids attended in Texas, so I'm sure there's a lot to learn."

"There's one more thing I need to ask you before we finish our tour. What's your placement preference?" Grace asked. "Would you like to have Mike and Mia placed in the same classroom or separated? Usually, we try to separate siblings so that one doesn't dominate or impede the other's learning progress. But your two seem to be quite self-sufficient and will likely make different friends and be drawn to different learning activities regardless of their placement."

"That's a fair assessment." Ian said. "At times, Mia acts as if she's the older sister, but Michael is his own person and has interests that are very different from Mia's. I think I'll just leave the decision of their placement up to you."

"Good," she said as she turned to the kids.

"Are you ready to continue the tour?" Grace called. Mia put her books back in the bin, and Michael placed his markers in the tray and brought his picture over to the adults. "Wow!" Grace exclaimed, "You are quite the artist!" Michael smiled proudly. Then the kids scampered down the hall anxious to see what was next.

"Now, here's our greenhouse." Grace said as she opened the door to the steamy plant-filled room. As they entered, they noticed a young woman bent over a tray of mums.

Grace greeted her warmly, "Why, hello, Peggy. I didn't know you were here this morning."

A tall, attractive, rather grubby young woman in faded cutoff shorts and a t-shirt rose from beneath one of counters holding a tray of mums. Wiping her hands on her shirt she gave a cheerful, "Hi! I'm Peggy Gerber, one of the directresses. Forgive my appearance, but I didn't expect to see anyone today. I just wanted to water these plants and make sure they would be OK until Tuesday. And who is this fine young man and lovely young lady?"

"Hi," said Mia, "you have dirt on your face."

"Now, Mia, that wasn't a kind thing to say," Ian responded quickly. As he turned toward the young teacher, he couldn't help but notice her long tanned legs and mop of blond hair tied haphazardly on top of her head. "Please, uh, please forgive my daughter," he stammered, taken aback. "I'm...I'm Ian Mahoney, the parent of these two hooligans. You've heard from Mia already...and this is my son, Michael. I'm...I'm glad to meet you...dirt and all!" Ian turned a bright shade of pink and wondered why in the world he had said THAT!

Peggy laughed gaily, "I LIKE dirt, Mia. Don't tell me YOU don't like to play in the dirt once and awhile, yourself! And what about you, Michael, do YOU like a little dirt on your face once in awhile?"

The kids relaxed and began chuckling themselves, "Yeah," Michael said, "love it!"

"I make a mean mud pie," Mia added.

"Well, then, it's settled," Peggy stated, shoving a loose lock of curly blond hair off her forehead. "We are mud buddies from now on!"

Grace chuckled as well. "As you can see, our staff relates well to kids! Peggy is an important part of our staff. She began as an aide while attending MSU and now is a directress. She's also an able gardener and supervises work in the greenhouse along with her regular classroom duties. Would you mind stopping by the office before you leave, Peg?"

"Of course, Grace." Peggy turned to the kids and squatted down to their eye level. "It was a pleasure to meet you both. I look forward to having you as part of our school family, Mia and Michael. I'm always happy to get some new mud buddies!" Standing she faced Ian. "It was very nice to meet you, Mr. Mahoney," she said as she offered her muddy hand – then quickly withdrew it with an infectious giggle. "I guess we'll save the handshake for later."

Smiling broadly, Ian responded, "It was great to meet you, too, Miss Peggy…and I'll take a raincheck on that handshake!" Embarrassed, again, Ian wondered how he could say something so stupid. What was the matter with him? He quickly turned to his children. "Now, kids, it's time for us to go and leave Miss Grace and Miss Peggy to their work. Thanks for the warm welcome and the fabulous tour. We'll look forward to seeing you both on Tuesday!"

"See 'ya Tuesday," Michael called as he headed for the door.

"Bye-bye, Miss Grace and Mud Buddy!" quipped Mia.

"MIA!" Ian said, reddening once again.

"It's okay," Peggy laughed, "I started it. Yes, kids, I'll see you Tuesday!" She waved cheerfully as the family left the greenhouse.

A few minutes later Peggy joined her boss in the latter's office. "Nice little family," she said. "Where was the mother?"

"I'm afraid there is no mother." Grace said. "According to their school in Texas, the children's mother was killed in a car accident about two years ago. So, it's been a difficult time for Dr. Mahoney...and those two little ones."

"Oh, how tragic! I'm sure it's been terribly hard for them all. My heart goes out to those little munchkins. Dr. Mahoney's a new professor at the University, right?" asked Peggy.

"That's right." Grace confirmed. "According to a friend of mine who works in his department, he's a highly regarded researcher working on biofuels. As I understand it, he had a number of offers at other universities, but chose MSU -- perhaps because he remembered a happy childhood here when his father was on the staff. He even attended this school for several years as a preschooler!"

"By the way, Peggy," Grace changed the subject, "did you have a good time at home this summer?"

"Yes, thanks for asking," she smiled. "It's always fun to be back on the farm. I was able to help Mom can a lot of tomatoes, put up some dilly beans and even make a few new clothes for school. Then my older brother J.R. and I spent part of a week camping in the Upper Peninsula. We're so much alike, it's always a fun time for both of us."

"Hey, a belated 'Happy Birthday' to you!" Grace said, giving Peggy a warm hug. "Did you do anything special to celebrate?"

"Yes, as a matter of fact I did," she answered. "J.R.'s school friend, Donn Bahler, invited us to be his guests for the last summer weekend at a posh hotel he manages in Traverse City."

"That must have been nice after roughing it in a tent," Grace muttered.

"It certainly was a change." Peggy chuckled. "On Friday night we attended a lovely concert at the Interlochen Music

Camp. Then on Saturday while the guys golfed, I was treated to an afternoon at the hotel's spa. I got the works -- massage, manicure, pedicure, facial and even a fancy up-do for my hair."

"That was some birthday present!"

"But that wasn't all," Peggy intimated. "You won't believe this, but Donn had a gorgeous royal blue cocktail dress and silver slippers waiting in the room for me to wear to the end-of-summer gala on Saturday night."

"Wow!" Grace responded with amazement. "How did he know your size…or what you might like? I can't imagine my hubby buying something like that for me…and we've been married 24 years! I'm sure that you looked lovely, though… you always do…even in cutoffs and dirt!"

Peggy laughed heartily, "I guess Donn thought so. I heard him say, 'The kid sister duckling has turned into a grown up swan.' Then he said, 'She might be a real fox, if she'd just do something with her wild hair and choose clothes that she didn't make herself.'"

"Hmmm," Grace mused, "Me thinks that the kid sister has become more of a 'love interest' than just 'the duckling next door.'"

"Yeah, maybe," Peggy frowned, "but I'm not sure that I welcome the change of status. But…I think I've probably bored you enough with my non-love life, Grace. I'd better get back to the greenhouse and leave you to your work."

"Hey, just a minute, Peggy." Grace touched Peggy's arm as she started to leave. "How would you feel about having the Mahoney twins in your class, since a couple of your students from last year have moved? We usually separate siblings, but their case seems to be different."

"Sure, that would be fine with me," she said agreeably. "I expect that they'll be a real handful…especially that little Mia.

You know I love the feisty ones. I'm sure I'll enjoy them."

As Peggy left the school and returned to her apartment, she thought about the family she had just met. Having a set of twins in class would be a new and challenging experience. "I wonder." she thought, "if they have a special language of their own and how I will handle it if they do. How will the other children react?"

And she wondered about their father, too. It was a little humorous how tongue-tied he became when little Mia spouted off after they first met. And was he actually checking her out…or was that just her imagination? "This whole thing with Donn has certainly affected my perception of things." Peggy thought.

Peggy was excited for the first day of school…as she was each year. She welcomed every year as a new challenge and was so thankful she had chosen this career. She couldn't imagine going to work each day, if you didn't love what you were doing. The prospect of not sharing her talent and passion as a Montessori teacher was beyond her comprehension.

In her recent conversations with Donn, he had remarked at how well she related to people – adults, in particular. Then, he went on to say that those qualities were just what he hoped to find in a wife. Someone that was comfortable in a variety of social and professional settings, someone who could "smooze" clients and guests. "Someone like that would be critical to furthering my career advancement," he had said. He intimated that she might just be the person to fill that role.

"It's true," Peggy reflected, "I do love people…all people… and I think people like me. I enjoy talking with just about anyone about anything. I'm interested in people's families, careers, interests. Actually, I'd have to say I'm interested in the lives of other people. Is that why Donn thinks of me as his perfect 'career partner?'

But could Peggy really see herself in that role? Or more importantly, did she even want to try considering it?

"After all," she thought, "I also love children and get my greatest pleasure from seeing their eyes light up when they connect with a new idea...or see beauty in the world around them."

In the past, Peggy had turned to God often. Her conversations with Him were personal and helped her sort out her thoughts. Always, those intimate, honest conversations had led her to decisions that were just right for her; so why worry now about a possible future with Donn? She would chat with God...she would turn to Him for guidance, and when the time came, she was confident that the answer would be there for her. In the meantime, she would ask God to help her nurture and sustain the two motherless children he had put into her life. She vowed to herself to do all in her power to see that they felt safe at school, that they were challenged to do their best and that they had warm and nurturing relationships with other children and adults at Ojibwa. Smiling and reassured, she turned her key in the lock of her apartment and went inside.

CHAPTER SEVEN

The next day the kids were up bright and early once again…ready for a new adventure.

"How about we spend an hour or two at my office this morning?" Ian suggested while washing up after a hearty pancake breakfast.

"Can we really go to your office, Daddy?" asked Michael in awe.

"Of course," Dad laughed, "just pack a few toys in your backpacks and let's get going."

The trip to the MSU campus took only a few minutes. As they drew up to the parking lot behind the Crop, Soils and Microbial Sciences Building, the children noticed the beautiful flower beds adjacent to the building. "Look at all those pretty flowers! There must be a gazillion of them!" shouted Mia.

"And who pulls all the weeds?" asked Michael.

"As I recall, that's actually a large test plot where they are experimenting with different kinds of seeds. There's also a big Children's Garden behind the building, I heard. We'll have to explore that when we have a little more time."

"What is a 'Children's Garden?'" the youngsters wanted to know. "Can only kids go there?"

"No," Dad chuckled, "but it was designed with children in mind. I read someplace that they asked groups of kids what should be included before they planted it. I think there's a pizza garden that includes all the good stuff you might put on a pizza as well as an ABC garden with plants whose names begin with all the letters of the alphabet. It will be fun to explore it. I think there are also climbing structures and other things to play with."

"Do you want me to help you carry some of your books?" Mike offered.

"I want to help, too," added Mia.

So off they went with their arms full of books and office supplies. Fortunately, the building was open, but Ian needed his key to get into the corner office on the second floor -- not far from the elevator. Already his name plate was attached to the wall beside the door. What a spacious office! It really seemed too grand for an associate professor. Ian wasn't accustomed to special attention and hoped it wouldn't cause trouble with other young professors.

The children wandered around Dad's office bouncing in the desk chair, looking in drawers, checking out the view from the window. "This is really a neat office, Daddy," Mia bubbled.

They finally settled at a round table in the corner where they unloaded their toys, books, paper and markers.

"I know, let's play professor," Mia suggested.

"Ok," Michael said, "I'll work on those new seeds for the gardens…you can be my helper."

"No way!!!!" cried Mia. "I have my own work…for the children's garden!" They got busy while their father arranged books on the shelves behind the desk and put away the supplies he had brought from home. It was surprising how content the children were playing at their table. He was touched that they were trying to imitate HIM!

"My, look at all the mail I have already!" Ian remarked to no one in particular. He decided to pile the accumulation in stacks according to their senders: items forwarded from Texas, letters from the university, departmental correspondence and finally miscellaneous items of questionable origin. "I'll leave some of this stuff here," he thought, "but I'll take the personal letters home to handle over the week-end." There was a welcome letter from the university president, an invitation to attend an orientation session for new faculty members, instructions on accessing the school's web site and a copy of the faculty and staff directory. "And so it begins," he sighed.

The department secretary had picked up a parking sticker for his car -- something he hadn't even thought about. He would have to remember to thank her on Tuesday. Also, in the stack was a calendar which listed faculty meetings and several fall social events, including one that invited family members. There was a note from the department head requesting that he make a short (no more than 20 minute) presentation about his research at a gathering of graduate students on Friday afternoon. That would be easy enough, since he was always eager to share information about his passion.

"Now what is this?" he wondered. There was a message from a reporter from University Relations who was requesting an interview for an article about new faculty hires. "I don't think so," he murmured to himself. "It would bring back too many sad memories."

He closed his eyes recalling a similar encounter when he was first appointed to the faculty of Texas A & M. That time he had responded, "Do come in" when there was a knock on the door to his cubicle. There stood a beautiful, dark-haired young woman with big dark eyes and a ready smile.

"Hi! I'm Laurie Calhoun from the University News Bureau. I'm here to interview you for an article we are doing on new faculty members. I'm sorry to interrupt, but I was hoping that I could have a few minutes of your time. If you're busy, I could come back at another time."

"Sure. Why not?" said the young prof, flattered by the sudden attention. "Come in and have a seat. I'm sorry this place is still a mess. I just moved here from the graduate student 'cage' where I've been working."

"How nice that you can stay in College Park now that you have finished your degree," Laurie prompted.

"Yes, it is a good feeling. I came here from Washington nearly five years ago, so it seems like home. I must say, though, it feels like the end of a long journey. I appreciate not having to do a job search, of course, but getting to know former professors as colleagues is an interesting new challenge."

"I'm local myself," Laurie offered, "I grew up on a small ranch in the next county. Will you be teaching as part of your assignment?"

"Just one course on research methodologies," he answered. "Most of my time will be spent on actually doing research. I enjoy interacting with students, but my passion has always been the search to discover new information. There is so much we need to learn to make this world a better place to live. I hope that my work can make a small dent in that information void."

"Maybe that's where we should focus our attention in the article," Laurie suggested. "Tell me about your research agenda. Please go slowly, though, because I am not really a science writer. The arts are usually my beat."

Ian liked the young woman's candor and her lovely smile. He really didn't know all that many young professional women, since he'd been so focused on studying to do much dating. Female classmates…were just classmates without gender implications for him. But this Laurie Calhoun was so personable, and something about her made him want to impress her. He wondered if she had a husband…or a boyfriend. She wasn't wearing a wedding or engagement ring, he observed.

"Well," he began, "I'm interested in plant genetics -- exploring what characteristics make a plant productive and deliver the desired quality in the end."

"You mean like a kind of corn that produces a lot of bushels per acre and is very sweet?" she asked.

"Exactly, if it's sweet corn one is studying," he responded.

"And do you happen to be studying sweet corn?" she continued.

"Well, no," he said, "I'm interested in field crops that can be used to produce biofuels."

"I thought corn could be used for ethanol…that's a biofuel, isn't it?" she asked.

"Well, that's true…but not sweet corn," he explained. "Field corn, as well as sugar cane and several other crops are used to produce ethanol…and soy beans are part of the picture if you are talking about biodiesel. But when the prices of such crops are high, using them for fuel doesn't make a lot of sense."

"And I've certainly read about the food plants versus fuel debate!" she added.

"Right again," Ian responded, warming to the conversation with this charming, knowledgeable reporter. "That's why I'm curious about the possibilities for plants that are not part of the food chain -- plants that may be growing wild rather than grown as a commercial food enterprise."

"Well that certainly makes sense," she said. "What kinds of plants might work?"

"The one that I'm studying is called Jatropha," he said getting excited about her apparent interest. "It grows fast, can be grown in all sorts of places, and some varieties have seeds that are rich in oil."

"I've never heard of it, and I'll bet our readers haven't either," Laurie noted.

"You're probably right about that," Ian chuckled. "About a decade ago, at the time when oil prices were soaring, it caught the attention of some scientists and investors who saw it as a viable biofuel option. It was thought that producing this plant might actually decrease transportation costs and reduce greenhouse gases at the same time. Unfortunately, their vision turned out to be a dead end. I'm hoping that further research can turn their dream into reality...and I've had some very promising results."

"This is all very exciting, Ian. Cutting edge stuff, really, but I'm not sure I can accurately explain your work. I'll do my best, but can I check back with you when the article is in draft form to be sure I have it right?"

"Sure," he said, thinking that would give him a chance to see this intriguing woman again. "Here is a bibliography and position paper I did recently. They might be helpful."

"Does this....Jatropha... grow in the United States?" Laurie asked.

"It could be cultivated here," he said, "but it's more likely to be grown in the developing world, since it can be raised without a lot of equipment and production expertise."

"Hmmmm, that sounds like it could be a life-changer!" Laurie said, warming to the possibilities, herself.

"My work actually correlates well with efforts underway in the African nation of Mozambique," Ian added. "The president there has had a lot of enthusiasm for Jatropha, so I'm hoping to do some exploratory work there."

"Wow," Laurie responded. "This is very exciting. I'm anxious to read about your work and write about it. I'll need to give you a draft to review by next Monday. Will that work?"

"Yes, of course," Ian said. "Just give me a call. Perhaps, we can go for a cup of coffee to discuss what you've written."

"I'd like that," Laurie said with a smile.

"Now why in the world did I suggest that?" he wondered. "I don't usually suggest meeting for a pseudo-date with someone I've just met -- not even if she's the most attractive woman I've talked to in…well….forever. This is certainly NOT like me!"

"Before I leave would you mind answering a few personal questions to add interest to your story?" Laurie asked, although she found herself more interested than usual in his answers.

"Sure, fire away," he offered.

"Are you married?" she asked, blushing slightly.

"Not even close," he responded, blushing, as well.

"You grew up in the State of Washington?" she continued.

"Yes," he said. "My dad was a faculty member at Washington State. Before that we lived in Michigan in another university community."

"Brothers and sisters?"

"Nope, you might say I'm something of a loner," Ian admitted. "I've always been a bit of a bookworm and never had much time for a social life."

"Now why did he tell her that?" he wondered.

"And hobbies? What about sports? I'll bet you played a lot of basketball given your height?" she observed.

"I like to travel, especially to foreign countries." Ian said. "I do some hiking and swimming, but basketball -- no -- not coordinated enough to make a team. How was it living on a ranch? You must be quite the horsewoman."

"Riding was fun…mucking out the stable…not so much," she laughed. "Perhaps I'll bore you with some 'cowgirl' stories when we meet on Monday. I'll give you a call and set up our meeting." With a quick "thanks a lot" and a friendly wave, she was off to her next assignment.

"What an amazing gal," the young professor thought. "Hmmm, I wonder what it was like growing up on a Texas ranch." He found himself looking forward to the Monday meeting, more than he would have guessed.

Ian roused himself from thinking about the first time he had met his precious Laurie. That meeting had led to a surprisingly short courtship and wedding. "Must move on," he sighed, watching Michael and Mia discussing their "flower research" animatedly.

Now he must deal with the MSU reporter's request. He turned on the computer and sent a brief message thanking the fellow for the invitation, but said he was doing no interviews at this time. Instead, he suggested the reporter attend the program for grad students on Friday afternoon and gather the information he needed for his article then. He concluded by saying that he would email a resume that would fill in the gaps about his background. Satisfied that he had resolved the matter, he shut off the computer and turned to the twins.

"So, what did you two discover in your research?" he asked his kids.

"I invented some flowers that you can EAT!" exclaimed Michael.

"And I put a mud kitchen in the children's garden, so kids can get dirty there!" Mia added excitedly.

"It looks like you guys drew pictures of your ideas," Dad said. "I love it! Can I hang those here in my office? They are just what I need to remind me about all the stuff we can come up with if we use our imaginations!"

"Yes!" the twins cried in unison.

"Let's put them over here, so you can see them from your desk!" Mia directed.

"And by the way, Mike," Dad added, "there actually ARE flowers that you can eat! Perhaps we'll find some next time we go to Meijer!"

Dad hung the pictures, as directed, then helped the kids pack up their stuff. "Time to go, you guys," he said to his two budding scientists. "How about a stop at the Dairy Store for some ice cream cones?"

"Yum! I want a chocolate cone," said Mike.

"I'd like one with nuts," added his twin.

So off they went to enjoy the perfect treat for a hot August afternoon.

"Well, that was a productive day," thought Ian as they made their way to the dairy store.

Ian looked forward to the start of the school year -- meeting colleagues and staff members as well as the students. This assignment was 100% research, but for him that meant working with graduate students in a variety of ways. His funding provided enough resources to hire several half-time assistants. He had already begun thinking about the skill-sets he would need to get the project underway. Next year, depending on this year's progress, he might need different capabilities. He had best take it one-year-at-a-time and make only one-year commitments to this year's hires.

He hoped that there might be an African student among the applicants, since he anticipated making a trip to Mozambique after the first of the year. At the risk of not being modest, he felt he was quite perceptive when it came to reading people. After all, he was Big Mike's son. Everyone credited the elder Mahoney as being one of the best when it came to personnel selections. Time would be a judge of whether Ian had inherited those skills or not.

"Hey, wait for me!" Ian shouted as he hustled after his children. "I want one scoop of strawberry and one scoop of chocolate!"

CHAPTER EIGHT

"Look, Daddy! There's a note sticking in the door," reported Mia as she scrambled out of the car.

""Who is it from? What does it say?" asked her brother.

"Just a minute," replied their Dad. "It is from Libby's mom giving me the information about some doctors I asked her about."

"Are you sick, Daddy?" Mia asked, concerned.

"No. But I want to be prepared if you fall and hurt yourselves or get a bad tummy ache. I need to know who to call or where to take you for help."

"Oh, we don't want you to be sick....or us either!" Mia added.

"She also says that a woman from her church is interested in talking with me about becoming our family helper. She can even meet with me tomorrow afternoon. Hopefully, Libby is free and can play with you during her visit."

Promptly at 2:00 Saturday afternoon, a late-model, gray Chevy sedan pulled into the driveway, and an athletic looking, older woman with short gray hair approached the front door. "Hi, there, I'm Ida Harding," she said in greeting. "We talked on the phone last evening."

"I'm glad to meet you, Mrs. Harding, I'm Ian Mahoney... but just call me Ian." Ian grasped her hand and shook it warmly. "Please come in. Let's sit out in the four-season room where there seems to be a breeze. Libby is watching the children next door so we can talk without interruption. Would you like a glass of iced tea?"

"Thank you, it is a warm one today…and please, call me Ida." she said as she followed Ian to the sunroom. "I've brought a short version of my resume and a letter of recommendation from the man who directs the Meals on Wheels Program where I volunteer and one from my former boss at the State of Michigan. I'm sure that Pastor Becky can tell you more about me than you care to know, since I am a charter member of her church and have known her for quite some time."

"Thanks, Ida. I appreciate your willingness to see me so quickly even on a holiday weekend." Ian led her to a comfortable chair near an open window.

"What a lovely view and that breeze is heavenly!" Ida remarked. "Actually, my sisters are here for a few days from Indiana, and they went to a movie I've already seen, so I was free to come over and discuss the position this afternoon."

Ian sat down in a chair next to her, and after a moment he opened his hands and shrugged. "I have to admit I'm rather new at this. Where we used to live, I had a service agency help with the house and kids. They actually told me what they would do rather than asked me what I needed. They were quite responsible, but we were never sure which worker would show up."

"That must have been difficult for the children to understand. How old are they now?"

"Yes it was, really," Ian admitted. "The twins, Michael and Mia, are almost four. They weren't quite two when their mother was killed in a car accident."

"I'm so sorry," Ida offered. "My husband, Frank, passed away just last year, and I still miss him terribly."

"I'm sorry to hear that, too…well, you certainly understand how overwhelming everything can be. Are you looking for full-time work?"

"No, more like part-to-half time," she said. "I did not retire voluntarily when I was 62. When the State's finances went into the dumper, those of us eligible to retire were pink slipped. I was an administrative assistant in the Department of Transportation for 25 years after being a stay-at-home mom when our daughter was growing up."

"That's a good place for us to begin. What were your special duties in Lansing?" Ian asked.

"In addition to the usual secretarial responsibilities, I was the person who managed the office and made sure everything ran smoothly. I kept the calendar, scheduled and organized meetings, purchased office supplies, monitored expenses and planned special events involving clients and staff members. Of course I also planned refreshments for our monthly birthday parties for staff members...the parties were my favorite part!" she laughed. "I liked the diversity of tasks and appreciated having a boss who didn't supervise my every move."

"Sounds like you have a lot of the practical skills we need around here…and more!" Ian said. "What about your daughter? Does she live in the area?"

"No, she, her husband and son moved to Denver about six months ago. I'm on my own now except for the Indiana sisters I mentioned," she said with a sigh. "I miss taking care of my grandson several days a week. Tommy is seven, a bit older than your two."

"Getting along with the twins is the most important part of the job," Ian began. "I want them to feel safe and loved. My schedule is rather relaxed, so I plan to take them to the Ojibwa Montessori School each day, but having someone pick them up in mid-afternoon and be with them until I get home shortly after five is important. It sounds like you are used to driving kids around, if you babysat your grandson every week."

"Yes, Frank always emphasized having our cars in good working order and well maintained. I can assure you that I am a very careful driver with no points on my record. I expect that must be especially important to you since your wife was killed in a car accident."

"That's certainly true," Ian agreed, "but in Laurie's case, the accident was caused by a drunk driver who ran a red light."

"How very tragic for you…and for those dear little ones!"

Moving away from the sensitive topic of Laurie, Ian continued, "I expect to do all of the heavy cleaning and yard work, but it would be really nice to come home to a home-cooked meal…perhaps something I could put in the oven or pop in the microwave…nothing too fancy. Fortunately, none of us is a picky eater. I'll admit, I'm not much of a cook and not very adept at doing laundry either, although we get along. Got to have something to wear, after all!"

"I love to cook and would be glad to do the grocery shopping…and laundry is something that you just pop in and out while doing other things…no problem."

Ida went on, "What hours were you thinking about? I would like to continue working Thursday mornings at the church where I prepare the bulletins for the Sunday service; and I hope to keep taking my turn every other week delivering Meals on Wheels to the home-bound on Tuesday mornings. It's always so satisfying to be greeted by smiles from seniors who don't get out much and have few visitors."

"That shouldn't be a problem. I was thinking four or five hours, five days a week. Of course that might have to change if one of the twins becomes ill or if there is a school cancellation." Ian changed the subject, "But tell me a little bit more about yourself. What kinds of things to you like to do? Do you have any hobbies?"

"Well, I try to swim one or two mornings a week at the YWCA. I belong to an evening quilting group and do my share of reading – mysteries, adventure stories and travel books, too. We did a fair amount of camping around the states in national parks when Alice was young, but going to Europe was on our bucket list. That never happened due to Frank's illness, but maybe someday I'll go on one of those Roads Scholar Programs that I hear so much about."

"Mrs. Harding – Ida – it sounds as if we may be a good fit. We need to discuss salary, of course."

"I am not looking for a high paying job. My home is paid for, and we've always lived simply and within our means. I have our retirement and Social Security income. Sadly, we did have to dip into our savings to cover medical expenses last year. But, really, I'm in a pretty safe place financially… not that a little extra wouldn't help each month." Ida paused, then added, "It's just that I have spare time on my hands and like to feel busy and valued. Being part of your family would be a real blessing. How would $200 a week sound to you?"

"Are you sure that's enough? Michigan wages seem to be higher than in many other states, perhaps because of all the unions. I just want to be fair."

"The $200 a week will be quite enough," she said. "Take some time to read through my resume and letters…then talk with Becky before you make a final decision. If everything is a go, I can begin on Tuesday. You can leave a key with Becky if you want me on board. There's just one more thing….I need to meet those two kiddos of yours!"

"That sounds great, Ida. I'll also leave $50 with Becky so you can grocery shop for meals for a few days. Here are the twins!"

The twins came barreling into the house and ran to their father.

"Libby's house is so cool, Daddy!!! You should see it!!!" Michael exclaimed excitedly.

"Hold on, a minute, Buddy," Ian laughed smiling at Libby. "Thanks, Libby, sounds like the kids had a ball. I'll settle with you later."

Turning, he indicated the kind-faced woman standing behind him. "Mia, Michael, this is Mrs. Harding. She may be our new family helper. We're hoping she will pick you up from school, play with you here at the house until I get home and help us get some things done around here."

"Hello, Mrs. Harding," said Michael shyly.

"That's cool! You look like a grandma. Are you one?" Mia bubbled.

"Do you know how to bake chocolate chip cookies?" asked Mike warming quickly.

"Yes to both of your questions," Ida chuckled. "I have a 7-year-old grandson, Tommy, but he lives in Colorado, and I don't get to see him much. I miss him a lot. He says I'm pretty good at Legos, and I like to play games outside, too. I also know how to make doll clothes."

"All our grandmas and grandpas live far away, too! We miss them a lot! Maybe we could be pretend grandkids, and you could be our pretend grandma! Then when they come here....you could meet the real ones!!!" Mia prattled on... instantly finding a solution to everyone's problem.

"That would be such a treat for me," Ida said, a small tear glistening in her eye. "I do know that whatever happens, we'll be friends. We may go to the same church, after all. I can't wait to see you both again, perhaps at church tomorrow or soon!"

Another answer to prayer, thought Ian as the three waved good-bye to the woman who was destined to become an important part of their lives. He would check on her references and touch base with her pastor -- just to make sure, but he had a feeling that she was a perfect fit for the Mahoney family.

How could things be falling into place so easily? The Montessori School visit had more than lived up to expectations. Having a good lead on a pediatrician was another step that seemed promising. He had always gotten along well with people at work – whether they were colleagues, secretarial staff, administrators, technology folks, students or custodians. He and Laurie had some good friends in Texas, too, but they had not developed close ties with their neighbors…who, like them, were renters, busy with their jobs and not inclined to stay long enough to establish real friendships.

This, he hoped, was going to be different. He was here to stay, and, hopefully, so were the Lanes. Mrs. Harding appeared to have roots in Okemos, as well, and he prayed she would like working for them. He knew that he would do everything he could to make the job pleasant and fulfilling for her. He could see that she and the twins already seemed to have a bond.

God certainly must have been guiding my every move these past few months. Otherwise, why would everything be falling into place so nicely? Ian closed his eyes and whispered a little prayer, "Thank you, Lord, I am truly overwhelmed with appreciation and praise!"

CHAPTER NINE

Having resolved his two critical issues, put his office in acceptable shape and completed the unpacking, Ian was ready for a quiet day at home before attending the neighborhood gathering Labor Day evening. The twins, too, were content to spend time in their rooms and play in the yard, running through the sprinkler and splashing in their plastic pool as Dad watered the lawn. Preparing a salad for the neighborhood picnic took very little time. There was even a chance for all three of them to lie down for a few minutes and drift into afternoon naps.

The twins' red wagon came in handy when it came time to load the folding chairs and picnic basket containing the salad, buns, hot dogs, paper plates and plastic silverware. Always trying to be prepared, Ian added a few bottles of water, in case no beverages were provided. The twins insisted on pulling and pushing the wagon as the three made their way to a circle of grills that had been set-up in the street. There were also a number of tables lined up for food.

They were immediately greeted by Libby, who invited the twins to join her and a group of other children she had corralled into playing games. Ian joined several men who were firing up the grills.

"Hi, there, I'm Rod, your next door neighbor, and you must be Ian," said a sandy-haired man, who reminded Ian of his Dad. I've been in Ohio the past few weeks helping the folks down-size and move into a retirement community near

Ohio State University. The lesson I learned was…don't save a lot of stuff you'll never need."

"I can identify with that," Ian laughed. "Moving here gave me an opportunity to donate a lot of stuff to Goodwill. Why we all have a tendency to become packrats, I'll never know."

"How about you, Ian? Are your parents still alive?" Rod looked at Ian, hoping that the answer was affirmative. He knew Ian was an only child and had lost his wife recently.

"Yes, thanks for asking. They are very much alive and live in a Dell Webb retirement community near Hilton Head, South Carolina. Dad can finally get his fill of golfing now that he is retired."

"Are you a golfer?" asked Rod.

"'Fraid not...never had the time. And you?"

"Not my thing either. Too bad since we live right on a golf course."

"Yeah, my Dad always wanted me to pick up the sport… but it just wasn't my thing," Ian added. "I understand that you are writing a book about Chief Okemos."

"Guilty as charged," Rod admitted. "There are a lot of myths floating around about the old guy, so I hope to get at the truth. He seems to have been a remarkable fellow. He, like all of us, was a fine person at times and then something of a problem on other occasions. I am thoroughly enjoying the research, though. It fits right in with my work as an American history teacher. I fear that too many of our young people don't know much about our amazing history and the men and women who made ours such a great country. I'm doing my best to change that situation."

"That's a noble calling, for sure. I'm glad my kids will have the benefit of your passion and knowledge when they get to high school," Ian said. "I understand you are also the neighborhood handyman."

"Yes, I do like to do home maintenance projects and help out the widows and others in the area."

"Widows…huh…how about next-door-neighbors who mistake a ratchet for a wrench? It sure is nice to know I have an expert close by, since I'm a total klutz when it comes to fixing just about anything. And since this is my first time as a homeowner, I bet I'll get a lot of opportunities to learn some things from you, if you're willing. Lucky me…a handy guy… and a teacher…right next door!"

"Hey, I'm always happy to help. Enjoy the challenge, really." Rod changed the subject, "I understand that you are a crop scientist working to develop the potential of a biofuel plant...in Africa, right? Global climate issues, fossil fuel use, saving the environment…those are areas many of us are concerned about. I look forward to hearing more about your work."

"You'll always find me eager to discuss it," Ian laughed, "sometimes too much!"

Rod began moving toward the grills, "I guess it is time to cook the meat. Good talking with you, Ian. Welcome to the neighborhood. I look forward to getting better acquainted."

"Likewise!" Ian said as he followed Rod toward the grills.

Libby returned with the twins and handed them some wipes to clean their hands before heading to the kids' table. Becky asked those assembled to form a circle and join hands for a short prayer. Ian noticed that Peggy, the Montessori Directress, had come to the picnic with the Lane family.

"I didn't know she lived in the area," he thought to himself. "How nice!"

Neighbors greeted each other, welcomed Ian and his family and filled their plates with picnic delights. As adults and children dug into their heaping plates of food, Becky also introduced Peggy to the neighbors. Becky explained that

Peggy had remained in town for the holiday weekend to get ready for the start of school the next day, so she was part of the Ottawa Drive "family" for the evening.

After dinner, it was time for Bob to bring out his guitar and lead the group in camp songs. He had a nice bass voice and easy manner with the group, many of whom joined enthusiastically in singing such old favorites as: "I've Been Working on the Railroad," "You Are My Sunshine," "Tell Me Why," "Let Me Call You Sweetheart" and even "Deep in the Heart of Texas" in honor of the Mahoneys.

Next it was story-teller Rod's turn. Everyone sat back, eager to hear his new tale about Indian Chief Okemos, whose name their village bore. Mia climbed on Ian's lap and Mike pulled a camp chair close by.

"Listen my children and you shall hear," he began. "Sorry...wrong story...." Everyone laughed and waited for him to begin again.

"This evening I want to share a little known story about the Chief. It is recorded in the journal of a white man named Theodore Potter, who lived near the Indians' camp. They actually planted corn in this area. Potter considered himself a friend of Chief Okemos and was amused that the Indian seemed to enjoy watching him work at hauling logs and clearing land with his oxen and primitive wagon."

The twins wiggled, eager to hear what their neighbor was saying. They wanted to know more about this special Indian.

"The Indian noticed that his white neighbor was working with bare feet. He pointed to his own feet and said, 'Squaw make moccasin; you need wear moccasin. That night the Chief took the white man to his wigwam where the squaws looked at the man's bare feet and began to shake with laughter. One of the other braves told Potter that the women were making fun of his bare feet. Soon one of the squaws handed the visitor a pair of nicely beaded moccasins and pointed to indicate he should put them on. The journal reported that an offer was made to pay for the gift, but the Chief refused. Potter's actual words were, 'I proudly walked around the wigwam to their delight. I am convinced that Okemos is the only Indian to give a present to a white man. I did not go barefoot again in the Lansing area and the surrounding community.' Those were amazing words from someone who actually knew the Chief firsthand. It certainly gives us a glimpse of the generous nature of Chief Okemos…and the proud heritage of the community we all call home."

Everyone clapped, having thoroughly enjoyed hearing this new story about their favorite Indian and looked forward to the next chapter of Rod's ongoing narrative.

Ian spoke up and said, "I have a little personal story to share. As a kid living here on Ottawa Drive, my father and I joined a number of dads and sons in forming a chapter of Indian Guides – our own form of "boy scouts." My friends and I were excited about getting Indian names, learning to make Indian crafts and hearing wonderful stories about the natives who had inhabited our part of Michigan. One of the fathers was named Shaven Head; you can guess why that was his choice. My Dad was Wounded Warrior, and I chose to be Growling Bear because the bear was the symbol on the Chief's totem pole. I've often wondered why that was his choice. We camped out, made fires, learned about local edible vegetation and other survival skills. It was a great time…and it all took place right here in this neighborhood."

"Wow," a neighbor responded. "It's fun to hear about ancient and recent neighborhood history. Just think…we are making history for the future right now. Someone should write down what we're doing, so neighbors ten and twenty years from now will know what it was like to live on Ottawa

Drive in 'the old days.' Thanks for sharing it with us, Ian, and welcome home!"

Ian found himself standing next to Peggy Gerber. She looked up at him and said softly, "What a wonderful memory for you, Ian. How very special that you are able to return to your family home to raise your own children. This is such an amazing neighborhood and community. You are truly blessed to be among such warm and generous people."

Ian felt the warmth of her presence and her words. "You are so right, Peggy. I had forgotten how important it is to have family outside our little threesome. These last few weeks have really taught me some important lessons. I'm blessed to be here, it's true. And I'm also glad that you could be part of our neighborhood family tonight." Ian blushed and once, again, wondered why he had said something so personal to someone he barely knew. They both turned as Bob called for everyone's attention.

"Ready for s'mores, everyone?" The embers were still glowing when Bob passed around pointed sticks, and Libby handed out marshmallows.

Instructions were given to the newbies and the roasting began. Soon gooey marshmallows were squeezed between graham crackers with chocolate squares inside. "Oh yummy!" shrieked the twins as they tasted the sweet sticky marshmallow treats. "More please," they begged, licking their fingers and smacking their lips. Everyone agreed that this was a fitting way to end the summer. The tired residents packed up their belongings and headed to their homes...enveloped with the warmth of friendship and optimism for the beginning of a new year.

"I had a great time, Daddy" remarked Michael. "I really like it here."

"So did I, and the s'mores were the best," added his sister.

"Let's jump in the tub, Guys, and get some of that chocolate and marshmallow off you...then into jammies and off to bed. Let's lay out the clothes you'd like to wear to school tomorrow, then you can each pick one book that you'd like me to read while I put away the picnic stuff."

The kids did as they were asked. After stories...Ian listened to their prayers, kissed each of them goodnight and tucked them into their cozy beds.

Taking a glass of ice tea to his desk, the Ian reviewed the notes he had prepared for the next day. He wanted to make certain that he knew the correct drop off protocol at the school. "Must start off on the right foot," he promised himself. He wondered if he'd see that Peggy Gerber again. It'd be great if she turned out to be the children's teacher. He had the impression that she was highly regarded by the pastor as well as by the school's administrator. Besides, the children already knew her. Hmmm, he thought, once again, I'm getting ahead of myself. I just have to learn to be patient and see what might be in store for me and my little family. Ian was beginning to think that "faith" might be something he needed to revisit after all.

CHAPTER TEN

The days and weeks seemed to fly by. The twins loved their new school and couldn't say enough about the friends they had made and the exciting things they had discovered at the school's learning centers. Their dad was amazed at how eager they were to share what was going on in their lives. Before, it had been like pulling teeth to get a few words out of them about their school day. Now, thanks to Miss Peggy's encouragement, they could actually participate in a meaningful conversation around the dinner table. How lucky he was to be able to place them in Ojibwa Montessori with its creative learning atmosphere!

Things on the home front were also going smoothly. Mrs. H – as Ian and the children called her, instead of Ida – fit right in. What a God-send she turned out to be! The laundry was taken care of and the house picked up before she left each day. Having wonderful meals ready for him to warm up was almost too good to be true. One night they feasted on her special ham loaf and scalloped potatoes – not the kind he'd made from a box. Another night it was baked chicken with spinach casserole on the side. The twins loved her spaghetti and meat balls, and grilling marinated salmon on Friday night made a nice change of pace, too. Of course, the refrigerator was always full of fresh veggies and a variety of fruit. So, thanks to Ida Harding, they were all very well-fed and cleanly dressed.

One afternoon, Mrs. H and the twins made a batch of the promised chocolate chip cookies. What a treat! The kids were in cookie heaven! Both youngsters loved their playtime with their surrogate Grandma. She was always thinking of fun, creative things to do. One day they stayed after school to watch some of the older children – those enrolled in the elementary program – participate in a yoga class designed just for them. Ida thought she would mention it to Ian as a possible activity for the twins in the future.

Mrs. H helped them build a gigantic Lego castle, complete with a moat, and she told them stories about the princess and evil sorcerer who lived in the castle. Another afternoon she taught them the game of "safe kick," an outdoor game she played with her grandson that required lots of running, kicking, dodging and ended with peals of laughter. She also brought Mia a small doll that had belonged to her daughter, and Mia cherished it…cuddling with it every night in her bed.

Work at the office was going well for Ian, too. Colleagues stopped by to welcome him, offer encouragement and express their enthusiasm for the new project he had brought to the department. Everyone seemed to be aware of the substantial grant. They were all hopeful that a positive outcome would bring national attention to the entire department and could mean additional funded proposals in the future for them all.

One of the older men recalled working on a university committee with Big Mike and spoke fondly of the provocative discussions the two had had. He also reminisced about the times they had played golf together on the campus links. He expressed an interest in reconnecting with Ian's Dad. In fact, he and his wife were planning a trip to Hilton Head during winter break and would love to catch up with Mike and Kate. Ian assured him that his mom and dad would enjoy reconnecting, as well.

He was somewhat puzzled, however, with the cool reception he had received from two younger faculty members – men about his own age. Kevin and Jay were courteous enough, but something in their demeanor belied their welcoming words. What was it that made them seem quite distant and even brusk?

Getting along with colleagues had never been a problem for Mahoney. In fact, the opposite had always been true. Even though he was not the most out-going fellow, others seemed to gravitate to his work station to chat, confer with him on some problem they were having in class or the lab or just to pass the time of day. He wished he could discuss his quandary with Laurie. She was always the wise one, with a keen perception about human nature.

In response to his invitation to attend his opening lecture, the fellow from University Relations arrived right on time. How different this fellow was from the pert brunette, Laurie, who had interviewed him after his faculty appointment in Texas! This man was older, wore heavy glasses and seemed to take copious notes. He asked several questions about his research, though, which Ian appreciated. The printed vitae had been received with thanks. Ian felt a bit "sheepish" for not having given the man his requested interview but still felt that doing so would have been quite painful. Later on, he thought he would get back in touch with him – maybe even invite him for coffee to further discuss the project that could have such significant ramifications for both the developing world and the U.S.A.

Previously, he had taken the twins to Sunday services at the large East Lansing church where he and the family had worshiped during their time in Michigan. It seemed to be a viable part of the campus community, offering a wide variety of interesting programs for all ages as well as community service opportunities each week. And, of course, the music was great.

But, he asked himself, might it not be a good idea to shop around before deciding whether to reunite with that congregation?   What about joining Pastor Becky's congregation that he assumed was a lot smaller and perhaps more intimate. It too – if its name was any indication – offered an interdenominational perspective that was to his liking. And besides, he mused, didn't Miss Peggy attend that church, too? Yes, he decided. "I think I'll check the paper and their web site about times and location," he said aloud, "and give it a look."

CHAPTER ELEVEN

The October morning was crisp and sunny. The smell of fall was in the air; leaves were starting to turn colors. Ian was glad that his mom had sent the twins some hand-knit woolen sweaters the week before. By turning up the sleeves a little, they fit just fine. They would be perfect to wear to church that morning. He had decided to visit Pastor Becky's church and see if he might prefer this smaller, probably less formal service to the large East Lansing campus church he had attended as a child and since he had resettled in Okemos.

The minister was waiting to greet all comers and seemed especially pleased to see her neighbors. Her welcome was certainly genuine as she told Ian that the twins would be staying with him in the sanctuary until after the Children's Moment, when they would go to their Sunday school class. She told him that Libby was helping with the program, so Mike and Mia should feel quite comfortable in the group.

The church was meeting in rented quarters in a converted office building on the outskirts of town where there were many new homes being built. No stained glass windows there; nor was there a massive pipe organ. Nevertheless, the sanctuary had a quieting grace about it with fresh flowers and a simple cross in the center of the open space. The pastor's words were clear and direct, and hearing the scripture reading from a different translation was thought provoking. Although the choir was not that big, the voices made a joyous sound as they sang a rousing spiritual as the anthem.

Ian noticed that the twin's Montessori directress was one of the singers, and he was pleased to see Mrs. Harding in the congregation along with several of his colleagues and neighbors.

All in all, it was a welcoming, meaningful religious experience for Mahoney. Likewise, the children were eager to tell Daddy about the Bible story they had heard and the fun they had had with the other children, one or two of whom they knew from the neighborhood or school.

As the family was leaving, Pastor Becky invited them to join several other families who were going to a local restaurant for brunch -- something she said they often did after the worship service. Ian gladly accepted the invitation, since it provided another opportunity to meet new people and share an intellectually-stimulating discussion with other Christian adults.

During the lively conversation that took place, he learned that Becky had formerly been on the staff of the East Lansing campus church. That congregation had, for the second time in its long history, been helpful in nurturing the start of a new church to meet the needs of those residing in new areas of the community. What a wonderful unselfish outreach!

"One more issue resolved," he thought. Becoming part of a church on the rise appealed to the young professor, and he hoped to find a niche where he could contribute. After all, bricks and mortar didn't make a church; it was the people who shared a love of God and were willing to put concern for others into action that counted. That seemed to be the spirit he felt that Sunday morning as he listened to their plans for the coming season.

After returning home, he noticed on his calendar that

he was scheduled for his first parent-teacher meeting at the children's school the following week. He had been looking forward to having a more in-depth conversation with Miss Peggy about the twins' progress. He was afraid that he was being a little over-confident in his own assessment. Besides, he looked forward to seeing their attractive teacher again. There was something about her that made him want to talk to her again…about the children, yes, but also, hopefully, a little about herself!

CHAPTER TWELVE

There were quite a few cars in the school's parking lot when Ian arrived for his meeting with Peggy Gerber. Knowing that other parents shared his interest in the learning activities of their children was always a positive sign that the school was well supported by the parents. He planned to get involved with the formal parent-guardian group before long.

Peggy Gerberr was all business as she ushered him to the faculty room for their visit. She certainly was an attractive young woman, he thought. Michael had it right when he said maybe they should, perhaps, call her "Miss Beauty" instead of Miss Peggy, because she was so pretty. Leave it to a youngster to be so perceptive.

"Well, what's the verdict?" he asked with a smile.

"That's easy to answer," was the quick response. "The twins are both doing beautifully!

They had a fine start at their Texas school and seem to have lost little over the summer -- even with the move."

"Glad to hear that," said their proud father. "I was afraid that the progress I thought I was seeing at home was more hopeful thinking than reality. It's hard to be impartial, when it's your kids – and I so much want them to be happy, well-adjusted and eager to learn."

"Rest assured. That's happening…for real," Peggy said earnestly. "They both have made some friends and go their separate ways discovering things of particular interest to each of them. Michael really has been eager to work with the beads and other math toys and was delighted when he was able to count to 1000 and even form sets of tens."

"Yes, I was amazed myself when he ran around the house counting paperclips, marbles and even the peas on his plate. It was rather amusing to hear his response when a friend of mine asked him about his counting achievement. Mike responded by stretching his hands and saying, "Do you mean like this?" indicating a line of beads, "or like this?" motioning a cube of beads.

Peggy chuckled and continued, "I can see him doing that. He also has learned to name and find all the continents on the globe, and he has shown special interest in geography and land forms. Combining those interests with the math will be an interesting trajectory to follow. But it's still early, of course, and there's so much more for him to explore. He really seems open to learning just about everything….a little sponge, really."

"And how about Miss Mia?"

"She really loves books and promises to be an early reader. Sometimes I wonder if she won't cause her little fingers to bleed…she rubs the sand paper letters so hard. She has an excellent memory and can retell stories and pretend read many of our books already. She is also the first one to comfort any child who falls down, feels sick or looks sad. She is very popular with her classmates."

"What is their reaction when other kids ask them to join a particular activity?" Ian asked.

"They are really quite different," Peggy responded. "Mia never says 'no,' but Mike may sometimes say, 'Not just now.' Both are very normal, but different responses."

"They seem to enjoy being with our family helper, Mrs. H, who always seems to plan special activities for them after school. She has been a real blessing. Previously, they seemed quite tense with the series of baby-sitters we had in Texas. I really appreciate the consistency that Ida provides."

"Well I know Ida very well from church and talk with her often," Peggy offered. "So I know that she is delighted to have something worthwhile to do afternoons, and she dearly loves the kids already! The extra cash will also help her make more trips to visit her daughter's family and perhaps even travel with her sisters abroad. I know that she and Frank never had that opportunity."

"Speaking of church," Ian interjected, "I was glad to see that you're a member of Pastor Becky's church. I've decided that it's probably the church we're going to attend on a regular basis, as well. I liked the feeling of intimacy that the smaller congregation provided and hope to find some ways to become active in church programs."

"Funny that you should mention that," Peggy smiled. "I have a friendly proposition for you. How handy are you with tools?"

"That depends. I can swing a nasty hammer at an unsuspecting nail…and I've been known to chop wood, but when it comes to electrical work or plumbing…you might as well call ServPro to assess the damage right now," Ian demurred. "What do you have in mind?"

"You might have heard about the program 'Christmas in July.' Well, we have our own version called 'Christmas in October.'" Peggy explained. "I help advise the youth group at church, and they have scheduled a 'work day' this Saturday. They plan to help an older couple repair their front steps and install a railing. Unfortunately, my co-advisor's wife just had a new baby, so he needs to stay home with his family. We have to get the work done before it gets icy and it becomes more likely they that they could slip and fall. I could really use your help if you are free and willing to get involved."

"If you don't need an architect to design the thing...I actually think that's something I could handle, and it would be fun to work with you and the young people," Ian answered, perhaps a little too eagerly. "I'll see if Mrs. H is free to stay with the twins. Having them underfoot would not be a good idea...they'd be all too eager to help, if you know what I mean. What time and where do we meet?"

"I really appreciate your help, Ian," Peggy said with obvious enthusiasm, then added quickly, "...and...and so will the teens...they know my limitations. We're meeting at the church at 9:00 Saturday morning. We should be able to finish by noon."

"Great! I look forward to seeing you then -- tools in hand!" Then he added sincerely, "and many thanks for filling me in on the twins' progress. I'm so impressed with the impact you have had on my children. They chatter excitedly about school every night...and especially about you! I so appreciate the challenging, caring learning environment that you have created for my munchkins. They really look forward to coming to school each morning and being 'afternooners,' as well!"

"Well, the feeling is mutual," Peggy said, cheeks turning a quick pink, "They are a joy to have in class, and they already have a special place in my heart. See you Saturday!"

There was a bounce to his step as Ian headed for the car. When he glanced in the rear-view mirror, the strained look that so often was present on his face had given way to a smile. Then, uncharacteristically, he actually chuckled out loud! "Yes, indeed," he thought, "things were moving quite nicely...in many arenas." He found himself humming as he steered his car toward home.

CHAPTER THIRTEEN

Ian was pleased with the progress of the research project. Last week, representatives from the Department of Energy, who funded the project, came to campus. The visit had gone extremely well. The visitors were very impressed with how swiftly Ian's group was moving toward their strategic goals. They were especially interested in the data collection and field investigation that was slated to take place after the first of the year in Mozambique.

They expressed an interest in becoming involved themselves and even joining the group traveling to Mozambique. In fact, they indicated that since they had arrived on campus, they had become so impressed with the humanitarian potential of Ian's project that they had conferred with several other federal agencies about identifying consultants who might also want to join them on the African trip if their finances can be approved. That is quite possible due to the interest in strengthening ties with Mozambique.

Locally, in addition to selecting and managing the work of three graduate student assistants in the department, Ian had met a number of times with faculty members in several other university units, including the African Study Center Director. Of particular help had been two men in the Department of Agriculture, Food and Resource Economics, who had just returned from extended stays in South Africa.

Although these researchers were not working in Mozambique, they had been there and were able to identify one or two faculty members at the country's main university who were interested in field crop improvement. They also had contacts with others who had prominent roles in the African Union, an organization in which Mozambique had membership. This type of inter-departmental interactions in cooperation have always been characteristic of MSU development outreach.

But, most noteworthy of all, was the fact that Dr. Mahoney had made a wise selection of three outstanding graduate students to help carry the investigative load. He had been surprised at the number of students who approached him after his initial presentation in September and expressed interest in being part of what some considered "out of the box" research. After a careful review of their credentials, in-depth interviews and consultations with faculty references, he had offered the positions to David Mason, Dana Walters and Christian Rosario.

To Ian, putting together the right team—a group who could work well together—was just as important as the skill sets each brought to the project. He was glad to see that as a team, they grew stronger each week. They certainly were a varied trio by any stretch of the imagination! He often wondered how he had been so fortunate.

David was the oldest of the group, a tall Texan working on his doctorate. He had transferred to MSU from Texas A & M after learning of Ian's appointment there. By training and experience he was a plant breeder. He had returned for graduate work after several years of employment with a prominent U.S. seed company. He loved problem-solving and didn't hesitate to spend long hours tracking the genes of the plant he was investigating. He was considered a traditional plant breeder but was eager to branch out into the more challenging work of genetic engineering.

His knowledge was invaluable to the group. Hopefully, work on the project would lead to his dissertation and later a promising career in academia. In a number of ways he resembled Ian, himself…in his work ethic, his ability to focus on flaws in the investigative process and his deep concern for improving agricultural productivity.

Dana, the daughter of a large Iowa corn and soy bean producer, was quite familiar with the biofuel industry. Her family had part ownership of a dry milling plant that used corn to produce ethanol. She had worked from time to time in the plant and felt strongly that there should be a closer, more complementary relationship between the production of ethanol and biodiesel. Why, she wondered, didn't the industry make more use of the oil by-product from ethanol production to make biodiesel?

Last summer, following the completion of her undergraduate work at Iowa State, Dana worked as an intern in the Washington D.C. office of her local congressman who chaired an important agricultural sub-committee. This insight into the workings of government would be extremely valuable as the Jatropha project progressed. Tracking legislative actions and awareness of biofuel targets were important factors in funding decisions of many agencies. Ian was well-aware that his current funding would have to be extended and even increased if their goals were to be achieved. Dana's background and working knowledge about biofuels coupled with her recent governmental/political experiences made her an instrumental part of the team. Currently undecided about earning a doctorate, work on the project might help her decide.

Finally, the third member of the team, Christian Rosario, actually grew up in Mozambique, although most of his adult years had been spent in Zimbabwe, where his father was a minister. Fluent in Portuguese, as well as English and Swahili, his language skills made him invaluable—especially since travel to Mozambique would be crucial to their data collection and suitability studies. Christian was focused on increasing the Gross Domestic Product (GDP) of African farmers via crop improvement practices. His undergraduate work had been in Agricultural Economics before coming to the states. Having a native speaker with an economic focus was the almost-too-perfect graduate student to round out Ian's highly-capable team. Hopefully, he too would remain at MSU for a doctorate.

Although Mozambique's annual average GDP has been among the world's highest, Christian had been distressed that the country ranks among the lowest in GDP per capita and other measures for quality of life. His Christian zeal to help others, made him determined to find ways to improve the lot of all Africans—not just those in Mozambique. This passion to assist those in need resonated with Ian, who had observed the same kind of dedication to relevancy and maximum population benefit in his dad's work. Indeed, Mike Mahoney had pursued a broadly-based outreach agenda throughout his professional life. Perhaps being raised with a passion for making a difference is why his son included this dimension in his own professional goals.

The weekly meetings with his team were both inspiring and challenging. No one hesitated to speak frankly when opinions differed; yet it was clear that there was mutual respect among members of the group. Various perspectives were offered, and each member of the team appreciated that every other member was capable and committed. Others in the department were aware of the closeness of this work group and perhaps more than a little jealous of the extent to which they had come together in such a short time. Ian's team was clearly a role model to be emulated! It was no wonder that expectations were high for the success of the project!

CHAPTER FOURTEEN

Ian was glad he had accepted Peggy's invitation to participate in the "Christmas in October" work day with the church youth group. It would provide a nice change of pace, and except for raking leaves he had not had much opportunity for exercise. He hoped that his somewhat limited skills would be sufficient for the step-repair job.

As he was gathering the tools he thought might be needed, Mrs. Harding arrived, carrying a basket of freshly baked muffins—her treat for the workers. She also insisted that her time with the twins this morning be a "freebie," since she, too, wanted to contribute to this church outreach project. The children welcomed her…running into her open arms, eager to take her up on her promise to bake snickerdoodles together.

Ian loaded the car and was off to pick up some of the kids who would be working on the home improvement project. Peggy was waiting with several thermos bottles of hot chocolate. They would caravan to the home of the couple who needed their help. It was not surprising that Libby from next door was part of the group.

"People are really so generous," Peggy remarked.

Ian nodded in agreement, "That speaks well of the community, especially when their gifts go unrecognized." A local businessman had provided new lumber to reinforce the front stairs as well as a sturdy metal railing and all the hardware for the project.

They decided to divide into two work groups. Peggy and her group would install the railing which would be attached to the house beside the steps. The repair on the steps, themselves was left to Ian and the others. Her team's job seemed to be the easier—determining the right placement of brackets to hold the railing, drilling holes and then screwing in the fasteners.

Ian shook his head as he looked at the sagging, deteriorating steps. They certainly needed to be reinforced; otherwise the older couple could easily trip on them or even break through, injuring their legs. Part of him thought it would be a lot easier to simply pile in the car, go to Home Depot and buy some already-built steps. But that was not in the game plan, so he consulted with his team and then began to reinforce the supports for each step. The tops would have to be replaced. Thank goodness for the pre-measured boards that had been provided! Nailing on the new planks was relatively easy, once the reinforcement supports were in place. Ian and his team were quite pleased with the end result.

Peggy's group had also been successful in installing the hand rail on the house. Libby, who had been in Peggy's group, looked at the refurbished steps and offered a suggestion. "Why don't we add a lower half step to make it even easier for the older couple and their guests to climb the steps?"

"Good idea, Lib," said one of the boys. Ian and Peggy agreed, so the entire group got together and figured out how to do what Libby had suggested. Pleased with their morning's work, they sat on the steps to relax for a moment before heading home.

The older couple had popped out often during the morning, liberally providing encouragement and appreciation. They offered water and snacks, as well. Teenagers, never willing to pass up food, readily accepted, nibbling on chips and crackers, as they worked. When the job was complete, the couple clapped their hands in delight and hugged each of the volunteers. Noting how sturdy the steps now were, the man observed, "We'll be so much safer now…thanks to your work." His wife seconded that opinion, adding, "You kids are certainly a blessing to us. I can't tell you how comforting it is to see young people give so freely of themselves. How reassuring that the future is in the hands of people such as yourselves. We can't thank you enough!" Peggy asked the couple to join them as they passed around Ida's muffins, hot chocolate, and a basket of fresh red apples.

It was a very satisfied group that returned to the church shortly before noon. The building project was a success, and the morning had certainly been a positive experience for all of them. For Ian's part, he was just grateful that he hadn't embarrassed himself by nailing his thumb to the step! Working alongside Peggy on a joint project seemed so relaxing and natural. He had thoroughly enjoyed doing something with her…something that made a difference. A warm, comforting feeling came over him as he watched her hug her kids and wave good-bye, thanking them and telling them, once again, how proud she was of them.

As they were climbing into their cars, Peggy turned and asked, "Have you taken the twins to a Spartan football game yet?"

"No," was his reply. "Many of the home games have been at night, making them too late for my two. We did watch the marching band practice a couple of times, though. That was fun. Those kids certainly work hard to prepare for their game-day performances."

"Yes, I know. One of my brothers played drums in the band when he was here at State. He said those late summer and early-fall practices were brutal…especially carrying drums! But he loved it, made great friends and counted it as one of the best parts of his college experience."

"I've avoided the campus on game days since there's so much traffic and congestion…fans, tailgaters, kids who have been partying…" Ian shrugged. "It's like a moving obstacle course over there."

"You've got that right," Peggy agreed. "Today's game starts at 3:30, I think. By now, traffic may have thinned out a bit. Don't you think the twins would like to see all the tents, blow-up Sparties, balloons, banners and stuff? It's quite the celebration and worth a walk through—at least once a year."

"Thanks for the suggestion," Ian said. "I think we just might make it part of our afternoon activity. A stop for ice cream cones at the Dairy Store will make it worth the trip for Mike and Mia—and for me too," he added with a smile.

The children certainly did enjoy the unexpected afternoon excursion. Enthusiastic fans, often with elaborate set-ups, were out in full force. The tents were of all shapes and sizes. Blow-up figures of Sparty were everywhere, and loud music competed with tooting horns and the sounds of happy game-goers. All of them were surprised at how many people were enjoying the afternoon sun and having huge pre-game feasts in so many places all over campus.

"Peggy was right," thought Ian. Then, suddenly, he smacked his forehead. "Why didn't I invite HER to join us?" he thought to himself, "It would have been a nice thank-you for this morning, and the kids would have loved it! Next time…." he mused, "I've just got to get better at seizing opportunities."

Traffic was moving smoothly by then, since most folks were at their tailgate parties or heading to the stadium…not on the road. For a change, even the Dairy Store was practically empty, so the three Mahoneys were able to order their cones immediately.

Licking dripping cones, Ian and the kids headed for the car.

As they drove back toward Ottawa Drive, Ian said, "I guess we're still getting to know our new home, Guys. It seems like there is always something or someplace new to explore."

"I really love it here, Daddy," offered Mia, as the family drove into their neighborhood.

"Me, too," added Michael. "I want to be in the band and play football and go to tailgate parties when I grow up. Can I, can I, Daddy?"

Ian laughed, "Michael, you and Mia can go wherever your heart takes you when you grow up. After all…that's how we all ended up here!" Ian smiled as he drove into the driveway of the place he now thought of as "home."

CHAPTER FIFTEEN

October turned into November with little change in the temperature, but Ian found that this was a good time for him to catch up on his reading. While he reviewed all the literature on Jatropha when he was developing the grant proposal, he had noticed over the past few months that scientists in other parts of the world were also looking at this crop with renewed interest. Leading the way was an expert on biofuels in the Netherlands. Several scientists in India and Latin America were also beginning to explore the plant's special properties. "There is so much still to learn," he thought as he began critically reviewing the newest research from around the globe.

Jatropha is one of approximately 170 species of succulent plants, shrubs and trees. It sometimes goes by the common name, "physic nut." Unfortunately, it often contains compounds that are highly toxic. On the positive side, though, it is resistant to drought and pests and produces seeds containing 27-40% oil. It is no wonder that in 2007 Goldman Sachs proclaimed it as one of the best candidates for future biodiesel production! Unfortunately, few species have been properly domesticated, and no one knows the long-term impact on the environment if it were to be produced on a large scale.

Some countries have used certain varieties of Jatropha to make dyes or special baskets; and occasionally some forms have been detoxified and used for fish and animal feed. But because it also can be life-threatening to humans, some countries have actually banned a number of species. Even so, its potential as a source of biomass to produce biodiesel fuel is very promising…especially since there is evidence its use over time can help reduce CO2 in the atmosphere.

"Yes," Ian told himself, "Jatropha does have promise…if we can just discover the keys that will allow it to become a truly viable renewable energy source!"

"Perhaps, and God willing," he thought, "we can just find a few of those keys in Mozambique, then we'll be on the right road to making this dream a reality."

Mozambique, officially the Republic of Mozambique, is a country in Southeast Africa bordered by the Indian Ocean and adjacent to a number of better-known African nations such as Tanzania, Malawi, Zambia, Zimbabwe, Swaziland and South Africa.

It was explored by Vasco da Gama in 1498 and colonized shortly thereafter by Portugal. It gained its independence in 1975, but like many countries, it had difficulty handling its freedom as a Republic and experienced a long protracted civil war. Since its first multi-party elections in 1994, it had remained as a relatively stable nation.

Mozambique is rich in natural resources; and while its economy is largely based on agriculture, it has also seen a growth in industry…from food processing to aluminum manufacturing to petroleum production. Tourism is also a growth industry. Although Portuguese is the official language of the country, it is spoken as a second language by only about half of the people…several native languages such as Swahili, Makhuwa and Sena remain the peoples' main languages.

Believe it or not, the largest religion in Mozambique is Christianity. Traditional African religions as well as Islam are practiced also. Its largest city, the capitol, is Maputo. Since the turn of the century, Mozambique's annual average Gross Domestic Product (GDP) growth has been among the world's highest. Yet, the country ranks among the lowest in GDP per capita. Its population is around 24 million.

Back in 2007 investors, thinking that Jatropha was the miracle tree, threw money at Jatropha projects. After all, they reasoned, it could grow easily on unused barren land and not compete with food production. Even the president of the country and many in the media encouraged people to plant Jatropha trees—and many did. But it soon became evident that the more productive the land, the higher level of oil that came from the seeds. So many farmers planted Jatropha instead of food and it created controversy in the press. During the world-wide economic crisis that occurred soon after, big money dried up; and the miracle plant ceased to be so miraculous.

Unfortunately, many of the farmers who had taken the risk of growing Jatropha in hopes of gaining high returns lost money. Still, in some villages, farmers continued to grow it on a smaller scale. If scientists such as Ian could—with high-tech methods—select plants that produced more and better seeds and turn the semi-wild plant into a real crop...who knows, in time it just might become a viable commercial product that does not compete with food production. Jatropha could take its place alongside corn and sugarcane as a renewable fuel source, one that is friendly to the environment and can be grown on presently uncultivated land.

Ian was willing to give it a try!

CHAPTER SIXTEEN

It seemed like just yesterday that everyone was busy decorating for Halloween and preparing for trick-or-treaters, and suddenly everyone was focusing on Thanksgiving. The twins, with Mrs. H's help, had become quite adept at constructing turkeys from pine cones, pipe cleaners and paper fans. The Lanes had already sent out invitations to the annual Thanksgiving feast at their home.

Of course the Mahoneys were on the guest list, as were several other neighborhood families and a young couple who had recently begun attending services at the Church. Ida Harding decided that the weather would probably be too unpredictable for her to risk driving to Indiana on her own, so she volunteered to do feast preparations in the Lane kitchen. She knew the pastor would be quite busy helping with a special community service. Knowing his limits as a cook, Ian quickly wrote a check to cover the cost of the turkey with a bit extra to cover the "fixins."

He asked Pastor Becky if his grad student, Christian, could join them, and she readily agreed.

The young couple from church offered to bring an old New England family dish of cranberry salad to the feast. One family promised to bring baked sweet potatoes topped with marshmallows, while another added the traditional green bean casserole. Everyone brought appetizers and snack foods, as well. Ida would roast the turkey and prepare the mashed potatoes and gravy—as well as at least two kinds of dressing. Peggy Gerber had also decided to stay in town for the holiday, and she said she would contribute chocolate cupcakes and bake a pecan pie—one of her mom's famous recipes. The hostess laughed and said she'd be the lazy one and buy a pumpkin pie at the local pie shop. Even Mia and her twin wanted to get into the act, so they baked and decorated a batch of cut-out sugar cookies in the shapes of turkeys and autumn leaves with Mrs. H.

When the day arrived, people could not believe it. What a feast! There was scarcely room on the table for the lovely floral arrangement that Mrs. Harding's sisters had sent from Indiana. As the guests began to arrive, they were greeted by their host; and Rod was quick to hand around cups of hot cider and pass a jar of specially spiced nuts, a contribution from Christian—a very special treat, since they had come from Africa.

Ian wondered just how Becky would orchestrate the "thanks" in Thanksgiving. He was sure she had a plan to involve everyone in some kind of meaningful activity. Sure enough, after everyone was seated, she asked everyone to hold hands while she offered a short prayer and then suggested everyone think either of a special Thanksgiving memory to share or tell why they were particularly grateful this Thanksgiving while enjoying their meals.

It was quiet for some time as the guests passed casseroles and sampled the mouth-watering dishes while they thought about what they might say. One of the neighbors responded first by saying that he was very grateful that once again he, the father of the family, was fully employed; another added appreciation that aging parents had improved health and were again able to maintain life on their own in the family home. Ian shared a memory of himself with his parents often serving Thanksgiving dinners at a homeless shelter rather than indulging in fancy meals at home with just the three of them.

The young couple expressed pleasure and thanksgiving for being so warmly welcomed in their new community even if their accents sounded strange. Michael broke into the conversation by saying, "I'm thankful for our school." Mia added, "...and especially for our teacher, Miss Peggy." Peggy blushed as the guests chuckled appreciatively. Rod reminded everyone about the first Thanksgiving and wondered aloud just how Chief Okemos and his family had celebrated the holiday—or if they did. He also joked that he recalled with pleasure the Thanksgiving football games when the Detroit Lions actually won.

Peggy said she was thankful that school had survived the tough economic times and expressed her joy in having a job that she loved very much. Libby said she remembered going to Thanksgiving parades and loved to watch them on TV... such a joy for children! Ida shared that this was her first Thanksgiving since the death of her husband, a sad time for sure, but also a joy because of her friends at church, volunteer activities and especially the precious time she got to spend with Mia and Michael. This caused the three Mahoneys to smile broadly, and Mia even threw her a kiss.

Bob laughed and confessed that he was grateful to be keeping his New Year's resolution—playing the guitar and leading the residents of a local nursing home in their favorite hymns and folk songs. His mother's big thanks was the successful expansion of church membership and the eagerness of members to learn what it means to be followers of Christ's teachings.

After everyone but Christian had contributed, there was a pause as everyone went to the dessert table to heap their plates with sweet treats. When everyone was again seated, Christian cleared his throat and began. "Well," he said softly, "I probably have the most for which to be thankful. Not only have you good people treated me warmly and invited me to share in this wonderful meal, but your nation has also been graciously open to my coming. Even more gratifying, though, is the fact that many years ago, missionaries came to the shores of southern Africa and introduced my people to Jesus Christ, a blessing that can never be repaid. Today nearly half of my countrymen are practicing followers of the Lord. My father is a minister like you, Pastor Rebecca. He and my mother named me Christian so that all would know of their faith and abiding love of God. For this I am most thankful!" There was a moment of silence, and then everyone responded with rousing exclamations, "Praise the Lord!" "Bless, you, Christian!" "We are blessed to have you among us!"

After the dishes were cleared and the left-overs put away, Bob brought out his guitar and led the group gathered around the fireplace in a number of well-known seasonal hymns and songs, such as "We Gather Together to Ask the Lord's Blessing" and "Over the River and through the Woods." What a joyous sound they made! As he was putting the instrument back, in its case one of the children asked, "Can we sing "Jingle Bells, pleeeease?"

"Of course, we can," laughed the young man. As a matter of fact it was the perfect transition to the next holiday season—since snow had begun to lightly fall and thoughts drifted toward the Christmas holiday to come.

What a special ending to another wondrous day in their new neighborhood. Ian was truly grateful on this day of thanksgiving that he had made the risky decision to move back to the Midwest. Ottawa Drive…where friendship was so readily extended to others, especially to those who were alone and perhaps from far away…he was indeed proud to call this place…home.

CHAPTER SEVENTEEN

Once Thanksgiving was behind them, the twins were eager to start getting ready for Christmas. Mimi and Papa Mahoney would fly in—not just for the day—but to be with them during the early part of January when Daddy was slated to go to Mozambique. Nana and Grandpa Calhoun would take over that assignment after the Mahoneys went back to South Carolina.

A flurry of hugs and kisses and "My how you've grown"s filled the airport arrival gate as the Mahoneys stepped out. Nostalgia filled the elder Mahoneys when they turned onto Ottawa Drive…Mimi felt happy tears sting her eyes as the children talked excitedly about the neighbors and how much they loved it here. After a quick tour of the old family home and an unloading of luggage and mysterious packages, the family hustled into the car and headed out to find just the right Christmas tree.

There were a number of signs around town directing them to local Christmas tree farms, each of which had special attractions appealing to young tree cutters. The Mahoneys joined the crowd on Saturday afternoon. When they reached the tree farm, the kids were delighted to see none other than Santa, himself, and a couple of elves in the warming barn! Ian and the elder Mahoneys were eagerly pulled over to the jolly old elf. Each child took a turn climbing onto Santa's ample lap and assuring him that he and she had been very good, indeed…and hoped for something very special on Christmas morning. "What would you like?" he asked.

Mia stated with assurance, "A Princess Elsa doll, if you have any at the North Pole." Michael requested pirate Legos. Both children solemnly promised to be very good, indeed and hugged Santa good-bye.

Chattering about their good fortune at actually seeing Santa, the crew stomped off through the newly-fallen snow to find the perfect tree. And there it was! Michael pointed out an especially well-formed Scotch pine. After struggling with the saw, hauling the tree and precariously tying it to the roof (amid laughter and teasing), the family headed home with their treasure. While Mimi and the kids sipped cups of hot cocoa and warmed themselves by the fireplace, Papa and Daddy set up the tree in the corner of the living room. Mimi looked around for the box of tree decorations. Suddenly they realized that there were none—no ornaments or tree decorations of any kind! "Why, Ian Mahoney!" exclaimed Mimi, "Whatever did you do with all the ornaments you had in Texas?"

Ian shrugged sheepishly, "I...I don't know. I tried to down-size before moving, I guess I must have left them at the Salvation Army by mistake with several other boxes of stuff."

Mimi shook her head and sighed, "Ian....Ian. Well, no problem," she said brightly, "I guess we just get to start anew!" A quick trip to the local Dollar Store made for a fun shopping excursion since Mike and Mia agreed that the decorations should follow a green and white Michigan State color scheme. Later they added chains of popcorn and made small folded paper lanterns with Mimi's help. How they loved all of the tiny white lights! When it was finished...and Mia had placed a sparkling star atop the tree, Ian turned off the lights, stood back, and they all admired their work. "Wow," murmured Mike. "I think Santa will love it!"

"What a special way to celebrate Jesus's birthday," Mimi said quietly. "Just think of all the people from all over the world, who are decorating trees and planning ways to remember when Baby Jesus was born in Bethlehem."

Exhausted, happy children hustled off for a quick bath, bedtime stories and even a couple of much-loved Mimi lullabies. It didn't take long for them to drift into dreams of reindeer, elves and Baby Jesus lying in a manger in a far-away place.

On Monday, since it was a holiday, Ian asked his folks if they would like to go to Frankenmuth, the home of the famous Christmas Store. It was a relatively short drive for a nice winter day, and Ian and his folks reminisced about going there when he was a child. Ian also recalled that each Christmas for many years his mother allowed him to select a special ornament for the tree—a nice tradition to begin with the twins, he thought.

The town was festive with holiday trimmings, and the parking lot at the huge store was full—even on a week day. "Traffic must really be something on week-ends. Thank goodness we are here on a Monday," he thought.

The twins could not believe their eyes. Christmas carols, coupled with the sound of bells, filled the air, and everywhere you looked there were decorations from all around the world. Blow-up snowmen competed with lighted reindeer for attention, and there were tables and tables of delicate ornaments as well as artificial trees and wreaths of all colors and sizes. The children marveled at the tiny figures of Baby Jesus, Mary, Joseph, shepherds and wise men surrounding realistic stables. There were stars and angels hanging from the ceiling and salespeople dressed as elves.

It was pretty overwhelming for four-year-olds…but they were truly in Christmas heaven! Ian invited the twins to each select one ornament for their tree, reminding them to be oh so careful since many of the items on display were very fragile as well as expensive. It didn't take them long to decide, once the children spotted the case with MSU ornaments. Mike picked out a Sparty with a football, and Mia chose a cute little cheerleader holding a megaphone.

Although the youngsters knew that the family gift for Mrs. Harding would be a gift of money that she could use to visit her daughter once the new baby arrived, they still wanted to get her something themselves. There was so much from which to choose, but when they spotted a colorful holiday half-apron decorated with a laughing snowman, their problem was solved. Mimi concurred…saying that she knew Mrs. H would love it. As they were about to enter the checkout counter, Michael pulled on Ian's sleeve, "Look, Daddy, see that pretty angel on the turning box."

"You mean that ceramic music box, son?" Ian asked.

"It's a music box?" asked Mia.

"Yes, replied their father. "See…I'll give it a crank so we can hear its song. Listen, it's playing 'Hark, the Herald Angels Sing.'"

"That's so pretty," said Mia, "and her dress is so sparkly!"

"Yeah, and she looks just like Miss Peggy!" Michael added.

"Can we buy it for Miss Peggy, Daddy, please?" the twins asked in unison.

It was a bit more pricey than Ian thought might be necessary, but the twins so seldom asked for things that he couldn't say no. And indeed they were right…the ceramic angel did look like Peggy Gerber. "Well, I guess so," he said. "After all, she has certainly found a special place in your hearts!" That telltale blush, once again spread up Ian's neck…as he realized that Miss Peggy had found a way of creeping into his mind, as well.

Mimi and Papa watched this exchange with bemused looks on their faces, then they turned to one another at the same time, and Mimi gave her husband a knowing wink and a little smile.

After a quick stop to watch the figures on the large glockenspiel on the huge clock topping one of the town's famous dining halls, the five of them stopped for a quick lunch of brats smothered with sauerkraut, a new treat for the two who had never eaten kraut before.

The family arrived home before dinner, chattering about the winter wonderland they had visited that day. Ian thought that a trip to Frankenmuth was definitely going to become a continuing tradition in the Mahoney family.

After unwrapping their purchases and hanging the new ornaments on the tree, Mimi and Papa went upstairs for a much-needed rest, and the kids retired to the play room and began pretending it was Christmas morning.

Ian felt that he was halfway home with his Christmas shopping. Peggy had recommended a couple of series of books that he found at the campus bookstore—both with Spartan connections. One was about a pout, pout fish that he chose for Mike. It was written by an MSU graduate. Three lovely picture books for Mia were the popular work of the wife of a former Spartan football coach. The only other gift he had been planning for the children was a pair of new little bikes. But after hearing his children's exchanges with Santa on Saturday, Ian knew a little more shopping was needed…for legos and a princess doll. "Which princess was it?" he struggle to recall. "Oh, yes, Elsa, that's right." He chuckled as he gave himself a mental pat on the back. "Santa doesn't make the mistake of bringing the wrong princess on Christmas morning."

Earlier, at the campus museum gift shop, he had found some unusual Petoskey stone jewelry that would appeal to his mother, since the two of them had often hunted for such stones on trips up north when the family lived in Michigan. Big Mike would certainly appreciate the newly-released album by the Spartan Marching Band, Men's Glee Club and the Town and Gown Choral Union—in which the older man had participated.

The Calhouns, Laurie's parents, were sent a box of assorted MSU cheeses, sold by the students' Dairy Club, a gift that would also be appropriate for the Lane family who had been so kind to the Mahoneys. The gifts had actually been quite easy. Laurie would have been proud that, for once, he was almost done shopping…and it wasn't even Christmas Eve!

Now he could concentrate on preparing for the trip to Mozambique. Having the two sets of grandparents cover for his absence was going to be a Godsend for him, and a wonderful treat for the twins, who had not seen any of them since leaving Texas. Mrs. Harding would also be on stand-by, if the need arose. He was relieved that everything had fallen into place, and he had no misgivings about being gone for approximately three weeks. His only worry was how much he was going to miss his little Munchkins!

CHAPTER EIGHTEEN

Ian did a quick job of mailing a few Christmas cards to colleagues and friends in Texas, informing them of his change of address. A trip to Toys 'R Us resulted in securing the coveted Elsa doll and the pirate legos, Santa was to bring. Ian was relieved to have avoided his usual last minute rush of taking care of holiday business. This freed him to concentrate on the multitude of details yet to be resolved concerning the African trip.

December had passed quickly. Fortunately, others were stepping up to handle the pre-Christmas chores. Mrs. H, with the help of the children, did some baking and stored cookies in the freezer – frosted cut outs, snickerdoodles, raisin oatmeal cookies and frosted chocolate drops. At school the children made lovely gifts for their parents and grandparents – personally decorated picture frames to hold the candid photos Miss Peggy took of each child.

Since the Mahoneys had arrived the week before Christmas and Mrs. Harding continued to stop by to help before leaving for her sister's house, grocery shopping was done early; and the refrigerator and cupboards were well stocked, and all was ready for the Christmas meal preparations.

The last day of school before Christmas vacation, Ian joined his son and daughter for a special holiday party. Since the school prided itself on its diversity, care was taken not to leave any child out of the festivities. Songs and traditions of many religions and cultures were featured during the winter holiday celebration. Gifts were exchanged. Miss Peggy had kept her knitting needles busy throughout the fall and managed to finish more than two dozen pairs of mittens for her students' little hands – just in time for the party. The Mahoney twins were thrilled that theirs were dark green, Mia's decorated with a Spartan "S" and Mike's with the outline of Sparty.

The twins were the last to leave that afternoon and shyly handed their gift to Miss Peggy. She carefully unwrapped the package. "Oh my goodness!" she exclaimed. "This is so beautiful! Thank you so much for choosing it for me. I will treasure it always and remember the two special elves who gave it to me."

"We thought she looked like you," responded the pair, as they gave her a hug. But it was only Dad who noticed the tear that appeared in the corner of her eye and slid silently down the woman's cheek.

"Have a good holiday," he said to Ms. Gerber, cheerfully. "We'll all look forward to seeing you in the new year!" Ian was curious about how she would spend her vacation. Did she have a boyfriend back home, he wondered.

Preparations for the BIG DAY were progressing nicely for everyone. Fortunately, the weather cooperated, and Mrs. Harding was able to make the trip to Indiana without fear of having to drive on icy pavement.

Mimi and Papa were glad that they had decided to come to Michigan well before the holidays. They had thought Ian might need their help in these last, frenzied days before Christmas…and they were right! There were happy to be here sharing this special time with the kids and were looking forward to spending an extra few weeks when Ian left for Mozambique. What a great time they would have!

After arriving home from school and excitedly telling their grandparents all about the holiday party, the children ran off to play before dinner. Kate was busy in the kitchen, and Ian began telling Mike about all he had to do to prepare for his upcoming trip. It did seem a little overwhelming. Mike was calm and reassuring, though. "Don't worry, son. Any dad who can single handedly manage two active little sprites while orchestrating a move across the country, a new job and a new home…can certainly plan a trip overseas!"

At the dinner table everyone enjoyed bowls of hot soup that had been simmering in the crock pot all day, fresh fruit, a tossed salad and Mimi's famous hot bread pudding for dessert. The kids entertained their grandparents with stories about Miss Peggy, school friends and the upcoming Christmas play at church. They eagerly chatted about Santa's upcoming arrival and wondered if he would remember to bring Elsa and pirate legos, like they had asked. Michael and Mia assured each other that they had, indeed, been very good this year… so surely Santa would remember.

By eight o'clock the children were nestled in their beds, and the adults agreed an early night was in order for them, as well. Everyone knew that there would be plenty of time tomorrow to complete last minute projects for Christmas and prepare for the children's Christmas Eve service at church.

Indeed, even the adults were "snug in their beds" before the clock in the hall struck ten.

If the house could talk, one wonders what it would recall of Christmas holidays past when the Mahoneys had resided there all those years ago. The child, Ian, had been just as excited about choosing and trimming a live tree as the twins. He, too, had enjoyed baking and decorating cut-out sugar cookies. He was just as impatient awaiting Santa's arrival as his own children now were. For the house Ottawa Drive having three generations together under its roof…celebrating Christmas, once again…must have been a true delight.

The senior Mahoneys were tired, for sure, but as they snuggled down under the covers before falling asleep, they confessed in whispers to each other how pleased they were at the way the family was managing. Gone was the gaunt look that had been on Ian's face since learning of Laurie's death. The twins were healthy, energetic, confident and totally happy in their new home.

Certainly the move to Michigan had been a positive one, although at the time, it had seemed risky for them to move so far away from the grandparents. Kate and Mike looked forward to meeting the Lane family who lived next door... they had certainly been supportive of the Ian and the children. Getting the twins into a Montessori program was also a blessing. The children seemed to adore their teacher, who sounded very caring and creative. How thoughtful of her to spend her spare time knitting unique mittens for each of the children in her class! That must have taken a lot of time and was truly a gift of love for her charges.

They were also pleased that Ian had found a new church home and become involved with its youth group. Working with teens was a change of pace for their son, but it was a good way for him to prepare himself to parent his own teen-agers in the future. Interesting, too, they mused, that the children's Montessori teacher was Ian's co-leader of the group. He and Miss Peggy seemed to be developing a nice friendship...or did they sense there was something more there? Hmmm... Kate and Mike looked forward to meeting her.

No matter their age – or how successful their children were – parents always seemed to worry about them. Now, though, after two years of nagging concern and many sleepless nights, Kate and Mike felt that their son had at last turned the page and moved on. It was an almost palpable relief. Ian was finally, once again, embracing life's journey and looking forward to what the future might hold for him and for his precious children. With those comforting thoughts…they fell into a sound peaceful sleep.

CHAPTER NINETEEN

The highway crews had spent much of the night clearing the roads, so when Peggy steered her Chevy Volt north, she gave a sigh of relief, knowing that the trip could be accomplished without incident. She really didn't mind winter driving – especially on bright sunny days with sparkling snow blanketing the countryside. Humming along with carols playing on the radio, she reflected on the past few months.

She always looked forward to each new year at her school. This year's class had been quick to settle in, and the children had seemed ready and eager to learn. The addition of the Mahoney twins had worked out well, and they had immediately become integral parts of the classroom community. They both continued to be well-liked by their peers.

The last day of school before winter break had been such fun. The children were so delighted with the personalized mittens she had made them. She was glad that she had done it, even though her fingers ached after the long hours of knitting. It had been quite time consuming, but after all…it wasn't as if she had a busy social life. She didn't!   And how excited the children were when they presented her with their gifts! She would never forget the bright smiles on the Mahoney's' faces when she unwrapped the ceramic angel music box. How very sweet that they thought she looked like that angel. The memory made her chuckle.

Arriving at home amid hugs and joyful greetings, it didn't take long for her mother to put Peg to work baking a variety of cookies to package and deliver to shut-ins. This was a task she had shared with her mother, Rosemary, for many years. The only difference now was that instead of placing the baked treats in salvaged shoe boxes wrapped in Christmas paper, the cookies were put in colorful holiday tins purchased at the dollar store. This year she noticed that there were only 12 tins to fill – sadly, several of their former recipients had passed away over the past year.

The next thing on the family agenda was the annual trek in their horse-drawn wagon through their woods to select the Christmas tree. Peggy, her brothers and her parents climbed in the wagon – armed with hatchets and saws and rope – and headed for the woods. Her dad always teased that the right one couldn't be found until Peggy and her mom got cold. The same was true this year. Having the whole family participate in the tree cutting was special for everyone…especially now that the family was scattered and was so seldom together.

Caroling with friends and the midnight candlelight service at church were again part of the Christmas routine for the Gerber family. This year, the gift-giving had been simplified. The four siblings drew names and concentrated on finding just one special gift rather than trying to please three family members. Peggy was the lucky one…she drew Sam's name. Her middle brother was the computer geek in the family and always had a list of new software and gadgets he needed. That made her shopping a breeze.

J.R. had drawn his sister's name. She was surprised and delighted with the warm pair of Uggs boots he had given her. What a perfect gift! How did he know? She had made a bright red, boiled wool jacket with matching hat and mittens for her mom who declared the fit to be perfect. For her dad, there was a dark green Spartan vest, which she knew he would wear when using the gift from his sons – two tickets for the

Michigan State vs the University of Michigan basketball game
and reservations at a lovely bed and breakfast in East Lansing
in January. Christmas was a wonderful traditional celebration
with the family, and, of course, it had to end all too soon.

While preparing to leave for her return to Okemos, Peggy
and her mother paused for a last cup of coffee and some
mother-daughter conversation. Peggy confided that her date
with Donn Bahler earlier in the week had not gone well; in fact
it had been upsetting for them both. She said sadly, "You're
not going to believe what happened, Mom."

She told her mom that Donn had seemed ill at ease the
entire evening even though dinner and the movie were great.

"Did you have any idea why that was?" asked Rosemary.

"Well, I didn't at the time," came Peggy's answer.
"But when we got back to his house, I gave him his gift, a
monogramed U of M scarf I knitted for him. He loved it,
and he liked the fur-lined gloves I gave him, too; but he was
distracted and acting very strangely. I started to get a weird
feeling in my gut."

"Ok, Pegs," her mom probed, "what happened next? I'm
getting that same weird feeling myself."

"Oh, Mom, you know me too well. Then Donn kissed me
and said that he had grown to love me, then handed me a
beautifully-wrapped box. My fingers were numb as I tried
to untie the ribbon. I sort of dreaded what might be in the
box….and yes, there it was…a huge, emerald-cut diamond
engagement ring!! I was floored! I had no idea that he was
going to make such a move, and I was speechless!"

"So…wat did you do?" her mom prompted.

"I didn't say anything at first...I couldn't. I just looked at
that beautiful ring and a flurry of emotions came over me,"
Peggy said sadly. "I guess I should have anticipated something
like this. He sort of hinted at a permanent relationship this

summer when J.R. and I spent my birthday weekend with him in Traverse City."

Her mom gave her a hug and whispered, "So, what DID you say to him?"

"After blinking, swallowing, and taking a deep breath, I told him how he had always been such an important part of my life…that we had been friends for as long as I could remember. I told him I was touched and honored and humbled by his offer to spend our lives together…and that it was truly the most beautiful ring I had ever seen."

"But…." Rosemary continued.

"But…although I cared for him…and even loved him like a brother, I just didn't think of him as a husband. I told him his offer meant the world to me, and I would always cherish him and his friendship. I said that someday I hoped to dance at his wedding…a celebration of his marriage to someone as special as he is…someone who would feel for him the same love he will feel for her."

"Oh, Peggy, I know how hard that must have been," her mom hugged her again. "Donn has been part of this family for such a long time. I know you didn't want to hurt him, but you have to be true to your own feelings. If he isn't the right one…he isn't the right one. How did he react to what you said?"

"He wasn't angry…I think he seemed more disappointed and shocked than sad, really. He asked if I might change my mind after giving it more thought." Peggy paused for a moment and wiped away a tear of her own. "I really hate to hurt people, Mom … especially Donn. But, I said, 'no' that we really are very different people. We look at life differently, we have different goals and plans for the future."

I gave him a big hug and tried to smile through my tears. I congratulated him on his big promotion and upcoming move to Chicago. I told him I knew he would be wildly successful, and I knew the perfect gal who shared his goals and values was out there just waiting for him to find her."

He actually hugged me back and said, "You know, Peg, I sort of knew you would turn me down…but I had to give it a try. You are so special, and I would have been so proud to have you by my side in Chicago."

"We both cried a little and hugged…" Peggy continued, "and then we ended up chuckling as we began to tell childhood and growing-up stories of times we had shared. I really think we're going to be okay. But, wow, Mom, that was one of the toughest conversations I've ever had in my life!"

"Oh, Pegs, no wonder you were so quiet for much of this visit," her mom said. "I didn't want to pry, but your dad and I have been so worried. Truthfully, while we have always enjoyed Donn and welcomed him into our home, I think you're right. You and Donn are truly two very different people."

"I just knew that it was not the right match for either of us, Mom," Peggy offered. "He wants glitz and glitter and a high-visibility social life. That's just not me. I want to be a wife and mother with my focus on my home and my family. I only hope that one day the right guy comes along who wants those things too. I know it's corny, Mom, but I have always believed I would find someone I love with all my heart… someone I don't want to live without. I've always believed that if that special person comes along…I'll know it."

Rosemary swiped at a tear that was beginning to slip down her cheek. "Oh, my dear Peggy …how could a mother be more proud of her daughter? Loving someone as you describe is not corny…and being loved and a mother is a wonderful gift! There is not a day that goes by that I don't thank the Lord-above that your father and I found each other. You dad and I have often said that you are truly special. The man that finds

you will be very lucky, indeed. I know he's out there…and
you are right…you will know it when he comes along."

The women hugged once more and Peggy headed off to pack.

Before climbing into her Volt, Peggy said, "Mom, before I
go, there is one more thing. I just want to tell you how much
I love the special cross-stitched wall hanging that you tucked
into my Christmas stocking. I know it took you forever to
make it, and I will cherish it always!   Where did you find
such a beautiful little prayer for teachers?"

Rosemary smiled, "It was printed in our program at
church one Sunday. I know it was intended for Sunday school
teachers, but I thought it applied to all teachers, especially a
teacher like you. I'm so glad you like it."

Together they read the four verses:

Thank you for compassionate teachers who reach out to
each student with dignity and respect, remembering that every
child has a story to tell.

Thank you for wise teachers who remember that children
learn more from who we are than what we say.

Thank you for loving teachers who reach out to children
on the margins, remembering that we see Jesus in the face of
the poor, the challenged, the rejected.

Thank you for strong teachers who carry heavy loads with
patience and good-humor, remembering that Jesus walked an
extra mile.

"I love that prayer, Mom!" Peggy said as she hugged her
mom good-bye. "I will cherish those words and try to live by
them every single day in my classroom!"

"You already do, my dear, you already do." Peggy's mom
whispered and she, Peggy's dad and remaining brothers
hugged and waved good-bye as she drove down the long
country drive. She was off…heading back to Okemos to face
a new year and the challenges and still unknown adventures

that awaited her there.

As Peggy drove away many thoughts swam through her mind: Donn's proposal, Christmas with the family, her mom's wise words, the teachers' prayer.

She also thought about how sorry she was to miss the Christmas-Eve service in the little restored church in Okemos and being part of the choir. But Christmas was a time for families. She was fortunate to have such a wonderful family and thankful that she was able to spend the holidays with them. Her thoughts drifted to the little Mahoney family.

She thought about how wonderful it was that the twins' grandparents had come all the way from South Carolina. She wondered if Mia and Michael even remembered that their mother had died just before Christmas...probably not...they were so young at the time. She knew the family had shared joyous times this year and made wonderful new memories together. She prayed that the sadness of that tragic event two years before had faded into warm happy memories of a very special and much-loved wife and mother...one who had brought much happiness and joy to her little family.

Peggy also thought about school and looked forward to seeing the children and hearing all their holiday stories. The school's upcoming calendar was full of interesting family activities. She knew her youngsters would make tremendous growth – academically socially and physically. They changed so quickly at this young age. Greeting her class after Christmas was always such a treat! She couldn't imagine a more satisfying job than being a Montessori Directress at Ojibway School. As she pulled into her driveway in Okemos, she whispered a little prayer of thanks for all her many blessings...in fact way too many blessings to count.

CHAPTER TWENTY

December 24th was a beautiful winter day. Remnants of a light snowfall glistened on the trees, and smoke rising from fireplaces in many homes made for a greeting-card scene. Late risers in the Mahoney house were happy to enjoy a leisurely chat over breakfast before starting the long list of activities planned for the day Santa was to arrive.

Kate got busy organizing the holiday dinner, the children were playing Santa's workshop in Mia's room, and Ian and his dad cozied up with extra mugs of coffee by the fireplace to discuss Ian's research and upcoming trip. Big Mike was delighted to hear how far his son had moved toward isolating the genes in the Jatropha plant that might enable it to become a renewable fuel source. While he had never done much research, himself, his work at the university gave him an appreciation for the long and arduous task that lay ahead for the young scientist and his crew.

Ian said, "Dad, you were so right! Choosing graduate students, who can really work together as a team, is critical to the success of this project. I look forward to your meeting my unusual crew…unusual, but extremely competent, hard-working and collaborative." Ian quickly gave his dad an overview of their skills and unique professional portfolios.

"I am so excited, Dad," Ian said. "It is my greatest hope that if the plant becomes a viable fuel source, there will be benefits for both the developed and developing worlds. Sadly, countries like Mozambique are suffering from exploding populations, lack of resources, serious health issues, political corruption to say nothing of friction between populations and even civil wars. In my opinion, none of those challenges can be resolved without adequate financial resources. Improving agriculture and making it profitable – especially in Africa – is one big piece of the puzzle."

"It warms my heart to hear you espousing the Land Grant philosophy, Ian," Mike said. "It was the belief that improving agriculture through research to help populations in the United States and around the world – that provided the foundation for Michigan State and other Land Grant Institutions! Your work is just one more example of how the land grant initiative is still impacting the world in positive ways. I'm so proud that you are trying to make a difference, son."

"Thanks, Dad, I do believe we can make a difference… sometimes I think I want it almost too much, if that makes any sense." Ian mused.

"As the Good Book says in so many ways, my boy, helping others is what this life is all about." Mike responded.

The rest of the day flew by…cooking, listening to carols, visiting neighbors, heading outside to build a snow-family, reading Christmas cards, making Christmas pictures and watching the "Miracle on 47thStreet" while sipping hot chocolate and nibbling on fresh Christmas cookies. Before long it was time to grab a sandwich and some fruit before getting ready for Christmas Eve service at church.

Kate had sent bright red vests for Michael and his dad well in advance of the holidays. And she had chosen a red velvet dress with matching holiday tights for Mia. Michael even sported a red bow tie. They all looked very Christmassy as they headed for the early Christmas Eve service, which was to be held in the little restored church in the Township's Historical Village. Lighted candles flickered in all of the windows, and strains of "Silent Night" welcomed the congregation as they made their way up the front steps.

The altar, banked with red poinsettia plants was a perfect backdrop for the simple white cross. As the service began, groups of children came up to the altar to perform traditional Christmas hymns. Then a teen-aged tenor sang a beautiful arrangement of "Oh, Holy Night." Pastor Becky's message was simple – easily understood by the children. She held everyone's attention as she told the story of the coming of the Christ Child and how His birth impacted the world and each one of us – even today. After her remarks, a short film of the Christmas story was shown – depicting Mary & Joseph in the stable in Bethlehem, the arrival of the shepherds and the three kings and ending with a rejoicing choir of angels.

Because of the historic nature of the little church, fire was always a hazard. So when the lights were dimmed, a group of eight, robed teenagers came down and lined the aisle with lighted candles while the congregation held candles with LED lights. Everyone began singing their much-loved "Silent Night." As always, many a tear was shed while voices young and old joined in the age-old carol.

The moment was especially poignant for Ian…he couldn't help but remember how much Laurie had adored the ending hymn on Christmas Eve. How she would have loved to see her precious darlings in their red velvet, singing her favorite song…their cherubic faces lighted by the flickering candles. As parishioners quietly left the church and moved toward their cars…Ian was actually comforted by the thought that Laurie was, indeed, there that night, looking down upon them…and sending her love and prayers for their safekeeping.

Christmas Eve was bustling with excitement for the Mahoney family. After a light evening meal of hot soup, hot chocolate, and, of course, Jesus's birthday cake, the children prepared a snack plate for Santa. "He will love the iced cookies!" exclaimed Michael.

"…and milk, too!" added Mia.

"Don't forget the reindeer," Mimi offered. "You know they will be hungry, too, after all that flying."

"What do reindeer eat?" asked Mia.

"How about carrots?" suggested Michael.

"Yes, indeed," Papa said, "and I heard that they really like sugar as a little sweet treat, too."

The children, Ian, and the grandparents gathered the snacks and placed them by the fireplace, where Santa would be sure to find them. The stockings were hung (by the chimney with care) so that Santa would see them right away, as well. Finally, the children were hustled off to their beds. After a Christmas bedtime story and Mimi singing "Away in a Manger" for her little ones, the children snuggled into their beds. Ian reminded them that they should close their eyes and think happy thoughts so that sweet dreams would find them soon. There were hugs and kisses and Merry Christmases all around, the lights went off. After placing the gifts under the tree (and taking a bite of Santa's cookie and the reindeer's carrot) it was time for the adults to retire, as well. Soon the Mahoney household was quiet…for at last, they had "all settled down for a long winter's nap."

As predicted the twins were "up with the birds" on Christmas morning and charged into the adults' bedrooms pleading that they get up and see if Santa had come during the night. He had of course.

As the children ran into the family room, shouts and shrieks of joy reverberated through the house.

"Look! He came!!!" squealed Mia.

"He ate the cookies….and the reindeer left paw prints in

the sugar!!!" exclaimed Michael.

"Can we open our presents, Daddy?" begged both children at once.

Dad laughed but said with mock seriousness, "You may open only what's in your stockings before breakfast."

"Oh, Daddy, no!"

"No, I mean it!" Dad said more firmly.

The twins seemed delighted with the small "treasures" that were tucked into their stockings and glad to sit down to the special breakfast of blueberry pancakes topped with frozen peaches that Mimi had prepared. There were foaming mugs of hot chocolate, too.

Tummies full, the twins were ready to see what was under the tree. The first thing they each opened was their package of books. Michael immediately started to read his first book about the Pout, Pout Fish. Mia was wide-eyed as she gazed at vibrant drawings that illustrated her books. "I want to draw birds and butterflies and animals and flowers and a wooly worm just like these!" she said holding up one of the books.

Next came the gifts from Nana and Grandpa Calhoun. They had sent Ian a copy of a recently published book about A & M University. Each of the grandchildren received a rather large money bank. Mike's was a red wooden fire engine and Mia's a sly-looking Siamese cat. Taped to the bottom of each was a new $50 bill.

"WOW!" cried Michael, "Now we're rich!" Everyone laughed. Only recently had Ian started to give them a weekly allowance of $.25. Now that they had their own cash, they were learning to put a nickel in their piggy banks, set a dime aside for Sunday School and keep the remaining $.10 to buy something they especially wanted to have.

"Never too young to start budgeting," remarked their papa, "but I must say that inflation has set in. Remember, Ian, your first allowance was only $.15? Who knows how much the tooth fairy will be expected to leave?"

Kate was surprised that her son had remembered her fondness for Petoskey stones – at least collecting them. She had never had any jewelry made from them so she was delighted to finally own a necklace and matching earrings made from her favorite stone. Big Mike, as his son had predicted, was truly thrilled with the special album of MSU performers. The expression on his face when he offered his thanks, told the whole story. He could hardly wait to listen to the various Spartan ensembles.

Ian's gift from his parents would certainly come in handy on his upcoming trip. They had given him a safari-type vest with more than a dozen zippered pockets. Just the thing in which to carry his passport, credit cards, compass, cell phone and who knows what else!

The children eyed two brightly-wrapped packages tucked behind the tree. "What about these, Daddy, can we open them?" asked Mia.

"Of course," Ian replied. "Who do you think they could be from?"

"Santa!!!" shouted both children at once.

Michael ripped off the paper and tore open the package to reveal a box of pirate Legos. "He did it!!" Michael shouted. "He remembered!! See...I TOLD you we were very good this year!!!" Michael pulled open the box and dumped the Legos all over the floor.

Ian laughed delightedly. "I guess you were, at that," he said. "And what about you, Mia, dear….what do you think Santa brought you?"

Mia carefully removed the ribbon and she said with a serious expression, "I hope he remembered what I wanted for

Christmas, too." The paper was removed and there…in all her glory…was Princess Elsa!

"Yes!!!" Mia exclaimed clutching Elsa and running to her Mimi to show her the sparkly dress and crown that adorned her brand new doll. "I love her!!!" Mia climbed up on Mimi's lap and began talking to, cuddling and kissing her coveted Elsa.

"Hey, guys," Ian interrupted, "There are still a couple of gifts under the tree." Sure enough, there were still two big boxes and two smaller ones. Mike and Mia hurried to pick up the two smaller ones and distributed one to their dad and the other to their grandparents. Sure enough! In each box was a delightful picture of the twins framed in their own creatively-fashioned frames. "What a beautiful picture!" "This is the best gift ever!!" the adults exclaimed. "Thank you so much for thinking of us!"

"We made one for Nana and Grandpa Calhoun too," reported one of the twins. "We made them at school!"

"Well, they are simply beautiful…and I can't wait to display them at home," said Mimi. "Every time I look at these pictures, I will think of my two little Christmas elves and remember what a great time we had visiting!"

"Now what do you suppose is in the other two boxes? Whose are they? Where did they come from?" asked Papa.

"Good question," observed Ian.

"Oh, come on, Papa…you know who they must be from." Mimi laughed. "You see, children, Papa and I sent a letter to Santa and suggested that the two of you deserved some new creative playthings. I guess this might be what he brought."

"But Santa already brought us what we asked for," observed Michael.

"Well," offered Papa, "sometimes, Santa likes to surprise children with things they didn't ask for."

"But the boxes don't have names on them," observed Michael. "How do we know who they're for?"

"Well, maybe that means we're supposed to share them," concluded Mia. "I'll open the one with the red bow, and you open the one with green ribbons." So that's exactly what they did.

"Look what's inside this one." said Mia. "It looks like little logs."

"That's exactly what they are," explained Mimi. "They're called Lincoln Logs, and you can build things with them. Your daddy had some just like it when he was a child."

"Do you think we can build a castle with them?" Mia asked.

"Sure," added Michael, "and a fort, too."

"Open the other box, Mike," said Mia, excitedly.

He ripped off the wrapping and a loud shriek escaped his lips as he saw what was inside. "Dinosaurs!!!" he shouted. "Look at all the dinosaurs!!"

"Hey, there are two of each kind," Mia noticed. "Do you know all of their names, Papa?" Of course, both children loved dinosaurs and had several books about them. "If you don't know them, we can teach you," Mia volunteered. "Mike, we can build a dinosaur castle with our new logs and put the dinosaurs in it."

"I'll get the Lincoln Logs....you grab the dinos," shouted Michael as he headed for an empty space on the floor in front of the fireplace.

"How pleased their mother would be," Ian reflected. Neither child was "sold" on gender-based toys. Mia, like her brother, loved to play with their train; and Michael seemed to also enjoy make-believe with dolls and stuffed animals.

Ian brought in a large waste basket to collect the wrappings, but suddenly he stopped. "Wait a minute. I think there may still be another surprise. Dad, will you please come with me into the garage? Just maybe Santa left something else out there." And the two left the room. Soon they returned – each pushing a shiny new bicycle.

"Oh my goodness," said Mimi. "Santa must have thought you were very good children this year!"

"Bikes!!!!" they shouted, "Our very own bikes!!!"

The twins raced to their dad and papa and immediately began climbing on their respective bikes – silver for Mike and purple for Mia – both had training wheels attached.

"They really have been great kids," thought Ian, pleased with their reaction to all their gifts. Early on they had learned not to ask for things when the three were out shopping. Ian remembered how when he was still quite young, Michael had stated emphatically, "'I want' gets nuffin!" They still seldom asked for things. There had been no nagging for new bikes, although they had commented on how cool it was that several of their friends were able to ride around the neighborhood on two-wheelers. So far, they had both been content with their scooters.

That night, after the children had said their prayers and were tucked in their beds, the adults sat around the fading embers in the fireplace and reflected on the day. They compared it with the almost physical pain of the previous two years. Ian surprised his folks by revealing what had happened to him the night before. "You know, during the service last night at church, I had the most comforting experience. I actually felt Laurie's presence. Do you remember how she loved the candle-lighting and singing of "Silent Night?"

"Oh, yes," Kate nodded, "she would always get misty… especially that first Christmas Eve service with the babies."

"Well, as we were singing," Ian continued. "A warm, comforting feeling came over me. It wasn't sadness, really, it was something else. It was like she was watching us. I actually pictured her smiling down on us. I thought of her praying for us! It was so comforting and reassuring. Last night as I lay in bed, I thought about that feeling. And do you know what I realized?"

"What, son?" his dad asked softly.

"I realized that God really does work in mysterious ways. I never thought I would feel anything but pain when I thought about Laurie…and here I was feeling comforted and reassured by what I now know is our Guardian Angel Laurie." Ian explained calmly. "All of a sudden, I don't feel sad anymore, I feel thankful that God gave me such a special person…and that the children and I were blessed to have her with us for as long as we did…and we are blessed to have her in our hearts forever."

Kate and Mike were speechless. Words failed them both. Quietly, Kate walked over and hugged her son. "I love you so much, Ian."

Mike walked over and hugged Ian, too. "I can't tell you how very proud I am of you, son."

They sat side-by-side-by side on the couch gazing at the fire for several minutes…just letting the happy memories of sweet Laurie flow over them all.

A few minutes later, Kate got up and announced, "Hey, I almost forgot. We have one more present for you, Ian." She left the room and returned a few minutes later carrying a wooden box and handed it to her son.

"What in the world?" he wondered.

Inside he found a dozen small objects carefully wrapped in tissue paper. "Oh, my gosh, Mother!" he exclaimed. "I didn't know you saved them all these years!"

Inside was the collection of Christmas ornaments that he had selected each year as he was growing up. "Why wouldn't

I have saved them?" his mother said. "We have always hung them on our tree. I had intended to give them to you and Laurie but never got around to doing it. When we were in Frankenmuth, it warmed my heart to see you start the same tradition with the twins this year…and the Spartan ornaments they picked look wonderful on the tree? When I saw that…I was so glad that I finally brought your ornaments home to you. This was the perfect year."

"I know that Mia and Mike will enjoy seeing my old ornaments when they wake up in the morning," Ian said. "They will add a nice touch to our tree, which still has plenty of room for additional ornaments."

They all got up from the couch, stretched, and walked around the family room collecting empty dishes which they carried to the kitchen.

"What a special Christmas, Mom," said Ian. "I'm so glad you and Dad were here to share it."

"This is a special Christmas, indeed, Ian," said his mother. "I guess we can think of it as a 'first' in many ways." She gave her son one more hug and started to head off to the bedroom to join her husband.

"Mom" Ian called. She stopped and looked back at her son. "Thank you for everything!"

"Good-night, my dear," she said. "But really…it is the good Lord that we should all be thanking on this holiest of nights." With that she closed her door and silence settled over the Mahoney household.

The next week seemingly flew by. The children were enthralled with their new toys and make-believe took on endless manifestations throughout the week. Elsa huddled with pirates in the Lego/Lincoln Log castle…while dinosaurs threatened them from outside the castle walls. Another time the pirates kidnapped a magic dinosaur and took him on their

Lego ship…only to be rescued by Princess Elsa…and returned to the castle unharmed. Mimi and Papa joined in the make-believe and reveled in the precious moments they shared with their grandchildren.

Ian had to go to his office, of course. There was so much to do to prepare for his upcoming trip. He was relieved that his parents were there to spend time with the kids.

Before they knew it, it was December 31. The senior Mahoneys were looking forward to spending New Year's Eve with the children. They said they were much too old to do much celebrating on New Year's Eve, and they were pleased that Ian had plans for the night…even if those plans involved supervising the church youth group.

The youth activity at the Chapel began with a light meal at 9:00. Former youth group members who were now in college were invited to join the high-school members. There were about 30 young people in all. After the meal, the young people played games and danced to lively music before welcoming the New Year.

Ian joined the Monopoly and Clue group while Peggy served as DJ for those who wanted to dance. They had chosen a variety of "oldies" as well as more contemporary music. At around 11:30, hats and noise makers were passed out to revelers. Game players joined the dancers on the dance floor. Close to midnight the dance tunes turned to slower more romantic melodies.

It had been years since Ian had danced. He always felt that he had two left feet, and since he was about 6'2" and Laurie barely five foot, dancing had always been somewhat awkward for them.

But as Ian watched DJ Peggy spin her tunes, he couldn't help but notice how pretty she was in her long black velvet dress with her hair in a cute knot on top of her head. She was tall and lithe and swaying to the music as she watched the kids with a smile on her face. He wasn't quite sure what came over him…but suddenly, he just took the plunge and walked right up to her and asked her to dance.

Peggy hadn't noticed him approaching…and jumped slightly when he touched her arm. "Why, Ian," she said, somewhat surprised. "Of course…we can't let these kids think we are old 'stick-in-the-muds!'" She grabbed his hand and off they went to the dance floor.

"You are an excellent dancer," Ian observed.

"Must be that you know how to lead," Peggy replied with a smile.

As the music continued on auto…the couple danced to several more tunes. They were totally at ease with one another, chuckling at the antics of some of the teenagers, and stumbling once or twice themselves. The two continued dancing until the clock began to signal the New Year. Bells around town started to ring. Everyone cheered, starting blowing horns and shaking noisemakers. Then everyone started hugging each other and passing around kisses. It seemed very natural for the two adults to join in the affectionate fun. After a quick hug, they exchanged a pleasant not-so-brief kiss. "My," thought Ian, "what was that?"

Peggy, for her part, was a little breathless as she gazed into Ian's eyes…really gazed into them for the very first time. Peggy was all tingly and blushed deeply. "Happy New Year, Ian," she whispered. "I hope this will be a very special year for you and those adorable children of yours. I wish you all nothing but the best."

"And to you, Miss Peggy Gerber," he said, also blushing slightly. "I hope that all your New Year's resolutions and dreams come true!"

Peggy smiled and closed her eyes. She said a silent prayer of thanks for the unexpected gift of this magical moment the two of them had shared. Just a moment in time, she told herself…but perhaps one that held promise…

The evening ended with a brief devotion led by Bob Lane and another college student. Dr. Mahoney was home and in bed before 1:00. As he drifted off to sleep, he thought of the very pleasant way the evening had ended. He was never much of a ladies' man, but the New Year's kiss with Peggy Gerber was quite an unexpected and pleasant surprise. He certainly did not regret approaching her…nor their short, but somehow intimate contact. In fact, he thought, he looked forward to seeing her again. Now, when was that next youth group meeting? He started to mentally count the days.

Peggy could not sleep that night. The unexpected, but welcome encounter with Ian Mahoney at midnight threw her off her game. "What was it about that man?" she wondered. He certainly was totally unlike Donn Bahler. He had no "come on." He seemed serious and a little stand-offish, and yet…he had asked her to dance…and kissed her! That kiss surprised her…and her reaction to it surprised her even more. She felt warm and tingly all over just remembering it.

"What is wrong with me?" she asked herself. "I'm reading way too much into a little New Year's Eve peck." But something inside her refused to deny the kiss was special. "And," she said to herself, "I know I saw something in his eyes that said it was special for him, too." With that thought… comforting and unsettling at the same time…she drifted off to sleep.

CHAPTER TWENTY-ONE

Kate was looking forward to spending time with her sweet grandchildren, helping them read their new books and build many creative structures with Lincoln Logs and Legos. Maybe if the weather was nice, they could take a walk around the neighborhood or spend some time playing in the snow.

Ian and his dad decided to head to campus. Most of the students were home for winter break, and many faculty members were gone, as well. The parking lot was almost empty, and the vacant hallways echoed with the sound of their footsteps as they made their way to Ian's office.

"This is some new building!" observed Mike. "It really makes a lot of sense to have the horticulture people here, along with the plant-and-soils staff. I always hoped that someday that would happen. That old horticulture building, while close to Agriculture Hall, was always far enough away to discourage ongoing, face-to-face conversations with those who needed to work together on joint projects."

"Here's the faculty directory, Dad, one of the few that's available. Everything's online now, but sometimes it's just easier to have a hard copy. I know I was grateful that they salvaged one for me when I got here. Take a look, perhaps some of your old cronies still have offices on campus and maybe one or two are even here today."

"Thanks, Son, I'll do that. I'd actually like to take a walk around and see how they've re-assigned offices and where they've placed the labs and classrooms now. Please don't feel that you have to entertain me. I'll just mosey around on my

own, and then perhaps we can grab a bite of lunch before
your meeting this afternoon. Like I said, there's plenty for
me to do...and lots to read here in your office." Mike waved
over his head as he headed down the hall to check out the new
building.

Left on his own, Ian prepared a list of questions that
needed to be discussed during the afternoon meeting. No
doubt Christian would have his own set of questions, also.

The departmental budget officer and the foreign-travel
coordinator would be attending the meeting this afternoon,
as well. Their help with financing, travel preparation and
overseas protocols would be invaluable to Christian and Ian.
He hoped the meeting wouldn't take more than two hours
so there would be plenty of time for him and Christian to
inventory all the supplies that had arrived over the past week.
Given the avalanche of holiday mailings, there was always
uncertainty about how fast December orders would be filled.

Ian decided that to save time, he'd order pizza for lunch
for himself, his dad and Christian. Shortly before noon, both
Mike and Christian arrived at his office, and the three had a
chance to visit while eating lunch. Ian was pleased to observe
how easily his father interacted with the young man from
Mozambique. Clearly, he had not lost his skill of drawing out
shy graduate students and learning about their interests. Ian
had always admired this ability of his father and tried to do
the same when dealing with students, himself.

Shortly before 1:30, Ian and Christian headed for an
adjacent conference room. The consultants arrived about
the same time. There was a lot to cover, so they kept the
pleasantries brief.

"Let me begin," said the travel coordinator. "Here are
your plane tickets, boarding passes and several copies of the

itinerary to get you from Michigan to Maputo, your first stop in Mozambique. You will also notice the confirmation for your five-night stay in what should be a satisfactory hotel. I spoke with the Office of African Studies before deciding where to have you stay. They suggested the Radisson Blu because it was close to the government offices, so you won't need to rent a car."

"I know where that hotel is located," noted Christian. "It should be quite convenient, and we will be able to walk to most offices as well as restaurants and other businesses." Then he shyly confessed that he had never stayed there, since it was far too pricey for him or his family.

"I know it's not cheap, but safety and convenience are always major concerns when we send people out of the country. The representatives from Washington who will be part of your group should feel that this hotel is up to their expectations, as well," she added.

The travel consultant then asked if the travelers had received all their vaccinations yet. Both men answered in the affirmative, but they went through the list of recommendations together one more time, just to make sure. Ian was glad that he had taken care of his well in advance of their anticipated departure; and Christian, as an African citizen, had met all his medical requirements even before arriving in the U.S. six month earlier.

A discussion about expected weather conditions followed. The plan had been to avoid the tourist season -- June, July, August and September – and hopefully escape the monsoon period. Those months were really the least desirable since that was the hottest part of the year, humidity was high and cyclones were quite common.

Temperatures in January averaged between 72 and 79 degrees. February temps were a little higher – up to 86 degrees. There was some rain during those two months, but it was relatively pleasant. There was "dazzling sunshine" in the capitol city, according to the tourist magazines. Ian was glad that they had selected January and February for their trip to the southern hemisphere.

Christian was helpful in talking about the appropriate clothing to take along. They would, of course, need some business attire for meetings with government officials in Maputo, but he assured the group that dress on campus was quite informal. For their travels into the country, they could wear short pants if they wished, but often long sleeved shirts and pants were a better choice since insects could be bothersome in low-lying areas. Of course, a broad-brimmed sun hat, sturdy walking shoes, an umbrella, light- weight, rain-proof jacket and sunscreen were also essential.

Next the group moved to financial procedures for the trip. Ian, as head of the party, was given a special university-issued credit card to cover his expenses and those of Christian. It would also cover costs of an interpreter and the driver they would hire, once they arrived in country. The D.C. participants would cover their own expenses. The budget officer had also arranged for some traveling money in the currency of Mozambique, known as (MZN) to take care of various other expenses upon arrival. He indicated that Ian was free to pick up the tab for meal and other expenses, during their interactions with locals. He cautioned, however, that Ian needed to document the reasons for meetings, record the number attending the event and itemize the costs involved. Before the meeting ended, he gave the travelers a small box containing suitable items to distribute as tokens of appreciation for their Mozambique hosts and contacts.

Ian and Christian thanked the two staff members for their help and heaved a joint sigh of relief, knowing that they were as prepared as was possible. Ian also told Christian that he had gotten an international drivers' license and special chargers and satellite access for his cell phone and laptop.

Ian and Christian then headed to the storage room where all recent shipments would have been placed. As they had anticipated, all their boxes were stacked in one section of the room. Out came Ian's checklist. "Good," he reported, "here are our rainproof, lightweight tents, along with a pair of sleeping bags. I know we will have to carry everything when we are in the bush, so it's a good thing they won't be too heavy."

"We can always pick up some inexpensive rubber boots if we need them," remarked the grad student. "What about the special lab materials we need? Have they arrived?"

"Fortunately, yes! I tried to keep the number down, since we'll have to backpack them. Most of the data will be recorded electronically, but we do have to carry several weather-controlled containers in which we'll ship live plant material home."

After finalizing their inventory, and wishing each other good luck with their final packing, the pair separated until their meeting on January 4th. That was the day when their trip to Christian's birth country and their research adventure would begin. In the meantime, both had plenty of material to review, since the onsite data collection was so crucial to the overall project and would guide their future course of action.

Satisfied that nothing more could be done, Ian joined his dad back in the office. On the drive home, he told his dad about the meeting.

"Things have really improved since I was a professor here," remarked the older Mahoney. "We had to figure out travel logistics on our own back then. It was rough going overseas when you were as inexperienced as many of us were our first foreign assignments. I think that because of former President Hannah's commitment to international work, the university learned to better-prepare those who were representing the university abroad."

"Lucky us!" responded his son, "I, for one, appreciate that you and others paved the way for seamless international experiences...both for student learning and for research. I'm so excited to get over there and start collecting data. I have to admit, though, I'm really going to miss the kids. Once, again, I'm so thankful that you and Mom are willing to stay with Mike and Mia."

"We are the thankful ones, My Boy," said his dad. "What an amazing gift your trip has turned out to be for us – an opportunity to be with our precious grandchildren for three whole weeks! Your mother and I can't wait, either!"

As they turned into the driveway, they were greeted by three snow-covered, tightly bundled snow bunnies.

"How do you like our fort, Dad?" Michael asked excitedly.

"Whoa!" exclaimed Ian. "That is quite a fortress! So... who did the heavy work? Did YOU roll those big snowballs, Mia?"

"Oh, Daddy," Mia laughed. "Mimi had to help us. Do you like it?"

"I can't wait to play in it myself," Dad said.

"Well, that will have to wait til later," Mimi announced. "We are frozen and our mittens are sopping. I think it's time for supper and some hot chocolate."

As they all trooped toward the house, Ian smiled to himself. "Yes," he thought, "the kids will be in the best hands while I'm gone. They'll have fun...Mom and Dad will revel in their time with their grandkids...and I won't have to worry about any of them."

"Hey, I want some of that cocoa, too," Ian shouted laughingly as he joined the snow-encrusted crew at the back door, and they all went inside to warm up.

CHAPTER TWENTY-TWO

The plane trip to Maputo was quite long, and the round trip ticket cost nearly $5,000, even though it was not in first class. The Michigan travelers, however, were able to get some sleep and were wide awake when the plane landed at the airport early the next morning. They collected their luggage and immediately hailed one of the mini-bus taxis called "chapas" to take them the short distance – 3 kilometers (1.9 miles) to the Radisson Blu Hotel.

After checking into their suite, the two men stepped outside to look around. Christian told his companion that the city had several popular names including "the Pearl of the Indian Ocean." It was, indeed, an interesting and exotic locale. Ian was anxious to get to know the city.

The other members of their party would be checking in later that day, so the two MSU representatives had plenty of time to unpack, discuss the agenda for the coming week, grab a bite to eat and take a brief walking tour of the city. They had time to stop at the Fisheries Museum, said to be the best museum in the city. After returning to the hotel, they were able to catch a nap before meeting the others for a 7:00 p.m. dinner meeting in a small conference room adjacent to the suite.

The two representatives from the U.S. Department of Energy, George Stone and Fred Miller, had met Ian and Chris during their visit to Michigan in the fall. However, they were not acquainted with the representatives from USAID's Bureau of Economic Growth, Agriculture and Trade Program and the

Office of the Director of Research of the Foreign Agriculture Service. Henry Holt and Dr. Andrew Worthington both had long resumes of government service and were well aware of the substantial work that had been undertaken in southern Africa.

Holt and Worthington had set up a series of meetings for the next two days with Mozambique government officials who were interested in expanding the growth and export of biofuels. These included the Ministers of Finance, Interior, Industry and Commerce along with the Minister of Foreign Affairs and Cooperation. They shared brief biographies of each of the officials, several of whom had studied in the U.S. or Canada. Unfortunately, there was no U.S. Agricultural Attaché in Mozambique at this time. A translator, part of the American Embassy staff, would be present for all sessions.

Ian took copious notes, as did Christian. It was agreed that Dr. Worthington would preside over the first day of meetings. Mr. Holt would chair the meetings on day two. Ian had prepared a brief summary of the project that had brought them to Mozambique. His report highlighted the work they expected to do when they visited the agricultural areas. If they were lucky, on day three they would have some time with the President's Special Assistant as well as several media representatives, who had actively supported Jatropha production in the past and appeared to be open to promoting it now and in the future. Tentative plans also included a day at the university exploring mutual interests with researchers there.

The meetings with the Mozambique officials went quite smoothly. Clearly the Ministers were skilled political appointees, eager to convey the impression that they looked favorably on America as a continuing partner in the economic development of their country. They went out of their way to assure their American guests that previous tenuous relations between their countries were in the past. Those tensions and the resulting withdrawal of some U.S. funds had been caused by human rights concerns…concerns which had been aggressively addressed under new government leadership.

Hearing about the nation's growing GDP brought favorable responses from the Americans, who were pleased to learn of the progress being made in the export of cashew nuts, cotton and prawns. When it came to the discussion about biofuel crops – particularly Jatropha – the Ministers expressed their grave disappointment in the failure of previous efforts to produce profitable results. Foreign investments had been withdrawn over the past five years, resulting in hardship for the small farmers who had hoped to benefit from what promised to be their salvation. The various government officials, like their counterparts in many parts of the world, tended to be risk-averse. They favored investments where the outcome was guaranteed. Who could blame them?

It was clear to everyone that there was still much to learn about modifying the wild Jatropha plant, and scientific research in Mozambique was very limited. Ian had his work cut out for him! Everyone agreed that there were issues existing in both the U.S. and Mozambique related to infrastructure. Many roads in Mozambique were in poor shape and some even impassable. The Americans admitted that many of their rural roads were not up to handling the heavy truck traffic required to transport huge quantities of biomass crops such switch grass and corn stover needed to produce ethanol. The lack of updated communications systems in rural Mozambique was identified as another potential challenge to converting a wild plant into an economically-viable biofuel.

Ian asked about the status of hard science research in their higher education institutions. The Ministers explained that although considerable progress had been made to increase literacy through mandated compulsory education for children and youth, emphasis on higher education lagged behind. An increasing number of public and private institutions were being created, but since presently the universities lacked scientific researchers and even facilities for conducting research, emphasis was currently being placed on graduate programs in education and diplomacy. The Ministers encouraged Christian to return to his homeland after completing his doctorate to help them begin to develop an institutional research focus and also extended an open invitation to Ian to return often.

That evening word came that a special assistant in the president's office, as well as several media representatives would see them the next day. Stone and Miller from the Department of Energy agreed to take the lead in those discussions. Christian and Ian would handle discussions when they moved out into the country to interview growers, both small farmers and those still attached to previous Jatropha plantations.

On day three the sessions were quite different from those held the previous two days. The aide said that the president was still optimistic about the future of Jatropha and said that even though he was not promoting it as vigorously as had his predecessor when the latter went from village to village telling people to plant Jatropha trees. At that time it was believed that this home-grown fuel could turn life around in small villages.

According to the aide, the current president's primary goal is to increase the GDP and thus improving human development, insuring equality and extending life expectancy. The President believes that agriculture remains at the top of the priorities on the national development agenda. The focus

is on both food security and income. That's why the current
President expects to launch a major agricultural campaign,
they were told.

The two members of the media were also optimistic about
the emphasis on agriculture. They confirmed their belief that
if – or when – scientists were able to deliver the promised
high oil-content Jatropha species that thrived on poor land,
the so-called miracle plant would again claim a profitable
position in the world market. They indicated that once they
saw positive results, they would be more than happy to
publicize its success. The challenge was in the hands of the
researchers such as Ian and his colleagues to find the species
that would return Jatropha to its former "economic savior"
status in Mozambique.

Although they had hoped to be able to share data and
research expectations with other scientists at the university,
the clear message that they picked up from the Ministers
suggested otherwise, so it was decided that only Ian and
Christian would visit the campus and only for a half day. The
others would spend the day reflecting on what they had learned
to date and develop a preliminary "After-Action Report."

While the MSU team was pleased to visit the Universidad
Eduardo Monoplane and interact with several professors, it
was clear that there was very little research underway that
would impact the Jatropha investigation. Perhaps in the future
professors could conduct follow-up visits with the small
farmers who were growing the crops or serve in some other
related capacity. Tracking the experiences of these producers
would be of value over time. For now, though, they were
happy to receive the professors' blessing for the project and
their offer of assistance wherever possible.

CHAPTER TWENTY-THREE

Meanwhile back on Ottawa Drive, things were going as planned. Papa had taken the children to the "Y" for several swimming lessons which they loved. They also delighted in hearing Mimi tell stories about when their daddy was a boy. Big Mike attended a breakfast with a group of his former colleagues, and Kate accepted an invitation to participate in the January meeting of a campus woman's club she had chaired during their time in Michigan. Although the group had changed its name to broaden membership, its focus continued to be on earning money for scholarships. So the "family" was settled in and everyone was very busy.

They were all looking forward to their skype visit with Ian from Mozambique, so they all gathered around as Papa read parts of Dad's long E-mail. In addition to telling stories about Africa the kids would enjoy, Ian described in detail the capitol city and early meetings the team had been having. Ian told them that he might have trouble sending messages once they moved into the rural areas since the telecommunications systems were not the most reliable.

The children and Mimi and Papa quickly composed a response telling Ian everything they had been doing in Okemos and sent it off.

Time flew by as they continued with their routines in the Mahoney household. Mimi began to get a little sad, as their departure date approached.

"How quickly the time here has passed," said Kate a few days before heading home.

"It's really been wonderful," agreed her husband. "I'm so glad that we were able to be here and allow Ian to do his work without worry about the children. He's doing an amazing job. Being successful under such challenging circumstances just shows how well he's able to focus and adapt. He is both knowledgeable and flexible. I'm so proud of him."

"Yes, and he's done an amazing job of parenting, as well. The twins seem so bright, happy and well adjusted," responded Kate. "I'm proud of him, too."

Sunday afternoon the four of them were invited to attend a special program at the Indian Cultural Center. Rod Lane, their neighbor, was presenting an interactive program based on the research he was doing for the Chief Okemos biography. Upon their arrival, they were surprised to be greeted by Peggy Gerber. The grandparents hadn't been aware that the twin's teacher was a regular volunteer at the Center. Mimi noted that Miss Gerber certainly appeared to be an active, involved, caring person. Her role that afternoon was hostess. She greeted the quartet warmly and gave each twin a little hug before escorting them to seats near the front of the gathering room.

Rod soon appeared, walking straight and tall. "Oh, look!" giggled Mia. "Mr. Rod is pretending to be an Indian." Sure enough, he was wearing beaded moccasins and a tan leather-like loose shirt. Around his forehead, he wore a leather band with a long feather standing straight up in the back.

"But he doesn't have on any war paint," remarked her brother.

Mr. Lane welcomed the group and described how the presentation would proceed. "Rather than lecture, I've decided to have a question-and-answer format today. So, to start, who can tell me whether or not Chief Okemos was born in our town?"

There was some disagreement about the answer.

"Actually, he wasn't. He was born in Shiawassee County in about 1775. That's east of here, but he loved to hunt and fish in this area. He's also said to have planted corn along the Red Cedar River. Can anyone tell me the name of his tribe?"

"I think he was a Mohawk," said one child.

"No, he was a Kiowa or an Ojibway," responded another older child.

"You are right," said the speaker. "He was actually an Ojibway or Chippewa; the two are really the same. Can anyone tell us where this tribe lived?"

"Sure," said a teenager, "they lived in Michigan."

That brought a laugh from everyone.

Rod laughed along, "I guess that was pretty obvious. But did you know they also lived in Minnesota and Wisconsin?"

"I think I knew that," replied one of the women, "and I seem to recall reading that they were also in some parts of Canada."

"Good! Now you have the picture," Rod continued. "The women farmed the land, and the men were trappers, hunters and fishermen. Sometimes the men went to war to protect their families. Does anyone know what kind of homes they had?"

"Either wigwams or tepees," came a reply.

"Yes, when they formed a more or less permanent village, they would build sturdy birch bark wigwams; but when they were on the move, they chose tepees made of animal hide, since they could be folded and were easier to carry."

"Did they have a real language?" asked a girl. "We usually only hear about Indians using hand motions and sort of grunting and saying "'ugh.'"

"That's another myth, promulgated by old movies, that I hope to denounce," Rod said patiently. "The tribe was probably an Algonkian-speaking tribe. Both men and women were said to be talented story-tellers, musicians and artists. They were especially well known for their beautiful beadwork, birch bark boxes and baskets, as well as sturdy birch bark canoes."

"Did the men ever wear big feather headdresses?" asked one young man.

"Traditionally, they wore headbands such as I'm wearing with just a single feather standing up in back," Rod indicated his own headband, "but in the 1800s some Chippewa chiefs began wearing long headdresses like the Sioux. Most men and women wore their hair in long braids, but a few men sometimes shaved their hair in the Mohawk style."

"What did they use for money or did they just barter for things they wanted?" asked one of the men.

"Actually, they crafted white and purple shells into what they called wampum and used it as currency," Ron explained.

Mike Mahoney raised his hand and asked, "When my son and I were members of Indian Guides, he chose the name Growling Bear because the bear was reportedly the symbol on the Chief's totem pole. Why was that? Did his tribe hold the bear to be sacred or something?"

"You raise an interesting question, Mike. That's still a bit of a mystery. Recently, I read about another tribe, the Kiowas. The bear was very special to them. Men who had 'bear' as a part of their names were believed to have special medicinal powers. Because they were thought to be blessed, when others spoke to them, they weren't even allowed to say the word 'bear.' A Kiowa was not to kill a bear, much less eat its flesh even if he was facing hunger."

"That's certainly interesting," added Mike, "especially since I believe that tribe was also located out west."

"Indeed it was," agreed Rod. "That's why I intend to research the matter further. Just why did Chief Okemos have a bear on his totem? Let's hope I can discover the truth. The Ojibwas called themselves 'The Original People' or 'The True People.' The translation of the word, 'Chippewa' is 'Puckered up.' We think that's because they traditionally wore moccasins with a puckered seam across the top."

"Didn't the Indians fight with the British during the Revolutionary War?" asked one of the adults.

"The Ojibwa sided with the French in the French and Indian Wars," the teacher explained, "because the French had treated them quite well in their growing fur trade. But as you rightly suggest, they later fought with the British against the Americans. Chief Okemos was severely injured in the Battle of Sandusky Bay. That battle left all of the Indians in their group dead except him and his cousin. Many Indians from the Detroit area chose to fight against the Americans because they feared that they would move into Indian-held lands."

Glancing at his watch, Rod said, "I can't believe the time has flown by so quickly. You've asked wonderful questions and given me much fuel for thought, and I appreciate your interest."

Peggy moved to the front of the room. "Thank you, Mr. Lane, for clearing up some of the myths about Indians and helping us get to know our town's namesake a little better. Now," said their hostess, "if there are no more questions, show Mr. Lane how much we appreciate his presentation and take a look at the special display that he has set up on the other side of the room. Do help yourself to nuts and dried fruit, typical foods you might eat, if you were an Indian hungry for an afternoon snack."

A round of applause followed, and the audience rose to take a look at the display of beaded necklaces and moccasins, birch bark boxes and baskets, strings of wampum and other small items decorated with feathers. They also helped themselves to the surprisingly tasty treats that were being offered.

"Do museums ever have collections of Indian bones," one teenager asked, munching on some dried apricots.

"Not anymore," Rod replied. "At one time, people thought they were relics worth salvaging and displaying, but eventually the government put a stop to the practice. Many bones were returned to their Indian descendants, so they could bury them in a sacred place. Every once in awhile we still read about bones being discovered as new ground is ploughed, but these bones are removed from the earth and taken to suitable Indian burial grounds, often on an Indian reservation. We do have such places here in Michigan, you know."

Soon people began to drift out of the Cultural Center.

"What an interesting way to spend an afternoon," thought Mike Mahoney as he drove everyone home to Ottawa Drive. "That cultural center adds so much to the community," he remarked. The kids bobbed their heads in agreement in the backseat. Yes, he would miss Okemos when they left, and being around the little ones, of course.

He and Kate had totally enjoyed their time in their old hometown, and they were also looking forward to spending a day with the Calhouns. Laurie's parents would arrive tomorrow so that they could take over babysitting duty when the Mahoneys left the following day. The two couples had become warm friends during the time their children were married, and they had not seen each other for several years.

Before retiring that night, Kate made lists indicating the twins' schedule, emergency phone numbers and several other hints she had picked up that would make the house run more smoothly when the other grandparents were in charge.

Little did she know that her carefully-planned schedule would fall apart and there would be complications that no one could have anticipated. Ian had been so careful to put back-up systems in place for the care of his children. But Ian was in rural Mozambique at the moment…and unable to communicate with his family. He certainly would have been horrified to know that his carefully-crafted plans were about to be trashed. He also didn't know at that moment, how God's grace would take over to ensure his precious children were safe and well-cared-for in his absence.

CHAPTER TWENTY-FOUR

Upon returning to the house after delivering the twins to school, Kate received a phone call that caused her momentary panic. Helen Calhoun, although a seasoned rider, had been thrown by her horse and broke her leg and wrist. Clearly, she and Hal would not be able to come to Michigan to relieve the Mahoneys.

Kate expressed deep concern for Helen's injuries and wished her a speedy recovery. She calmly assured Hal that even though she and Mike had to leave, Ian had made alternative arrangements with the twins regular nanny, so the twins would be in good hands.

But on the inside, Kate was extremely upset that she and Mike couldn't stay beyond their scheduled departure date. Fortunately, thank the Good Lord, Mrs. Harding was on stand-by for just such an eventuality.

"Mrs. Harding," she said, when Ida answered her call on the second ring. "This is Kate Mahoney. I hope you've been having a great time with your sisters...and I hate to bother you there, but we have an emergency here. Ian told us that you had to be our back-up for the children, if the need arose. I just learned that the Calhouns, the twins other grandparents, aren't able to come to Michigan. Mrs. Calhoun was seriously injured in a fall from her horse. Is there any way you can get back to take over the care of the children when we leave the day after tomorrow?"

"Oh, my, I hope she's going to be okay!" Ida responded. "Of course, I'll come to help! I know it won't be the same as having their grandparents on duty, but frankly, I've been missing the little ones, and they're used to me being with them. I know we'll be fine until their dad returns."

"Great! You are a Godsend to us all, Ida," sighed Kate in a relieved tone. "Now I know why Ian has such trust in you. We'll go ahead with our return as planned. I'll try to leave the house in good shape and see that the refrigerator and cupboards are well-stocked."

The twins were sorry that they wouldn't be seeing Grandpa and Nana, but Mimi assured them that the Calhouns would make the trip as soon as Nana was feeling better.

Mrs. Harding arrived from her visit in Indiana, and the Mahoneys left for South Carolina on schedule; life continued in an almost normal fashion—at least for several more days. Then another unexpected event derailed everything! Around noon on Friday, Ida received a frightening phone call from her son-in-law in Colorado.

"Mom," exclaimed the upset young man, "we just got some very bad news. Alice has to stay in bed for the rest of the pregnancy, since there's been a dangerous rise in her blood pressure and several other alarming conditions. Of course, I have to work...and I'm worried about Alice and Tommy. What in the world are we going to do?"

""Please calm down, Rick, let me get this straight," replied the usually-calm Ida. "Did you just see her doctor? Is that who diagnosed the problem? Will she and the baby be alright?"

"It was just supposed to be a routine appointment," Rick explained. "We had no idea that there were any problems. Her doctor feels quite sure that bed-rest until she reaches term will ensure that both she and the baby will be fine. She also said that this happens more often than we realized."

"That is a comfort," Ida soothed. "What can I do, Rick? You know I'll do anything I can to help."

"I hate to ask," Rick said hesitantly, "but would it be possible for you to come and stay with us until the little one arrives—probably in another five or six weeks? Unfortunately, I can't take time off from my job, and we don't have anyone to stay with Tommy or to take care of Alice. I know that you're staying with the Mahoney youngsters until their father returns from Africa so I really hate to ask, but I just don't know what else to do. I'm so worried!"

"I'll do my best to get there as soon as possible, Rick," assured his mother-in-law, sounding much more confident than she felt. "Tell Alice and Tommy that Grandma loves them and will be in Denver soon."

She hung up the phone and closed her eyes, "Now what in the world am I going to do? No wonder the Bible says that sometimes the really tough decisions are between the good and the good – not necessarily between good and evil."

"Well," she said to herself, "I've always believed that when things get tough…call your minister." So it was natural that the first call she made was to Pastor Becky. After hearing about the problem, the pastor immediately dropped everything and headed over to the Mahoney's.

The two women began to explore possible options. Clearly, they couldn't ask the Mahoneys to return from South Carolina. How about neighbors? Was there a family in the neighborhood with whom the children could stay? Probably not, since the Mahoneys really didn't know the neighbors that well yet.

"Too bad," said the pastor, "that Gladys Mason, a retired nurse in the congregation, was spending the winter in Florida. Gladys would have been the perfect answer – another grandmother the children knew as one of their Sunday school teachers."

Hiring a stranger was not even a consideration, both women agreed.

"Well," suggested Becky, "since our family lives next door, and we are probably Ian's closest friends, we will just have to step in and cover all bases until he returns. I can take Mike and Mia to school, and Rod can collect them in the afternoon. Lib – and even at times Bob – can keep them occupied 'til suppertime. Then either Rod or I will spend the night with them. Sleeping in their own beds would seem to be best. What do you think? Will that work?"

"That would certainly take care of things," Ida said, "and it is so kind of you to disrupt your lives like that to help out. But, really, that would put quite a strain on your family. That's more of a burden than you should be expected to carry. I wish that I could think of a better solution."

"I know that if the Lane family needed help in an emergency," Becky replied, "you and others of the congregation would be just as willing to step up and help out. After all, it is just following the teachings of Jesus to help others in need. It's decided, then. I think I'll give Peggy Gerber a call and have her meet with me this afternoon to fill her in on the plan. I'll be happy to pick the kids up from school this afternoon. Meanwhile, you get on the phone and arrange to fly to Colorado as soon as possible. How are you fixed financially? That can be an expensive ticket at the last minute."

"That's no problem," Ida said, relieved, "thanks to the big bonus that Mr. Mahoney gave me as a Christmas gift."

Peggy greeted her pastor warmly when the latter arrived to collect the twins. The four then went to the faculty breakroom where a plate of chocolate chip cookies waited on the table.

"Mrs. Harding has to go to Colorado unexpectedly," Pastor Becky explained. "Her daughter's had some pregnancy complications, and the family needs her."

"But what about us?" asked Michael nervously.

"Daddy won't let us stay alone, even in the daytime," chimed in Mia as they were trying to understand what was happening.

"Of course not," said Pastor Becky. "You will become part of our family for awhile."

"But you have to work and go to school!" responded Mia.

"You won't have time to take care of us," said Michael, his lower lip beginning to tremble as both children tried to hold back the tears.

"We'll be just like orphans," whispered Mia, remembering a story they'd read recently.

"That's not true, sweetheart," said Peggy, gathering the children in her arms. "You have a daddy and two sets of grandparents who love you! Just think of all the other church and school friends and neighbors who care about you and are really like family, too."

"Of course, you'll have to get used to my cooking," laughed Becky. "I'm certainly not a chef like Mrs. Harding. Mr. Lane and I will take turns spending nights with you, and both Libby and/or Bob can be your companions after school. You'll be able to sleep in your own beds in your own house until your daddy gets home. Won't that work?"

There was silence all around for what seemed like a long time. Then Michael wrinkled his forehead and proposed another solution.

"What about you, Miss Peggy?" Michael proposed. "Couldn't you be our substitute nanny until Daddy gets back home? We would be really good and help a lot…could you do it, please?"

"Yes, Yes!" exclaimed Mia. "We'll make our beds, pick up toys and go to bed at 8:00 without fussing! Please, Miss

Peggy, please?"

The two women looked at one another in surprise. It was strange that neither of them had come up with that particular solution. Peggy chuckled and said with a smile, "You know what…I think that sounds like a fine idea. Once when Mother and Dad were ill with the flu and nobody was home but me and my two younger brothers, I had to play Mom. That was a lot harder than being your substitute nanny. Let's do it! I'll go home and pick up some extra clothes and be with you by 5:30. Okay?"

Rebecca returned the pair to their home. On the way there, the twins talked excitedly about Miss Peggy coming to stay with them. Mia told Pastor Becky that she knew Miss Peggy would be a mommy someday. "This way, she can get some practice…with us!" she said brightly.

The older woman smiled and said nothing. "Who knows," she thought, "there may be more truth to their thinking than even they know."

So for the next week, a new family unit was created. Mia said that her room would be Peggy's, and she would sleep on the spare bunk in her brother's room – which was the way they worked it when Mrs. H or the grandparents spent the night. They were surprised when Miss Peggy joined them on her knees as they said their bed-time prayers that evening. They knew that grownups, including their father, prayed, but no one had actually knelt with them when they said their prayers before.

"Thank you, God," said Mia, "for bringing Miss Peggy to stay with us."

"Thanks for giving me the great idea," added Michael.

Peggy smiled as she looked down at the two sweet cherubs. She was enjoying every minute of her time with these two adorable little beings. What a blessing this unexpected emergency turned out to be for her!

The days passed quickly. Libby came several afternoons to free Peggy to run errands and enjoy a bit of freedom from her charges. Rod took them for a swim on Saturday morning, and one of the neighbors invited the pair for a "play date" Sunday afternoon. The only thing that troubled their caregiver was the fact that several times one of the children had a nightmare and called out for Daddy. She knew she was keeping them safe, but she hoped and prayed that she was making them feel secure, as well. Little did any of them know at the time, how Mother Nature in far-off Mozambique might complicate their lives even further.

While marriage and starting a family of her own had always been part of Peggy's long-term plan, it had not been an immediate priority for the single woman. Rather, it had been on hold as she began her career as a Montessori educator. After all, she was still young and needed to meet her obligation to be a Directress at Ojibwa for five years, a promise she'd made to the Board who funded her certification program. This year would fulfill that commitment…just as she was approaching her 30th birthday. Spending time with these munchkins made her start thinking about her future as a mom. "Yes," she thought, "I do look forward to nurturing and caring for my own little ones someday. It's just in my blood. I know I will love being a mom."

With that, she said a little prayer, "Thank you, God, for giving me these beautiful weeks with the Mahoney children. And please, help me find the path that will someday lead me to the perfect life-mate and a family of my own."

CHAPTER TWENTY-FIVE

Meanwhile, the weather in Mozambique had deteriorated. The rains that came were heavy and steady. The group of travelers had some concerns about the conditions they would face as they traveled inland to rural areas. They reached the first stop at a former Jatropha plantation in late afternoon. After a night at a small local guesthouse, they prepared for a meeting with the retainer, or caretaker, who had been left by the investment group to look after the property.

They met in what had been the main office of the operation. The hectares that had once been green with rows of growing Jatropha trees or bushes lay fallow, awaiting the next agricultural venture, if one was ever to come again. The retainer said that he sincerely doubted any rational investor would gamble on a business as risky as the last one. He felt the previous investors had known very little about agriculture and were only interested in making a quick profit.

Realizing that they would not get additional useful feedback from that retainer, the group thanked him for his time and pushed on. The next site was some distance away, and they had to negotiate extremely muddy roads caused by flooding from the substantial rain. Some roads had such deep ruts that they were practically impassable and no longer safe. Fortunately, the local driver was used to these road conditions; and the van, while rather old, seemed to be well maintained. The driver chose to take a longer, alternative route to keep the vehicle from becoming mired in the mud. That road was slightly better, and they finally arrived at their destination; but many daylight hours were lost.

Ian hoped that the hot, wet, humid weather and bumpy roads would not be too uncomfortable for his older traveling companions. Fortunately, all had come prepared with rain gear, and he had extra insect repellant to share. He crossed his fingers that the food supplies would be sufficient.

The second visit proved to be more helpful. There the retainer was an agronomist, who was more aware of what had gone wrong with the earlier Jatropha enterprise. He echoed the concerns the researchers had already observed on their own. Infrastructure, such as roads and equipment was, perhaps the biggest problem. But the retainer also expressed concerns about the seeds, themselves. He had actually done some soil research on his own. He explained that during the plantation's short operation, he had set aside several small sections where the crop could be planted in different soil types. His hypothesis had been that soil type would have little impact on the quality of the seeds produced or the yield per hectare.

However, he had been wrong. Soil type did make a difference. The better the soil, the better the quality and quantity of oil seeds that were produced. His soil experiment indicated that the entire premise of the project had been wrong. That, in fact, the Jatropha seeds they used produced a plant that would have to compete with food production for the better soils in order to be profitable. It was the fact that Jatropha could be grown anywhere that had made it such a promising source for bio-fuels. According to his limited research…this simply did not appear to be true.

Unlike the retainer at the previous plantation, this man was a Mozambique native and was committed to finding another viable export product for his homeland. He was quite aware that several groups of investors were again considering capital ventures with existing Jatropha plantations, because of promising research on new hybrid seeds that would produce higher yields. He wondered if these hybrids would thrive in the less desirable soils where most Mozambique plantations were located. He certainly hoped that would prove to be true.

Ian shared information that he knew about two such ventures: a large California conglomerate, CA Biofuels, claimed that after five years of research, they had developed hybrid seeds that would yield more than the typical 5.5 tons per hectare. They were now establishing plantations in India, Guatemala and Brazil.

Mr. Holt observed that unfortunately, since this was a private enterprise, their research was privileged and not in the public domain.

Of greater interest, however, was a smaller project slated for Togo. Dr. Worthington explained that recently a Singapore plant producer had signed an agreement with a West African agribusiness company to start a plantation in one location in Togo. That project was focusing on producing higher yields in less desirable soil. That project could have some positive results.

The consensus, however, was that in most cases the seed-stock emerging from private labs would grow well only in the best soils with high input costs and mechanized production methods…in other words…biofuel crops that would have to compete with the production of food. It seemed as if the vision of a "green fuel crop" that could be produced in poor soil still seemed like a distant scenario.

At the end of the day, Dr. Worthington and Mr. Miller decided to return to the capitol and then back to Washington. The others would meet with one more local retainer before slogging their way further into the African bush to conduct a modest survey with farmers who were actually growing

Jatropha.

The rains continued. Driving was hazardous, especially since a number of bridges had been washed out, requiring them to take time-consuming detours. The travelers who remained were tired and drenched by the time they arrived at their final scheduled appointment. Their host welcomed them warmly and was eager to discuss what he was doing and to encourage their efforts.

Here, instead of owning and planting a sizable plantation, an investor had opted to sign contracts with quite a few small farmers, each of whom had attempted to follow the prescribed cropping systems and produce an acceptable product. Some were still cooperating, with modest success. The project coordinator was encouraged by the limited success of some of the local farmers, but he expressed concern about the obstacles they had encountered along the way…the farmers' lack of agricultural knowhow, very poor roads and enough vehicles to transport the seeds that were produced. In spite of the challenges, however, the coordinator still felt that working with small farmers was a positive option for the future. The visitors agreed and promised to continue exploring the small-farm concept as an option.

Before they left, Ian had asked Dr. Worthington and Mr. Miller to contact his department back at Michigan State when they got to Washington. He asked them to explain to his department chair what the situation was like on the ground in Mozambique. He was anxious to get word to his family, via the department, that their return would probably be delayed due to dreadful weather and poor road conditions. He wanted to let his in-laws and his children know that although he could not communicate with them directly, he was thinking of them and sending his love. Ian hoped that word would reach his family soon. His effort to use the cell phone had failed recently although some in the area seemed to be making local calls.

Once they reached their final destination, they realized how far from civilization they actually were. Finding suitable lodging was impossible, and they were planning to be there for several days. There was not even a hostel, let alone a guesthouse or hotel anywhere. Finally, in desperation – since it was much too wet to camp, Christian suggested that they inquire at the small church they had passed awhile back, to see if the pastor might have a suggestion for them. He was confident that no Christian minister would ignore strangers in need.

Christian was certainly correct in his assumption. Fortunately, he was able to explain their predicament in several languages.

"How do you do, sir," Christian said in Portuguese. "My name is Christian Rosario. This is my colleague from American, Dr. Ian Mahoney. I was born in a village not far from Maputo, but have lived most of my life in Zimbabwe. Now I am studying in the United States." Then he went on to explain, "We are a group of men examining the potential of the Jatropha crop in this country. The rain has made it difficult to travel and conduct our meetings with local farmers. Could you please suggest a place where we might find lodging or even a dry place to camp for several nights?"

"Welcome home, young man…and to our country, Dr. Mahoney," said the Pastor gripping their hands and shaking them vigorously. "Our country needs more of its bright young scholars to return and help their homeland."

"I can certainly understand your lodging problem," he continued. "We don't get many visitors here…but, perhaps I can help. By the way, I once met a Simon Rosario at an African Ministerial Conference. Was he by any chance a relative of yours?"

"Really?" exclaimed Chris, as always, amazed at the unexpected ways God worked. "He is my father and like you a minister of the gospel! I know he would never turn someone away, and it was for that reason we decided to stop here for help."

"Son, you made the right decision. I remember your father well. We spent several pleasant hours talking together. He is a remarkable man. Unfortunately, there is not public lodging anywhere around this remote area. However, like I know your father would, I welcome you to stay at our house of worship. It is modest, for sure, but it is warm and dry, and there is running water that is safe to drink. You are welcome to put your bedrolls on our meeting room floor or feel free to stretch out on the benches."

Christian relayed the message to his traveling companions, who nodded vigorously and showed their appreciation as best they could in the few words of Portuguese they knew, "Ohbrigado," they said in unison, each warmly shaking the hand of this kind minister.

"As the Bible tells us," the Pastor said, "strangers are always welcome in God's house. Do come in and dry off. My wife has just prepared a big kettle of bean soup. May I offer you some? By the way, just call me Pastor John."

The team was overwhelmed by the hospitality of the pastor and began salivating at the thought of something hot to eat. They didn't know what they were going do about an evening meal, since their provisions were becoming somewhat sparse and clearly a campfire was out of the question. When the group arranged themselves cross-legged on the floor to eat the bowls of hot soup, Ian asked their host to join them while he offered a prayer before starting the meal. Regardless of the humble and unexpected setting, the gratitude of the visitors was enormous! Ian's simple grace clearly reflected that fact.

The next morning, while the men ate a modest breakfast of dried fruit, cheese and crackers; Ian led a discussion about how to approach the local farmers. "Getting answers will be difficult, according to the reports of other MSU faculty who had surveyed farmers elsewhere in southern Africa," he explained. "There could be uncertainty about how much land an individual is actually cultivating. In many cases the estimates might be too high, so it will be difficult to estimate the true value of the seeds they're producing. But we have to do the best we can and ask questions in several ways to get the most accurate data we can."

"The nature of our questions could also be problematic," Ian continued. "Trust can be an issue, since we represent the 'dreaded foreigners' who they might believe are here to buy or even take their precious land. This has happened to them before. Many farmers will not understand that the government supports their efforts, and clearly few will appreciate the actual impact they could have on the national GDP."

Christian was nodding his head. "What Ian is saying is true. These are hard-working farmers, trying to make a living for their families. They are more concerned with their daily chores and this year's crop than long-term, sustainable revenue sources, hybrid seeds…or certainly the national GDP. In fact, few would even know what "Gross Domestic Product even is…nor would they care."

Ian went on to explain that in spite of that, from all reports, farmers were generally willing to sit for several hours to discuss their agricultural practices, hoping to learn how to improve them. Ian wanted to make sure that his group would avoid one of the mistakes that other researchers and visitors had made. Often when "big time" researchers or investors come to remote villages, farmers do not receive feedback from their foreign interviewers. Although many of these visitors are experts in agricultural practices, seldom do visitors take the time to share information or give advice to those they are questioning. The farmers are eager to hear about how they can be more efficient in their farming practices. They want advice about inputs and harvesting suggestions. In short, farmers have been disrespected by foreign visitors. It is no wonder the farmers are leery of foreigners who are perceived as self-serving and disinterested in helping the farmers, themselves.

Ian emphasized to his group that this was not how they would operate. "We are here to give-and-take," Ian said emphatically. "These farmers have knowledge and data we need…but we can help them, too. We must make sure that each one of us takes the time to listen and respond to the questions and concerns of the local farmers. We need to provide them with as much helpful information we can."

Christian, again, agreed, "You will find the people here to be open and eager to share, but Ian is right. They have been disrespected in the past, so a healthy exchange of ideas will go a long way toward helping us meet our data goals…and at the same time, make a difference for these people. I know this isn't easy. Translating makes conversation difficult…but if each of you has patience and listens carefully, watching the body language of the speaker…we will do just fine. Thank you, Ian, for bringing up this critical issue."

Throughout the day, visits with local farmers went quite well. Even the rain stopped for short periods in the morning. It became clear that there was limited agronomic knowledge among the farmers. Low literacy and educational levels were partially to blame, but foreign investors had done nothing to remedy the situation, offering little advice on how best to plant, grow, maintain and harvest Jatropha. Farmers also complained about the poor condition of existing roads and felt that local governments did not have the resources or desire to help. The researchers found these challenges to be common across most of the farms they visited. They were determined, however, to conduct at least several dozen interviews in three or four different locations before ending their stay in Africa. Their findings were consistent throughout.

They also found that they were able to respond to many of the basic cultivation issues that the farmers raised. They were able to give demonstrations on how planting could be simplified, readily-available fertilizers and other inputs that could improve their crops and suggestions on how to handle the harvested plants. The farmers were very appreciative of the interest, concern and suggestions Ian and his group offered.

The more they interacted with farmers, the more certain they became certain that in order for these small land owners to succeed, there would have to be a way to reduce transportation costs and risk. Finding a way to provide the farmers with training on best agricultural practices was also going to be critical. Lack of telecommunications was a problem, as well. Based on their conversation with the Ministers of Interior and Industry and Commerce, perhaps consideration of credit and subsidies could be possible…a way to minimize the risk that small land owners could ill afford to take.

It also seemed clear that the idea of contract farming had appeal even though the concept was not fully understood by many of the growers. With contract farming, farmers would have a reliable buyer for the crop they produced. Since there was no well-developed market structure in small communities, ensuring that their products would be sold would be a strong incentive for those eager to continue growing Jatropha. Even if the quality and quantity of their crops were poor, in most cases – since cultivation cost little time or money – they could still make a modest profit.

Ian's research goal – to engineer plants that produce higher- yielding oil seeds – was critical for the success of any undertaking in Mozambique or elsewhere in the world. They would also have to consider soil type when engineering hybrids…and work on developing seed stock that could thrive in all types of soil. Concentrating on lab work must be his main focus in the months ahead.

After meeting with farmers during the day, Ian and his team gathered to engage in vigorous discussions well into the night. They talked about the fact that previous researchers, investors, government officials or even producers had given little thought to the byproducts that remained after the Jatropha seeds were harvested. The team began exploring the possibility of converting that "waste" into marketable products, also."

What about the "cake" that remained after the oil was extracted, they wondered, could it perhaps be used for fish or animal feed – if detoxified? What about the biomass feed stock, like leaves, stems and roots? Could it be used to power electricity plants or as biogas? Could the residuals be used as fertilizer, or even as bio-pesticide? The question of how to use the byproducts of biofuel vegetation effectively has been an issue plaguing American researchers and entrepreneurs for years. The team agreed that finding profitable uses for Jatropha byproducts would be another area to explore…one that could have major benefits for a developing nation such as Mozambique.

Ian's team bubbled with ideas and suggestions about what could be done to help the people of this developing country. They all agreed that given the status of many roads in the country, infrastructure was definitely a challenge to be addressed by the government. But if genetic improvements were made to the Jatropha plant, and its oil became a viable export, there would be incentive to improve rural infrastructure. And if parallel investigation could be undertaken to capitalize on the plant's byproducts, there could be even greater economic potential for this country. The possibilities were real and achievable, but it would require major cooperation of government, universities and investors.

Since others at MSU had been generous in sharing their insights and African survey results, Ian and Chris were careful to take detailed notes that they could pass along to the other researchers upon their return. True, they had surveyed relatively few farmers, but given the depth of those interactions, their observations might be helpful to others doing follow-up surveys in that part of the globe. They were anxious to talk about the possibilities for other related research with their MSU colleagues, as well. If others could secure funding for research on Jatropha byproducts, for instance, the possibilities for cooperation and collaboration on projects in this area were immense.

Ian was glad that in spite of the less than pleasant conditions – constant dirt, sweat and insects, none of their group got sick. Moreover, their positive attitudes were a blessing. "What a great crew," he thought.

Using the small church as their base, the group continued their investigation as planned, often slogging through knee-deep mud to meet at the property of their contacts. Throughout their stay, church members had joined their pastor in providing something hot for their evening meals, even though it was evident that they had little to share. The warm and generous people of this small, rural community certainly demonstrated Christian outreach at its best. Ian was determined to see that their kindness was repaid.

The glimmerings of an idea began to form in Ian's mind. "Wouldn't it be wonderful," he thought, "if our home church

could adopt this small church in Mozambique?   What a
meaningful partnership that might become!" He could hardly
wait to suggest the idea to Pastor Rebecca.

Given weather conditions, Ian knew he would not return
home on schedule. It was troubling, to be sure, but he was
relieved that the Calhouns had assured him that their return
date was flexible. And, of course, there was Mrs. Harding who
had agreed to step in, if the need arose. So, the young father
relaxed, trusted that all was well, and reconciled himself to
the delay.

CHAPTER TWENTY-SIX

One evening later that week, Ian's Department Chair stopped by the Mahoney home to give the family a report about Ian. He assured Peggy and the children that Ian was just fine, although his group was going to be delayed because of the extremely heavy rainfall and extensive damage to roads and bridges in their area. The trip was going extremely well for Ian and his researchers, in spite of frequently being soaking wet. He also gave the twins a special message from their dad and told them he would be home very soon.

Peggy thanked him for the long-awaited news about the travelers. She, the grandparents, neighbors, and especially the children had been terribly worried. They had been following media reports on the internet of torrential rain, washed-out bridges and extreme flooding in Mozambique. "It will certainly be good to have them back home," she confided to the messenger with a huge sigh of relief.

The children seemed to relax more now that they knew their dad was okay and was thinking about them. However, the delay of his return was tough on both children. Peggy was glad that from the time she arrived, she had encouraged both to keep journals in which they drew pictures of their daily activities, and she helped them by writing their descriptions of those activities. "That way," she told them, "your daddy won't miss out on the important things that you're doing each day." Since both children liked to draw, they were delighted to have this daily assignment.

Others in the church and community stepped in to assist the "blessing nanny," as some thought of her. Neighbors invited the twins for several play-dates, the Lanes had them over for a meal or two, and Rod continued to take them for swimming lessons. For her part, Peggy tried to plan special outings for the children. She often took them to the sliding hill, had snow picnics, and one day she surprised them with an after-school trip to Impression Five, a local interactive children's museum. Peggy was very sensitive to the fact that these precious children had lost their mother unexpectedly.... one day she just didn't come home. She did not want them to worry that the same thing would happen to their dad. She even discussed it with Pastor Becky...and they both watched for signs of depression or grief in the children. But the children continued to be quite content and while they missed their dad, they were too busy to focus on his absence.

At the outset of the new arrangement, Miss Peggy had suggested that they not talk about their home situation too much at school. "This is our special arrangement," she explained. "While we are at home, I'm your nanny, but when we're at school I'm your teacher, and you are my students. The same thing is true for teachers who have their own children in class. That teacher is 'mom' at home....and 'teacher' at school."

The children had readily accepted the new relationship parameters and fallen easily into the teacher/nanny arrangement. It had been working out well both at home and at school. The children loved being with Peggy...and Miss Peggy enjoyed it even more than she thought she might. The Mahoney twins were becoming a very special part of her life. She had to admit that she would miss caring for, comforting, laughing and just relaxing with these dear children when Dr. Mahoney returned. She was thankful that they were in her class at school...at least she would continue to see them every day.

The children talked with Nana Calhoun and were pleased that her injuries were healing.

Their grandmother promised that she and Grandpa would come to see them at Easter. Nana said that they were looking forward to meeting their friends and visiting the school they had been hearing so much about. The twins marked the kitchen calendar to keep track of the days until they would see their Nana and Grandpa.

"Maybe you can take them to the university farms and see what horses in Michigan look like," Miss Peggy suggested. The children eagerly agreed and decided to draw some horse pictures to send to their grandparents.

Before the start of classes one morning, Miss Grace, Peggy's mentor and friend, asked her how the arrangement was working out. Peggy replied that the children seemed content to have her as their caregiver as well as teacher, and they had proved to be quite capable of differentiating the two roles. She added that she was totally enjoying the experience.

"Well," said the older woman, "that's because you have made them feel so comfortable and safe. I'm not surprised, of course. But...how about you, Peg? It's easy to become attached to young children when you're with them all day every day. Do you think it will be difficult for you to revert to your former 'teacher only' role when their father gets home? And didn't I get the impression that perhaps you were developing some special feelings for him, as well? I sure don't want you to get hurt."

"Ian Mahoney is a very remarkable man, and a wonderful parent. He and I are simply friends. We attend the same church and actually co-advise the church youth group...but that's as far as it goes." She then told Grace about their joint efforts on the "Christmas in October" project.

The older woman just nodded and smiled inwardly. "Yes, so you say," she thought to herself, "but I wonder if she is beginning to hope the relationship becomes something more. Peggy would be such a wonderful wife and mother." As far as anyone at school knew, the young woman didn't have a serious man in her life – at least she never spoke of seeing anyone or going out on dates. There was that friend of her brother...but Peggy was certainly not overly-enthusiastic about him.

After her talk with Grace, Peggy began to wonder if she had become too transparent in her admiration for the professor. There had never been any indication that he felt anything more for her than respect as the children's directress and co-volunteer at church. "Well," she mused to herself, "except for that one, probably-fluke moment on New Year's Eve."

For her part, she had to admit that she found him quite attractive and appreciated his quiet, genuine way of relating to people. He still talked lovingly of his deceased wife. Each of the children had a collage of photos of her that they displayed in their rooms. They always remembered her in their prayers, also. Her parents were still considered part of the Mahoney family and were expected to come for a spring visit. Ian was still in love with her...probably always would be. But would he be ready for a new relationship at some point? Hard to tell. She was determined to not think – or hope? – beyond their easy cordial relationship as friends. Besides, she was quite sure she was not ready for any complicated relationships, either.

Not knowing how much longer the travelers would be gone made it difficult to plan ahead. The Montessori parents were slated to attend a Sunday afternoon Spartan women's basketball game. It was a fun get-together that the group had held annually for the past few years. Peggy had never attended, but this year she bought four tickets so that she and a friend could take the twins, who seemed excited about going. Many of the group would gather for pizza after the game.

The night before the game, Peggy tucked the twins in with a hug and a kiss good-night. The kids were excited about the game and had a hard time falling asleep. Once the children were asleep, though, Peggy realized she was pretty tired herself, so she went to bed early. As usual, she left the bedroom door open so she could hear if she was needed during the night.

Sometime after midnight, Ian arrived home. "What in the world," he wondered, "is Peggy Gerber's Volt doing in our driveway?" He tiptoed down the hall and peaked into Michael's room. He and Mia were sleeping soundly in the twin beds. Next door he discovered a startling sight – neither the Calhouns nor Ida Harding was stretched out there. Instead, he eyed a sleeping Peggy Gerber, mop of blond curls cascading over the pillow. He was jet-lagged and a more than a little perplexed. What was going on? Even in his confusion, though, Ian couldn't help but admire the innocent beauty of a sleeping Peggy. "Michael sure is right," he thought, "she is a beautiful woman."

Shaking his head…and smiling…way too tired to question the woman's unexpected presence; Ian went to his room, dropped his luggage, climbed into bed and was instantly asleep. Tomorrow would be soon enough to ask WHY?

The next morning, of course, it never occurred to Peggy that the homeowner might have returned in the night. The door to his bedroom was closed as usual. She quickly took a shower and dressed for church before waking the children. As the three of them sat down for breakfast, Mia spotted a suitcase in the hall. "Look," she screamed, "Daddy's home!" She and Michael fell over themselves racing to their dad's bedroom. "Daddy! Daddy!" they shouted. Sure enough, Daddy was home!

Ian roused and was immediately engulfed by four little arms and cascading kisses. "Daddy, Daddy, you're home!!!!"

the children chorused, jumping on the bed. "When did you get here? Miss Peggy's here! We're going to a basketball game today!! We're SO GLAD you're back!!!" they bubbled without a breath. "Come on, Daddy...Miss Peggy made French toast for breakfast, and you know how much you love French toast!!!" They jumped off the bed pulling a groggy daddy behind them.

Their father grabbed his robe and followed his children into the kitchen. "Well, well, what have we here? This is certainly a surprise," he said, smoothing his erratic hair that sprung back up the minute he removed his hand.

"Good morning," Peggy said brightly. "I guess this is a surprise for us all! So, when did you get home? We weren't sure when you'd arrive back in the states." Peggy unconsciously smoothed her own hair before grabbing another plate from the cupboard.

"You must be hungry. Do sit down. Coffee is ready, and I'll get you some juice and start your toast," stammered the astonished cook.

"Miss Peggy has been our nanny, Daddy!" Mia blurted.

"Yea," Michael added in a rush. "Mrs. H had to go to her daughter's 'cause she's sick and having a baby, and Mrs. H has to take care of Tommy til the baby's born, so Miss Peggy's here. She's still our teacher, and it's really fun."

"I see," said his father nodding, but not really understanding. Did Nana and Grandpa Calhoun have to leave early?"

"Didn't you know, Daddy?" asked Mia incredulously. "Nana fell off her horse and broke her leg and wrist, so they couldn't come. Mrs. H stayed with us for a few days, but then she had to leave, so we asked Miss Peggy to be our nanny. She's our nanny and our teacher!"

"She's a really good nanny!" Michael added. "She took us sledding...to the museum...we made snowmen....and we even had snow picnics!   We love her, Daddy…and she loves us too! I guess we really surprised you!!"

It was almost too much for their father to assimilate. "I…I…don't even know what to say," Ian spluttered, turning to Peggy. He did not have any idea where to begin. Clearly, this was not the time to ask questions and there was no way to even begin to express his overwhelming appreciation for her priceless gift of care for his precious children. He gazed back at his laughing children…safe, healthy, happy…thanks to this amazing woman. He could begin to feel the prickle of a tear at the back of his eye. What a blessing to have a friend like her! Without thinking, Ian grabbed Peggy's hand and squeezed it between both of his. "You are, indeed, an angel…" he said thickly. "I will never ever forget this moment and all you have done for us."

"Daddy, Daddy," exclaimed Michael, bringing the moment to an end. "This afternoon we're going to a Spartan basketball game! Can you come with us?"

Ian looked at the other adult in the room and asked, "What's all this about?"

"Well," began Peggy, trying to reign in her own emotions after Ian's unexpected display of unbridled admiration and appreciation, "for the past few years, the school has sponsored a field trip-of-sorts to a Spartan woman's game as a fun event for the whole family. We get a special rate on the tickets, and it's an event that requires no work from either the staff or parents. The game begins at 2:00. Many of the families go for pizza after the game. I've never gone, but thought the twins would enjoy it."

"Hey, it sounds great!" Ian said, "I'd love to join the group! How do I get tickets?"

"Actually, I bought tickets in advance and have an extra one you can use," Peggy offered.

"Hey, you've done so much already! You probably want to take your stuff home, relax, and start getting back to normal," Ian suggested.

"No, Daddy!" Michael exclaimed, "Miss Peggy has to come!"

"Please, Miss Peggy, please come with us…" begged Mia.

Peggy laughed. "Well, of course I'll come." She turned to Ian, "I think that I'll just tag along. The kids have had so many sudden adjustments in their living situation recently. Perhaps it would be good for them to ease out of our nanny arrangement and back into normalcy, rather than having another abrupt change. I think the game might be the perfect transition for them."

"We were just about to head to church. Do you want to take a quick shower and join us?" Peggy asked.

"You know, that's a great idea," Ian said. "I had almost forgotten it was Sunday."

"You go ahead and get ready while the kids finish breakfast and I clean up the kitchen."

"Great idea," Ian admitted. "I'll be done in a jiff." Pastor Becky and the other church members were delighted that Professor Mahoney had returned safely since they too had been concerned about his safety. They had said prayers for him at church after hearing about the treacherous weather conditions in Mozambique. A couple of friends even asked that he consider giving a presentation about his trip and the people he had met in such a far-away land.

After church and a quick lunch, the little group donned their Spartan gear for the game.

"Would you mind driving, Peggy," Ian asked, "since I don't really trust myself behind the wheel until I get a little more sleep. The game will be a good way for me to begin returning to a normal life. Let me tell you, our last week was anything but normal."

The trip to the women's basketball game was a fun time for the entire Montessori community. Peggy's friend was glad to give up her ticket so the professor could attend with his children. Per usual, the scoreboard recognized the attendance by the Ojibwa group and had special badges for each of the children. To add to the pleasure of the afternoon, the Lady Spartans won a close game in overtime.

Joining the other families for pizza and conversation after the game only added to the day's fun. Peggy was pleased to see how well Ian related to the other parents, most of whom he had never met. The twins were more energetic than usual... they had had a lot of excitement that day, but they were well-behaved, as usual. Several of the mothers commented on how polite they were and how well they got along with all the other children. As their substitute nanny, Peg could only nod and smile, basking in a warm feeling of pride for her charges.

After returning to the Mahoney home, Peggy packed her bag, gathered her teaching satchel, and hugged the children good-bye. "I look forward to seeing you two tomorrow," she said. She turned to Ian. "I know you are jet-lagged and little overwhelmed right now," she said, "but I just want you to know...these last weeks with your wonderful children have truly been a blessing for me, too. Do not feel indebted...just accept that God took care of both you and all of us over the past month. I look forward to seeing you all soon!" With that she rushed out the door and into her Volt. As she drove away, she saw Ian and the children waving from the porch, and it caused her throat to tighten and her eyes to cloud with tears.

Peggy reflected on how readily the twins had accepted her as a part of their family. "Being with all of them really did feel quite natural," she thought. She remembered how Ian had looked earlier that morning with a heavy growth of beard, a tousled head of red hair and a groggy smile. He had been a wondrous sight to behold...and it had warmed her heart to see the children race into his arms.

Being part of the children's lives for these past weeks, and the Mahoney family today – was an experience she would cherish...cherish forever.

CHAPTER: TWENTY-SEVEN

After preparing his After-Action Report on the Mozambique trip, Ian was finally able to take some time to reflect on what had happened on the home front during his absence. The senior Mahoneys had said they loved spending time with the twins and renewing some of their old friendships. They had also been delighted to meet the Lane family and were pleased that Ian and the children had found such a satisfying church home. Now, although he and the kids missed Ida…the threesome was managing reasonably well without her. He had to admit though, they were all looking forward to her return.

Ian was thoroughly enjoying the pictorial journals the children had made for him during the time that Peggy had been their nanny. What a thoughtful idea and wonderful way to ensure that he did not miss out on any of their special activities! Sending Peggy a few flowers was hardly adequate repayment for all she had done for his family. He wondered if taking her out for a nice dinner would be an appropriate thing for him to do.

"When in doubt," he thought to himself, "ask your mother." And so he did.

"Mom, I need your advice," he said to Katie when he called her later that evening."

"Of course, Dear, how can I help?" responded his mother.

"I've been wondering if it would be appropriate for me to invite Peggy Gerber out for a nice dinner as repayment for her time caring for the twins in my absence. I did send her some flowers, but that hardly seems sufficient. She was quite adamant about not receiving any payment for her time with the children."

"Why in the world are you hesitating, Ian?" his mom asked.

"Uh, you know…it wouldn't be like…asking her for a date, would it? As you know only too well, my social life before Laurie was…well… nil. So, I'm really pretty naive about dealing with single women. We are good friends and seem to have a lot in common, but I'm not sure I want to give the impression that I'm looking for a relationship. Although I must confess…I really enjoy spending time with her at church and with the youth group. And besides, I don't even know if she's seeing anyone else right now."

"Ian, is it Laurie that's still holding you back? I think you know in your heart that Laurie would want you to get on with your life, develop new relationships and, if it happens, find new love. It's amazing how often love is built on solid friendship. I'm not saying that person in Peggy. But taking her out for a meal to thank her for caring for your children in an emergency seems like the very least you could do. Besides, Peggy seems like the kind of woman who would accept your dinner invitation as it is intended, a Thank You for her gift and nothing more. Do invite her for a nice evening out, and try to take her someplace very nice where neither of you has been… so it will be special for you both."

"Oh, Mom," Ian sighed, "You always have a way of making things seem so natural and obvious. Of course, you are so right about Laurie. In fact, I can almost hear her encouraging me to just take the plunge and go out with someone! I'm pretty sure Peggy will accept, and we'll have a great time. Thanks for the listening ear, Mom. You never let me down. How did I get so lucky to have you and Dad for parents? One more question…

do you have any suggestions about where we might go?"

"Well, when we were in Michigan, several of our friends spoke about going to a charming place in Eaton Rapids that had an interesting history. We hoped to go there for dinner, but the time passed too quickly. I understand that the food is excellent and the ambiance is like an English country house."

"Sounds like the perfect choice, Mom. I'll go online and check it out. And thanks Mom," he added, "for always being there when I need you. Love you lots!"

"Love you back!" she laughed.

After hanging up, Ian went online and discovered that the English Inn and Pub got high marks from travelers as well as locals who often hosted special events there or wanted to treat the family to a special meal. So he promptly picked up the phone and called Peggy.

"Hi, Peg. Ian here," he began.

"Well World Traveler….how's the jetlag?" Peggy responded.

"I've totally adjusted to the time and a real bed," Ian laughed, "and it's great to be back with my little hooligans. I really wanted to call you earlier, but I've been swamped."

"Ian, thank you so much for the beautiful flowers! They brighten my spirits and bring a breath of freshness into this winter-bound apartment!" Peggy gushed. "It was really very sweet of you to do that."

"Well, I'm glad you like them," he continued. "Actually, I've been wanting to invite you out for dinner ever since I got back from Africa, but I got a little bogged down completing reports and paperwork on the trip. You'll never know how much I appreciate you stepping in when Ida was called away, and the Calhouns couldn't make the trip to Michigan. Having the twins keep daily journals was a touch of genius on your part. I am just so grateful! My mother and I were talking recently, and she mentioned an interesting place in Eaton Rapids. They hope to go there on their next trip to Michigan, so I thought maybe you could join me in giving the place a try. Are you free this Saturday evening, if I can get a reservation? No twins, of course."

"What a lovely idea! Thank you, but you know, the time in your home with the twins was very special for me, too – a special treat really," Peggy responded. "And, yes, I'm free on Saturday, and I'd love to accept your invitation. I think you must be talking about the English Inn. I've never been there but passed it a number of times and wondered about the interior. I've heard the food there is fabulous! It'll be a lot of fun…I'll look forward to it."

"As will I," laughed Ian, "I'll pick you up around 6:30, then."

"Perfect! I'll see you then!"

On Saturday evening, Ian decided to wear his best suit and a bright pink tie. He was glad he did, when he saw how lovely Peggy looked in a beautiful blue sheath the color of her eyes. The ambiance of the Inn was lovely, the food and service perfect, and the couple had a great conversation about the kids, their jobs and their lives prior to meeting.

Ian confessed that he'd never had much of a social life, not that he didn't like girls when he was growing up, but he always felt somewhat shy about approaching them for dates. He always wished he'd had an older sister to guide him. Laurie was really the only woman he had dated seriously, since he had always been so busy studying.

Peggy laughed and said that having three brothers and their friends around made it easy for her to be viewed as their Tom-boy buddy rather than a potential girlfriend. She admitted, however, that recently one of her brother's friends had changed his mind and now saw her in a different light.

"Did you always want to be a teacher?" he asked.

"Yes, as long as I can remember," she confessed. "This is my fifth year at Ojibwa, and I have finally fulfilled my obligation to the Board who funded my certification training in Italy. I love working with children, especially your two who are really creative, are kind to others and have endless energy."

"That they do!" he raised his hands in surrender. "I can't tell you how much I've enjoyed reading about their antics in the journals they kept in my absence. They really had fun with Mother and Dad, too, and delighted in showing off their swimming skills and ability to ride their new bikes."

"I wish that the enormous fort they built from Lincoln logs would have survived 'til you returned," she said. "It took them several long tedious hours to build it in front of the fireplace. They engaged in numerous heated discussions about the right architectural features to include. I think in the end they both knew it was a terrific accomplishment, because they ended up using ideas from both. Who knows, you may have a budding architect – or two – in your family."

"I think that Michael's developing a nice sense of humor and has learned how to get under his sister's skin in rather amusing ways," he chuckled. "She, on the other hand, is not going to be bossed around by any boy, much less her brother."

"What a joy they both are!" laughed Peggy.

"It's still an early evening…and not too cold…how about a walk around the grounds? Ian asked. "I've been thinking that this might be a nice place to hold a meeting with the funders from D.C. Since it's also a B & B, they could stay here and enjoy the change of scene from Washington."

"Great idea…let me grab my boots from the car. I really don't want to tackle the snowmelt in my 3-inch heels!" she said, donning her wool coat.

As they walked around and inspected the grounds, conversation was easy; and they both seemed to laugh a lot. How nice it was to share ideas, stories and future dreams with a good listener. Someone who really seemed to understand!

"Oh, look!" exclaimed Peggy. "There's a shooting star! Do you believe that if you wish on a shooting star your wish comes true?"

Of course, Peggy KNEW that this was true, if you really believe, but Ian was probably rolling his eyes in skepticism. Nevertheless, she asked Ian to close his eyes and make a wish. She promised to do likewise. Then she reminded him that they could not tell anyone what they had wished for.

Ian found himself drawn to this woman. Being with her brought back the feelings he had first experienced on New Year's Eve when they shared a hug and brief kiss. As he gazed at her with her eyes closed making her wish, he was moved by her beauty, honesty and giving spirit – the very things that had been missing in his life for way too long.

Ian was so moved by her beauty…their closeness…some inner warmth… that he gently took Peggy into his arms and kissed her softly. Peggy moved into him, responded tentatively, then eagerly, and their kiss deepened. Both became breathless, and they quickly separated and laughed nervously.

"Well," she said, "that was unexpected!"

Ian stammered, "Unexpected, maybe, but --"

Peggy saved what could have been an embarrassing moment by taking his hand and saying, "Ian, you are a very special person – a great dad, a successful professional and a guy trying to create a life for himself and his family in a new place. I don't want to presume too much, just because tonight was so special. But, you have so much on your plate right now – so much to think about. What you don't need are complications. Believe me, I understand and would never want to be the cause of added stress in your life."

Ian was rather baffled by her response, didn't know what to think of her words and was speechless himself. Was she trying to tell him that she had another man in her life or that he had too much baggage for her; or was there some other hidden message in her words. So he just laughed nervously – embarrassed – and said, "I guess you're right."

Peggy's eyes clouded over and her smile faded slightly because that was certainly NOT what she hoped he would say. But, once again, she saved the moment by grabbing his arm and hurrying him along laughing, "Okay, friend, let's get going. We both have an early morning tomorrow. And I need my sleep if I'm going to be in good voice for the choir. It has really been a special, even magical evening, Ian. Thank you so very much for sharing it with me. Now don't forget your falling-star wish, Dr. Mahoney…and don't tell anyone what it was….or it won't come true!"

"Mom was right," Ian thought as he drove toward home after dropping Peggy off at her apartment. "It is time for me to start looking at the future. She was also right about the English Inn. It was the perfect spot for a new beginning. Asking a woman out really wasn't all that tough – even for a duffer like me. Of course, that was probably because the woman was Peggy Gerber! She asked me not to forget my wish…as if I could!" He smiled inwardly as he pulled into his driveway.

CHAPTER TWENTY-EIGHT

Peggy stretched and thought how nice it was to sleep in on a Saturday morning, the one day of the week when she had time for a jog around the apartment complex. School and church prevented her going for a run other mornings, since she was never an early riser even as a kid on the farm. This promised to be a really good day. She was going to have a long lunch with her former college roommate, Jodie Allen, who had moved back to Michigan after Christmas with her husband and young son. Peggy couldn't wait!

The two had met their freshman year at Michigan State when both were representatives on the Dorm Council. Jodie was a nursing student from a small town in the Upper Peninsula. They hit it off immediately and became inseparable. After their freshman year, the two decided to room together. They were best friends then, and they had remained best friends ever since. Pursuing a career in medicine seemed a natural for Jodie, since her father was a small town doctor and her mother was his nurse. Her older sister had been a first year medical student when Jodie met Peggy. Jodie wanted to become a nurse practitioner. During her time at State, she had worked part time as a nanny for a faculty couple and later as an aide in the children's ward of the local hospital.

Their interest in children was one of the things that had brought the two women together, and they had great fun sharing stories about the little ones they met on the job – a nice break from the routine of crowded academic schedules. After graduation, both women had gone on to fulfill their dreams.

Peggy went to Italy for her Montessori certification, and Jodie enrolled at Duke University to become a nurse practitioner, as she had planned.

While at Duke, she met Ben Allen, who was focused on becoming an orthopedic surgeon, aiding children with genetic physical disabilities. Peggy had been the Maid of Honor in their wedding...and they had only seen each other once, after baby Ben was born...and Peggy flew out to attend the baby's baptism. She was to be his godmother, after all. But the two had not seen each other much since then. They kept in touch, for sure, via email, text, facetime, social media and frequent hour-long phone calls; but they had missed being together. The best gift Peggy received at Christmas was a phone call from Jodie...sharing the good news that the Allens would be moving to East Lansing! She and Ben had decided to leave their positions at a Shriners' Hospital for Children and move back to Michigan to be closer to their families. They had accepted positions with a small medical group located in East Lansing and affiliated with MSU.

Peggy had seen Jodie and Ben several times, since their arrival in January, including the day they arrived when Peggy brought over a house-warming meal of hot soup, salad, and fresh cookies. She and Jodie had also squeezed in a short visit or two with the twins and Benjy. But both their schedules were impossible, so today's luncheon was going to be a treat for them both. Peggy and Jodie rushed into each other's arms when they arrived at the restaurant. As always, it seemed as if they had never been apart. Their conversation just picked up where it had left off the last time they talked.

Where to begin? So much had happened in such a short time. They quickly ordered food and got busy catching up. The Allens were living in a temporary rental apartment until they could find a suitable house to purchase. Jodie was not working at the moment, since they had yet to find child care for three-year-old Benjy, known as B.J.

"Hey, Jod," Peggy began, "why don't you think about enrolling him at my school? We have a great three-year-old program…and next year….he'd have me for his teacher!!" She laughed heartily as Jodie rolled her eyes.

"But, If we did that…we'd want to get a really GOOD teacher for our brilliant B.J., not some old slouch like you!" Jodie said laughingly lifting her pinky in hoity-toity fashion. "Actually, Ben and I have talked about just that a number of times. Not only do I know all about Montessori from you… but several of our friends have had their kids in Montessori schools and have been very pleased with them. But…that doesn't help us now…we're nearing the end of the year."

"At Ojibway, we usually have quite a waiting list for fall entries," Peggy explained, "but this time of year it's sometimes easier to get in. We like to enroll children throughout the school year, which isn't typical of many programs."

Jodie nodded slowly. "No kidding! Well….I'll talk to Ben, again. We really hadn't even considered that option for now…we were just trying to find a babysitter or nanny that could come to our house. Finding just the right person is not as easy as you may think."

"But, let's talk about you," Jodie changed the subject abruptly. "I know you're busy with the youth group; and you seemed to have a glorious time playing substitute nanny for Michael and Mia, but what's the deal with Dr. Ian, hmmm?"

Peggy blushed, "Oh, Jodie, I have to admit that staying with the kids was truly an amazing experience. Caring for them, comforting them, even scolding them…just seemed so natural. It really made me realize what I was missing!"

Jodie nodded, "You know, I always thought it would be you who'd marry first and quickly became the mommy of several adorable children. You're a natural!! Of course, that's why you're such a fabulous teacher! I mean, I've always loved kids, too, of course, and B.J. has taught me lots…but it sure wasn't always easy…and there was only one of him! Weren't you absolutely exhausted by the end of the day dealing with twins?? I can't even imagine dealing with two four-year-olds all day, every day."

"No, actually the whole thing was energizing," Peggy said thoughtfully. "Michael and Mia were very sweet and helpful. They got along well and listened to me when I asked them to do things. Church friends also stepped in to give me a little breathing space, now and then."

"I have to admit, though," Peggy chuckled. "It was quite something to see the look on Ian's face, when he realized that I had been the substitute nanny for his kids while he was gone."

"So, what is the latest with the professor?" Jodie prodded.

"Well, like I've told you," Peggy began ticking off attributes, "he's clearly very smart and highly regarded in his profession. He's on the quiet side, a good listener, from a lovely family, a great father and a willing volunteer at our church."

"Okay, so he's Mr. all-round great….but does he have a social life…and is he fun?" asked her friend.

Peggy pondered this, "I really doubt that he's made many friends except at work and church; he's simply been too busy. Remember, I actually conned him into helping me with the church youth group last fall when he happened to mention at the kids' parent/teacher conference that he wanted to get involved in some kind of volunteer work."

"Well, we know that has worked out well," Jodie smiled innocently. "Wasn't it chaperoning the youth group that got you together on New Year's Eve?"

"Oh, Jodie," Peggy rolled her eyes and shook her head.

"The truth is, he relates well to the kids. Even though he was an only child, his rapport with young people is terrific. He really listens to their questions and opinions, he talks with them not to them….and they genuinely like him. He is a good role model…and heaven knows we need more Christian men to spend time with young people and be their friends."

"Ok, Pegster, I know you have tremendous respect for him," Jodie shrugged, "but what's happening on the romantic front? I remember that not-so-casual peck on New Year's Eve. Has Mr. Mahoney made any moves lately? Fess up Peg 'o My Heart, this is old buddy Jodie asking. I sense that there may be more to this relationship than either one of you wants to admit. Well….has he asked you out on a date, yet?"

SILENCE!

"Geez, Jod…! You haven't changed a whit! You sure don't hesitate to get to the nitty gritty!" Peggy shook her head resignedly. "The truth is…I've been dying to talk to you about this….keeping it inside has been killing me. My feelings toward this guy actually scare the living be-geebers out of me. I'm usually so centered when it comes to guys… but Ian Mahoney is different. I can't stop thinking about him. I haven't said much about him to Mom, since she would worry about me….and I sure can't talk to folks at work about it…. not with the his kids in my class!"

Jodie folded her arms and bobbed her head, "I knew it! You can't hide from the Jod-meister!! I'm just so glad that God brought us back to Michigan! I knew that moving close to family (and you are my family, Miss Peggy) was important… and this is why. Now, my friend, help me understand what's going on between the two of you. Has he talked much about the twins' mother?"

"No, not really," Peg admitted. "They weren't married very long. She was a journalist, employed on the Texas A

& M campus where he attended graduate school and had his first teaching job. After the twins arrived, she became a stay-at-home mom and did volunteer work at church and at a local hospital. She's still a presence in the twin's lives – even though it's unlikely they can actually remember her. After all, they weren't even two yet, when she was killed."

"How do you know that?" Jodie asked.

"They have several delightful candid photos of her playing with them in their rooms, and they always remember her in their bed-time prayers."

"How does their Dad treat you? Like another guy? Does he even notice that you are gorgeous?" Jodie continued.

Laughing, Peggy replied, "Oh, Jodie… Well….until recently, he treated me more like a good friend and neighbor. We're very comfortable with each other. We laugh at the antics of the twins, talk about our work and the kids in youth group. I think he has deep faith, although I suspect that was shaken when his wife was taken from him so suddenly. He harbors deep sadness about that, I think…understandably. You know about our New Year's Eve kiss…but I thought that might have just been a fluke, since everyone was hugging and kissing. It was New Year's Eve, after all! Then, he left almost immediately for Africa."

"And…since he's been back…?" prompted Jodie.

"Well, maybe it's changed a little…" she began. "The day after his return from Mozambique, he, the children, and I went to a school family-day activity. It was a fun afternoon at a MSU women's basketball game followed by a pizza party with other parents and children. It all seemed so natural. It was a good opportunity for him to meet the parents of the twins' friends, and nobody seemed surprised or questioned that I was there with the Mahoneys."

"That sounds like progress…but I know there's more… keep talking…" Jodie prodded.

Smiling, shaking her head, and responding to her friend's gentle pressure, "Actually, there is. Last Saturday night, Ian took me out to dinner as a 'thank you' for staying with the kids. Now mind you…he had already sent me a beautiful, thank-you floral arrangement. Obviously, I refused any payment for babysitting, since it was a treat for me to spend time with two of my favorite four-year-olds. I had loved it, as you know."

"Okay….so back to the good stuff… Where did you go?" Jodie pressed. "Did anything happen?"

Smiling with forbearance, Peggy continued, "We went to a lovely, country house in Eaton Rapids, built perhaps in the 20s for some important business person. It's now a classic restaurant and inn with added facilities for banquets, weddings and conferences. The grounds are lovely year-round, the ambiance gracious and the food gourmet."

"That sounds very romantic," Jodie sang suggestively.

Peggy nodded, "It actually was. Neither of us had been there before. We had a wonderful open conversation during dinner, sharing thoughts about our jobs, chatting about the kids, revealing bits about our growing up years and sharing our hopes for the future. It was just so comfortable…for both of us, I think."

"What happened after dinner? Do I have to pull it all out of you?" Jodie grabbed her friend by the arm. "You haven't changed a bit! You still like to keep me in suspense as long as possible! Shame! Shame! Shame on you!"

"Oh, Jodie," Peggy laughed…then got serious as she placed her hand atop that of her friend and squeezed gently. "I really do want to talk about the rest of the evening and get your advice on how I should act when we next meet, which will no doubt be tomorrow at church. This is all so new for me. You, of all people, can understand why I'm more than a little nervous – fearful of making a mistake. I would hate to lose him…as a friend."

"A friend…sure…." Jodie mumbled.

"After dinner we took a short walk. Ian thought the inn might be a nice venue for his next meeting with his project funders. He took my arm so I wouldn't fall on the icy pebble walk-way. Then, all at once…I saw a shooting star, so of course I had to react."

Jodie continued for her, "And you asked if he believed in wishing on shooting stars. I wonder how many times you and I did that when we were students here? And guess what? Ben and I still do it, because like you…I'm convinced it is true if you really believe."

"Of course it is! And guess what…he did it!!! We both did." She shut her eyes, remembering then continued softly, "…and then, unexpectedly, he gently pulled me into his arms and kissed me. Kissed…well…I would say it was more like we both became lost in one beautiful, romantic moment."

"And then?" asked Jodie breathlessly.

Laughing, Peggy continued, "And then we were both quite embarrassed. I made some comment about how unexpected that was – and he agreed."

""Moments like that can be quite difficult, since one never knows quite what to say or how to act afterwards…" Jodie agreed.

"Then I grabbed his hand and said that he was a very special person, a great dad, a successful professional and a guy trying to create a life for himself and his family in a new place." Peggy went on. "He nodded, so I added that he had a full plate and much to think about without added complications."

"What??? What did you say that for???" Jodie asked indignantly. "And how did he respond?"

"He was quiet for what seemed like a long time, looked embarrassed and finally indicated that I was probably right, whatever that meant." Peggy looked crestfallen.

"Well, I'm glad that you responded first," Jodie said soothingly, trying to reassure her friend, "but your words may have confused him…as much as his response confused you."

"I wasn't trying to scare him off…really," Peggy pleaded.

"I know, sweet Peggy," Jodie hugged her friend. "You were just trying to protect him from getting in too deep… even though that is exactly what you wanted him to do."

Peggy hugged her friend back. "Oh, Jods, you know me so well…. Anyway, I tried to save the awkward moment by laughing and suggesting we hurry along, since the next day was Sunday and I needed my sleep so I'd be in good singing voice for the choir."

"No good night kiss at the door?" asked Jodie.

"No, he just patted me on the arm when I thanked him for the very special evening and said he'd see me in church."

"So how did church go the next day?" Jodie asked.

"We really didn't get much of a chance to talk. I was in the choir, and he had to drop off and pick up the kids. He and the kids didn't join our group after church either…I think they must have other plans that day. I sure hope he wasn't avoiding me!" Peggy moaned.

"Oh, don't worry about that," soothed Jodie. You'll see him often…your lives are interconnected now. The question is…how to act next time you are together."

"Exactly!"

"I wish Ben could meet him. He's so perceptive about people," Jodie said thoughtfully. "Do you mind if I tell Ben about it and get his take on what you should do, if you're really serious about this man?"

"Not at all…You know I think the world of Ben. I wish he could meet Ian…I just know they'd become great friends." Then Peggy added shrugging. "I need all the help I can get… this is such a new place for me…love? Really? Yikes…that is scary!!"

"So what would be the best way for the men to meet?" Jodie wondered.

"Have you found a church home, yet?" Peggy asked. "If you haven't, you might want to visit our church. It's a relatively small congregation. The church just began three years ago. We meet in what was once a store near a strip mall on Jolly Road. It's called the Okemos Interfaith Chapel; The minister is a woman, Rebecca Lane. She and her family live next door to the Mahoneys. Most Sundays many of us, including Ian and the twins, go out for brunch after church to discuss the sermon and share ideas. Would you and your pair of men want to join us tomorrow?"

"That sounds possible. We've been talking about visiting churches, but haven't begun the process yet. Is there a nursery or toddler room where we could leave B.J.?" Jodie asked.

"Yes, there's excellent child care as well as Sunday School classes. In fact, he would be in the 3-4 year-old class with Michael and Mia, so he would have friends there, already," Peggy offered. "Your coming would seem like a natural follow-up to our lunch today, and the men could meet without it looking like a put-up job."

Jodie began putting on her coat and grabbing her purse. "I'll check with Ben when he gets home. He took Benjy to get some new shoes this afternoon. I'm sure it'll be fine, but I'll give you a call to let you know for sure and get the particulars about the service – time and exact location."

"Great. I'll be waiting for your call," Peggy said buttoning her own coat, then giving her friend a quick hug. "Having lunch with you has been wonderful! You can't begin to know how much I've missed you these past years. You are always so positive, so grounded, so fun….how lucky I am to have you for my friend. I thank the Lord that you are back here, again, Jodie Allen. I'm not sure I ever told you how much I love you, Babe!"

"I guess not, but I love you back and always have," Jodie hugged her friend even tighter. "True friends are hard to find, so we both have much to be thankful for! Bye for now, Miss Margaret Ann."

"Hope to see you in the morning. Bye, bye!"

And the two parted, grinning from ear to ear.

CHAPTER TWENTY-NINE

Ian and Christian's return to campus caused quite a stir. Everyone in the department wanted to hear about the trip to Mozambique and learn as much as possible about their impressions of the possibility of the future of Jatropha as a fuel stock. The two men tried to be as positive as seemed reasonable but knew in their hearts that success – as once imagined – would be a long time in coming.

Ian knew that he and others had many long hours ahead of them in the lab before they found the still-hidden gene that would mean increased quality in the oil seeds. That was one part of the puzzle that was in his hands. To succeed, however, he would need to find a way to interest others in joining him and David Mason in the search. Surely, he hoped, other colleagues would want to get caught up in the quest. He knew for a fact that there were at least a half dozen other professionals in the unit who had interest and experience in plant breeding. The challenge would be to get them involved in what was seen as his project.

The department chair, himself, was a big supporter of the project. He wanted to get other faculty members involved... and had promised to devote at least ten hours a week himself to the project. That was a start; and at the next department meeting when the chair reported that he was going to be personally involved in the project, several others immediately agreed to do likewise. This was in spite of the fact that everyone was carrying a heavy load due to an increase in student enrollment.

After the meeting, Kevin and Jay, the two who had been anything but hospitable to Ian when he arrived, asked to speak with him privately in his office. "Now what?" wondered Ian as the three walked silently back to the corner office.

"Please sit down, Kevin, Jay...how may I help you?" Ian began companionably.

"Kevin, you go first," suggested Jay.

"Well, Ian," the younger man began, clearing his throat. "This is a little difficult for us. As you were probably aware, neither of us was too happy when you came aboard with what we considered unnecessary fanfare. You aren't much older than the two of us. We've been here for more years than we like to remember, and we are still only assistant professors without tenure and rather inadequate office space."

Mahoney nodded slightly, not sure how to reply.

"To make matters worse," continued Jay, "you brought with you a large grant that enabled you to hire three graduate students to assist you. Frankly, that really ticked us off. We haven't been able to attract outside funding, even though we've submitted, revised, and resubmitted our proposal several times for funding. The truth is...we both seem to be in limbo. Then, you move into this big office...and, to be honest, we got our noses a little out of joint."

"Kevin cut in, "In addition to that, you seemed to be a pretty straight shooter...friendly, modest...and you treated us with respect. You were genuinely interested in what we were doing. Even the secretaries thought you could do no wrong. That really ticked us off! The truth is...we both avoided you... and, honestly, you were the topic of more than one animated conversation between us."

Ian just stared at the two of them, speechless.

"We're here to apologize to you, Ian." Jay went on. "It's

pretty embarrassing now to recall how petty and inhospitable we were…we really are sorry, Ian."

"While you were away, slogging through the rain and mud of Mozambique," Kevin continued, "we learned that it was you who provided the input on our draft proposal that was so badly needed. We couldn't believe that you actually took the time to carefully review our proposal and make thoughtful, specific recommendations for improvement…while you were so swamped with your own work! We're quite optimistic that by incorporating your suggestions, our proposal will finally be funded this time around. We just want you to know how sorry we both are and how much we appreciate what you did for us."

Ian stood and went over to his colleagues. "Jay, Kevin, I fully understand how you must have felt, when I came here. Something like that actually happened to me when I was at A & M…and I felt just as you did. Also…I was pretty busy at home at first, so I really didn't go out of my way to be that collegial, myself…and I'm the one that must apologize for that. By the way…I really like what you're proposing to do, and the suggestions I offered…were things I learned from one of my mentors back at A & M when I was trying to figure out the best way to evaluate outcomes. His ideas really helped me…and they seemed to fit with what you were trying to do, as well."

"You're being very gracious, Ian, and we appreciate that. It's not easy to admit that you've been acting like jerks." Kevin said.

"I think perhaps we need to go out for a beer sometime soon…get to know more about each other…clear the air… what do you say, Ian?" Jay asked.

"Love to…I think I need a break from Jatropha…I feel like it is taking permanent residence in my psyche!" Ian laughed.

Kevin cleared his throat. "There's something else, Ian. We both would like to join your team of volunteers...not just because we're feeling guilty...we think this proposal might really make a difference. It can be a game changer, if we can unlock that genetic key. Besides, if anyone can finally solve this puzzle, it's our group at MSU."

"Yes," added Jay, eagerly. "Let's get busy and find that sucker and turn Jatropha into the miracle weed that many believed it to be not all that long ago."

"That's terrific, you two! I welcome your expertise and willingness to help. I have a feeling that working with our MSU team...we just might figure this one out!" Ian smiled broadly as he stepped over to shake their hands. Ian knew that both Kevin and Jay had solid backgrounds in plant breeding, and their enthusiasm for the project would be more than welcome by the entire team. "Let's get that beer soon!"

Ian could hardly wait to share the good news with his dad, who had always believed that faculty squabbles were common...but easily resolved. "Kill them with kindness," he had told his son more than once. "It'll bring them around every time."

This turn of events made the younger Mahoney determined to do what he could to assist the other two in preparing for their upcoming tenure reviews. He really did know how it felt to be shoved aside by some "bright, new hotshot," although he certainly had never thought of himself as that guy! He was so relieved that Kevin and Jay had come in. It took both courage and humility to do that. He admired them for being honest...and who knew...perhaps they would eventually become close personal friends. Not a bad idea, since all three would probably be on the staff together for a long time to come. Having so much departmental support was really going to make a difference for his project. It would be good for the department, too, of course. Having a comfortable, congenial, respectful work environment where everyone does his/her best to support each other…is ultimately what breeds success.

The following Sunday, Ian invited Christian to join him for his short presentation to the congregation about their recent trip to Mozambique. Church members were fascinated by their adventures…especially the story of the little church in the middle of rural Africa. They were warmed to hear about the hospitality that members of that tiny congregation had extended to Ian and his team…total strangers, wet and bedraggled who had wandered into their village. Not only had they provided the travelers with a warm place to sleep, they had been like the poor woman in the Bible, who had "shared her tiny mite." It was quite possible that the food they shared with the men during their several nights' stay was actually part of their own evening meals. It had been such a blessing that Christian could speak the language of the pastor, who, in turn, was eager to share Christian charity with strangers! Ian felt certain that even without their asking, Pastor John would have sensed their need and offered them food and refuge.

Pastor Rebecca was intrigued about becoming partners with the small congregation in that distant place. At its very next meeting, the Board of Elders – with unanimous consent – asked the pastor to explore an official partnership. They moved to send proceeds from the next special offering at the Chapel to that church as a token of appreciation for taking in a group of Christian "brothers." That motion also passed with unanimous consent. Ian could hardly wait to deliver the news to Christian, who was such an integral part of forging the cross-culture friendship that had developed in a tiny village, deep in sub-Saharan Africa.

Peggy, like others who knew Ian, was pleased to learn more about his trip to Mozambique. She appreciated how that difficult and challenging trip could lay the groundwork for a meaningful relationship between the US and that developing nation. While some in the congregation were not big "green agenda" advocates, of course, even they supported things that decreased emissions of the millions of busses, trucks and trains in this country. After all, who wouldn't support changes that saved money while reducing smog.

After his presentation, Peg decided to learn more about the weed Jatropha…and Mozambique. The topic intrigued her. She was a farm girl, after all. Besides, she talked with the professor often, and knowing a little more about his work might help her understand him better. She knew that he didn't have too many close friends outside of his department and the Lanes. So it would be nice for him to be able to talk with someone outside work about his passion. They had done some of that while out to dinner in Eaton Rapids, but it had only piqued her interest. After his presentation, she definitely wanted to get more involved.

She had already told Pastor Becky that she wanted to help the pastor make contact with the little church in Africa. What a heart-warming story that was about how they opened their arms to American strangers…truly the spirit of Christianity in a faraway land. She thought about the children in that little village. They probably had few resources for things like paper, markers, crayons, picture books, and so many other learning tools and toys. Wouldn't it be wonderful to gather donations of such items…new and used…to share with the children of that village? Peggy's mind was alive with the possibilities… as she left the church that day, heading for brunch.

She was looking forward to introducing Ian to Ben and Jodie. She was glad that Benjy, Mia, and Michael had been together during Sunday School…it would allow them to continue their already-comfortable interactions over scrambled eggs and bacon. She couldn't wait to hear what Ben thought about Ian…and what advice he might have for her. A bit nervously, she turned into the parking lot of the restaurant. "Here it goes," she sighed as she stepped out of her car.

CHAPTER THIRTY

Ian was looking forward to the meeting with the youth group at church. "I've certainly enjoyed interacting with those kids," he thought. "Little did I realize when Peggy invited me to help out last October that this would turn out to be such a meaningful experience. Those kids are really a great bunch of teenagers – bright, caring, fun and amazingly aware of current issues! Serving as one of their advisors has been a challenge, but sharing the responsibility with someone like Peggy has made it a lot of fun...and fulfilling."

Tonight was the briefing for the upcoming mission trip to the Pine Ridge Indian Reservation in the southwestern corner of South Dakota. How he wished that he could go with them on what could turn out to be a life-changing experience for some of them. Of course, his being gone for another week was out of the question. Maybe when the twins were older and could even participate, he would be able to spend spring break doing that kind of activity. Fortunately, Rod Lane was able to accompany the group in his place. Considering his extensive knowledge of Native American history and culture and his excellent carpentry skills...Rod was a welcome addition to the team.

Originally part of the Great Sioux Reservation, Pine Ridge was the eighth largest reservation in the country, and it had one of the lowest per-capita incomes. It made Ian cringe when he thought about the how these people lived – nearly 80% were unemployed, almost 50% of the families were below the Federal poverty level, and they had a school dropout rate of 70%! Many of their homes were without electricity, heat, telephone service or even running water. Alcohol use, depression, drugs, diabetes – all contributed to low life-expectancy rates. In 2007, life expectancy of people living on the reservation was 48 years for men and 52 for women.

During their time at Pine Ridge, the young people would help with a variety of construction and clean-up projects, conduct a daily Bible school program for young children, assist in gardening classes and support the residents in every way possible. They would be joined by several other church groups from around Michigan, who were also using their spring breaks for mission trips to aid those in need.

As the meeting in the Chapel's gathering room got under way, several students began spreading out the items they had collected for distribution on the reservation. A local pharmacy had given them a quantity of band-aids in different sizes, along with some over-the counter ointments. A dentist in the congregation contributed four dozen tooth brushes and tubes of tooth paste. Children in Sunday school classes had collected a wide assortment of crayons, magic markers, coloring books and small drawing pads. A sporting goods store that was going out of business sold them a dozen footballs, basketballs and soccer balls for $1 each. The Men's Bible Class donated vegetable seeds and a number of small tools to assist with the gardening project. Finally, there was a large bag of hotel soaps, shampoos and body lotions contributed by church members.

Peggy called the meeting to order. Rod passed around copies of their itinerary and a packing list. "You'll have to pack light," he began, "our van has to carry twelve of us… and our luggage. So bring sturdy shoes and old work clothes and no more than one nicer outfit to wear in case we get a chance to go out some night while on the road. If possible, use a duffle instead of a suitcase." Peggy went on to explain that they would assign duties once they learned more about what those in charge wanted them to do. Since many of the group had experience as Sunday school teachers and helpers, that would help with the Bible School duties. Peggy added that they would be taking a box of teaching aids to use with the children. The adults answered as many of the kids' questions as they could, but they understood that this would be a new experience for all of them, and they would just have to be flexible and take things as they came.

"Moving on," Peggy continued. "It's time for 'open chat.' Does anyone have an issue he or she would like to discuss tonight?" As a part of each regular meeting, the group had an open discussion of issues that concerned them. Sometimes, they dealt with such things as food safety, bullying or drugs and alcohol. At other times they had been concerned with restrictions of their right to free speech at school. The issue this evening pertained to their school's mascot, the "Okemos Chiefs." To date, there had been no strong advocacy for changing the name, but they wondered if using the name in some way maligned the Native Americans who had lived in this area. And even if it offended no one…was it really the image they wanted to give about their school? Recent controversies over professional and even collegiate team names had made them consider the name of their own school teams, and their upcoming visit to a Native American reservation made it even more relevant.

"The teams at Central Michigan are called the Chippewas," said one young man. "I don't hear any cries to change that name."

"Actually, there was a controversy there," corrected another student, "they are now referred to as the 'Chips.'"

"That's true," said yet another, "and I think the University of Illinois chose to give up their Indian Chief mascot who used to perform at their games."

"I don't see that Chiefs is any more derogatory than names such as Spartans or Trojans," added another.

"What do you think, Doc? "asked Libby Lane.

"Well, I guess I think it's probably a good idea to see how local Native Americans feel about the name," he replied. "Of course, that might be a hard thing to do, since my guess is that there are very few native Americans living in Meridian Township these days, let alone in Okemos. It might also be a good idea for some of you to do some reading about the issue…bring up some pros and cons…and perhaps after the trip, we can have a debate on the topic."

"Actually, that's a discussion we may want to have with young people who we meet in Pine Ridge," Peggy suggested. "They will certainly have some feelings and opinions about the matter. I understand that some tribes resent being referred to as 'Redskins' or 'Braves' and others do not. I, for one, will be interested in what our hosts think about the issue. Their insight may come in useful for our post-trip debate. Having facts as well as opinions is important."

"I agree," Ian said. "Let's plan on doing just that at our next regular meeting. Let's get some volunteers to do that pro and con research." Several kids raised their hands and volunteered to do some reading on the subject.

Peggy glanced down at her watch, "I hate to break up this discussion, my friends, but it is a school night and we need to have our closing devotions. Libby, I believe you volunteered to lead them tonight. The floor is yours."

Libby stepped forward. "I can't think of a better scripture than the one that reminds us to do unto others as we would have them do unto us…and remembering that the least of us is precious in the Lord's sight." With that Libby offered an

Indian prayer poem to close the meeting. The group began to gather their things and move toward the door. The kids were eager for the start of spring break and the adventure that awaited them. They would set out before dawn on Saturday morning and head to South Dakota for a week of volunteer service. For many, it would change them in ways that they couldn't begin to imagine.

The time spent on the reservation was a week of stark reality, hard labor, mind-stretching discussions and friendship building. Coming from a prosperous suburban community, the young people were shocked by the primitive living conditions of the residents of Pine Ridge. They had never been exposed to such abject poverty. Their own accommodations were meager....their meals basic....and their surroundings bleak.

Peggy and Rod were proud of their group, however. No one complained...they worked hard...they soldiered on. In fact, they seemed to thrive and be more and more energized with each passing day.

They talked about the joy they saw on the faces of the children during their singing and worship sessions. They laughed and played with the children and teens who lived there, as they developed personal relationships with the residents. Rod and Peg treasured the talks the group had each evening as they recounted what they had experienced that day. The construction and clean-up projects were much appreciated by their hosts, who saw how hard the kids worked. It was amazing how much the teens looked forward to their icy shift showers each day...and were thankful for a chance to just rinse off some of the dust and sweat.

A highlight of the week was a special program mid-week when an Elder spoke with the visitors. He talked about the desire of many on the reservation who were eager to bring back their native language so the young people would not lose sight of their heritage. Retaining aspects of their culture including dance and craftsmanship were also important parts of Indian life for the younger generation to remember. He also explained the connection between Indian spirituality and Christianity and how the Great Spirit and one God were united in creating the world.

One of the boys noticed a disabled older man who was always bare-footed. He had brought along a new pair of Nikes (despite Rod's admonition about limited space), but they were something he had saved for and been eager to wear. Before the group left to return home, he consulted with Rod and then offered his brand new shoes to the man whose feet seemed to be about the same size as his own. "I have my work shoes along," he told Mr. Lane, "so I won't have to go barefoot on the way home."

His gift brought a tear to the old man's eye as he grabbed the boy's hand and whispered, "Bless you, my son." It was a moment the young man would never forget.

Peggy was glad that they had encouraged the kids to keep journals that would highlight their experiences and help them recall incidents that they might otherwise forget. It was also a way to remember how they felt during their time on the reservation. For her part, Peggy fell in love with the beautiful little infants she was able to hold and cuddle. It was obvious that many of their mothers were very young themselves and knew little about the care and nutrition of babies; but their tenderness, love and pride in the little ones was evident in the gentle smiling way they held, fed and sang to their children.

Saying good-bye to the friends they had made…both on the reservation and among the other youth volunteers… was harder than any of them had expected. They found the warmth, openness, appreciation and congeniality of their hosts to be overwhelming. They found the work ethic, deep compassion, light-heartedness and optimism of their other young volunteers inspiring. Many friendships were forged... and plans to stay in touch were confirmed.

The group was busy on the trip back to Michigan planning how to share their experiences with the congregation. Many of the congregants had helped to cover the travel costs of the trip, provided items to be distributed and prayed for the well-being of the young people. They would be eager to hear how the adventure had unfolded. The teens struggled with how they could possibly thank the congregation for supporting their trip...and how they could put into words what this incredible experience had meant to them. It had shocked, challenged, vitalized and transformed them. Peggy and Rod smiled at each other as they listened to their young friends chatter about what the week at Pine Ridge had meant to them. It had impacted Peggy and Rod, too. They suspected that this experience would have special meaning to all of them...not just in the weeks and months ahead...but for the rest of their lives.

As Peggy reflected on the week's experience, she hoped that the young people would never forget or minimize the gift they had been given. It was such a meaningful exchange! Who would forget the glorious sunset over the desert? Who would not realize the cultural gift that had been shared by their hosts? Though "poor" in many respects, the artistry of the jewelry makers, painters and weavers were awesome.

CHAPTER THIRTY-ONE

Peggy could hardly wait to return home after the youth group meeting to give Jodie a call. The two hadn't been in contact since the brunch after church.

Jodie picked up on the first ring. "Hi, there, Girlfriend. How's it going?"

"Great!" Peggy responded. "I just got back from the youth group meeting with Ian and couldn't wait to hear what you and Ben thought about him!"

There was a pause.

"Jodie, did you hear my question?" Peggy asked, nervously.

"Of course, Silly. You couldn't wait to ask, could you?" Jodie laughed. "We really appreciated being invited to the Sunday service and the brunch afterwards. We loved the Pastor's remarks and couldn't believe that the people were so friendly and welcoming. We're thinking we might plan to attend regularly. A smaller church really seems to fit our family right now."

"I'm glad to hear that. And what did you think about Dr. Mahoney?" Peggy pressed. "You know I value your opinion… and Ben's"

"The long and short of it is…we think Ian is great!" Jodie said enthusiastically. "For starters, we were both very impressed with Ian's parenting style. He is so aware of the twins – their behavior and needs. Not all that many dads are so responsive to little ones! And they're quite a delightful two-some! I only hope B.J. turns out as well. I have a suspicion that in the short time you've known them, you've had something to do with that, too."

"Well, I don't know about that," Peggy demurred, "but the children have both been leaders in their class and have grown a lot – both socially and intellectually – since they arrived last August. And what did you think about Ian…the man?"

"Simply put," Jodie said earnestly, "we liked him a lot! He's so genuine and responsive to what others are saying. As you know, Ben's a little on the shy/reserved side and is seldom very open about his work and interests."

"I know that about Ben, of course, especially around those he doesn't know very well," Peggy said, "but his concern for others and his depth of knowledge about so many things makes it worth the effort to draw him out."

"Because Ben is like that," Jodie continued, "I can't believe how open he was in responding to Ian's questions about his work. Conversation between them seemed so natural and easy, almost as if they were old friends."

It warmed Peggy's heart to hear her friend talk about Ian that way. "Perhaps because Ian was an only child, he learned to relate to others easily…you know…question them about their interests and activities because he really wanted to connect with them. He sort of had to do it, because he didn't have the ready-made friends that siblings can be."

"Ian really listens when someone talks and seems to be sincerely interested in what that person has to say. I certainly appreciate it when people really look you in the eye when the two of you are talking," Jodie said, "and Ian does that."

"I can't believe you noticed that after only meeting him once," Peggy observed. "You know, Ian hasn't made a lot of man-friends since moving here. There hasn't really been a lot of time for him to do 'guy things.' I know he's made collegial connections at the office, but other than interactions with Rod

Lane, the pastor's husband, I don't know if he's developed any strong male friendships. I haven't heard him mention doing things with anyone…and he doesn't play golf."

"I sure hope that he and Ben can become close friends, Pegs. It would be great for both of them…and for us!" Jodie laughed. "By the way, can you believe Ben and Ian actually have a mutual friend? One of Ian's undergraduate friends in Washington was a Duke Med School classmate and lab partner of Ben's!"

"It really is a small world," Peggy agreed.

"Ben also said that he thought you and Ian have a special… chemistry – probably more than either of you realize."

"What led him to that conclusion?" Peggy pressed.

"Body language, non-verbals, I would guess," Jodie explained. "Ben's very perceptive about such things. We both noticed that Ian always smiled when he looked at you or responded to things you said. He also nodded a lot when you were talking."

"Hmmm, I never noticed that." Peggy reddened at the thought and was glad her friend couldn't see her right now. She knew that Jodie would tease her for blushing. She just calmly went on, "That's good to know. Did you two come up with any ideas on what I should do, so I don't scare him away or destroy our friendship? I'd sure hate to lose him as a friend."

"Yeah, I can see that, although we both know that friendship is not the end game in this scenario!" Jodie chided her friend. "I really don't have any suggestions, Peg. Just keep on being your open, personable, caring self – the lovely woman Ian clearly respects and counts on. He obviously values your friendship, your amazing relationship with his children…and I suspect a bit more than that."

"Yeah, we have a lot of fun doing stuff together like laughing at the antics of Mike and Mia and fielding challenging questions from the teens in our youth group, and we do share basic Christian beliefs and values, that's important to me," Peggy said tactfully avoiding any comments about their shared physical attraction.

"Well, those certainly form a great foundation upon which to build a lasting relationship!" Jodie agreed, also avoiding the feelings discussion for the moment. "What are his parents like?"

"Oh, I liked them immediately when I met them at Christmas." Peggy quickly responded before they got on the thin ice of romance talk. "They've always been active in their church and community, and they adore the grandkids. His dad is a retired professor, but I think he and Dad share a similar view of the world. I know that they both believe in outreach and helping others…so I think they would get along great together."

"And his mom?" prompted Jodie.

Peggy smiled widely, "She's energetic, fun and a logistical wizard. She can multi-task and have fun doing it. She's also very perceptive. I could tell by the way she looked at Ian and me that she suspected we might be more than friends…and she was so warm and accepting of me. I loved her immediately. I think she and my mom would click, too. Katie Mahoney was an elementary teacher, and you know Mom was a Home Economics teacher. They're about the same age and both dote on their families. My folks never warmed up to Donn Bahler's parents; they marched to different drums for sure…but I think this would be different."

"Well, sounds like there are a lot of stars aligned in this relationship…so let's stop avoiding the big question…do you love him?" Her best friend finally stopped beating around the bush and laid it right out there.

"I…I…" Peggy stammered. "You are so bad, My Friend, you know I've never loved anyone before…and the truth is I'm afraid to admit – even to myself – that I might actually love this man. If thinking about him all the time, wanting to be with him constantly, getting all tingly when he touches me and thinking of the future with him means I love him…then YES!…I guess I do love him. There! Are you happy?? You finally made me say the words!"

Jodie laughed heartily, "Oh, Pegster…I knew you loved him from the moment I saw you with him. You get that dreamy look in your eyes when you see him, you're so proud of him when he talks about his work and his kids, you laugh when he jokes, you blush whenever there's a suggestion of anything more than friendship…and when you told me about the times he held you and kissed you…it's just so obvious you're in love with Ian Mahoney! So there, we can stop pretending it's just friendship!"

"Oh, Jodie, leave it to you," Peggy laughed, "I guess that's what I wanted to hear. And actually, it's such a relief to finally admit that this is the man I truly want to be with…perhaps forever. So help me, My Friend, what do you suggest I do now? I've done my best to avoid romantic involvement so far...probably because I'm afraid."

"Afraid of losing him?" Jodie asked.

"Yes, I guess I really am."

"Well, let me tell you something, Peg, new love is like that. When you care for someone so deeply, you do worry that perhaps he doesn't feel the same or that maybe it won't work out…but take it from me…it's worth the risk to find out," the sage Jodie explained.

Peggy took a deep breath and sighed loudly, "Okay, you're right. I need to stop denying myself…and let the chips fall where they may. So where do I go from here?"

"Well, let's see. Here's one idea," Jodie offered.

"What's that?"

"You and I are kind of 'touchy/feely' people. My sense is that Ian doesn't get many hugs or pats on the back these days, something we all need. I have the sense that the professor would welcome your little touches now and then. Those little signs of caring are so important in a relationship and come more easily for women than men."

"That's no doubt true, and something I've never thought about," Peggy considered. "Our family does a lot of hugging and kissing. Even when Sam and I had our differences we always made up with a big bear hug. And I know Kate Mahoney is like that, too."

"You've talked about Ian's obvious love for his wife and her loving nature, so I suspect she may have been a hugger too. He probably really misses that kind of connection," Jodie added. "I think you should stop holding back and just do what comes naturally. And by the way…next time there's a romantic moment…don't try to make a joke or spare Ian…my sense is he doesn't need you to protect him from involvement. In fact, he probably worries that you are afraid of involvement. Again, just do what comes naturally. That will be $50, please…pretty cheap for such monumental love advice, I'd say."

"Hey, Peg," Jodie interrupted herself, "I hear B.J. stirring from his nap. I'm going to have to run. Keep me in the loop, My Friend. I can't wait to hear what happens next!"

"I knew I could count on you, Jodiemeister…many thanks for waking me up and pointing me in the right direction!" Peggy said gratefully. "You are, indeed, my forever friend… and I love you for being you!"

"Back to you, Peggy, Dear," Jodie smiled. "Hey, before I let you go, I have to tell you that B.J. and I have a meeting tomorrow with Grace Foster, the administrator at Ojibwa. I sure hope there's a spot for him so he can begin at the school soon. He really needs to be in a more structured environment and have a chance to interact with other kids his age."

"That's great! Be sure to peek into my room when you're there. I'll be eager to hear what Grace has to say. Oh, by the way, did you know that Ben invited Ian to join him in a 5K race on behalf of disabled children?"

"No, that's wonderful," Jodie said. "Perhaps they'll do some training together and then maybe start an exercise routine…I know Ben has wanted to find someone to work out with."

"Bye for now, Dear One…and thank the Lord for giving me a friend like you!" Peggy said before hanging up.

"We'll keep you in our prayers," Jodie responded. "Bye for now!"

Peggy mouthed a silent prayer. She was so thankful to have her dear friend close by. She had missed the special bond they shared. Although she had many friends and acquaintances, Jodie was special…one of a kind…and her dearest friend in the world. She really did thank the Lord above for bringing that special person home to her.

CHAPTER THIRTY-TWO

The children were excited – only a few more days until Grandpa and Nana would arrive from Texas. Michael and Mia knew they were coming soon, since every day they marked off the days on the calendar. It had been over nine months since they had seen these grandparents.

Mrs. Harding had returned to Michigan ten days earlier. Both her daughter and new granddaughter, Molly, were doing well. Mrs. H had finally felt comfortable leaving them and returning home.

"We're so glad to have you back!" Ian had said when he saw her. "Now things can finally get back to normal!"

The older woman had helped get the house ready for the visitors and made a point to restock the pantry and refrigerator, so the Calhouns would be able to manage without her.

It was Good Friday, and the twins were out of school, so they were able to go with their dad to the airport to pick up their grandparents. Grandpa and Nana were elated that the whole family was there to welcome them. Nana scooped the twins into her arms, wiping away a quick tear.

"My goodness!" said Nana; "Just look at the two of you! I can't believe you're so grown up! You don't even look like our Mike and Mia. Isn't that right, Hal?"

Their grandfather gave them each a big bear hug before he replied, "Right you are, my dear…what do you think happened to those toddlers we left in Texas? Pretty soon we'll have to put these two out to work to earn their keep." Everybody laughed at the thought of the not yet five-year-olds having to support themselves. Grandpa was always such a big tease.

The Texans had never been to Michigan, so they enjoyed the trip from the airport to Okemos. "What a nice place to live," remarked Helen. "Everything is so green, and I see that you have daffodils and even tulips starting to bloom. I expected it to be much colder."

"Well, spring is just around the corner, that's for sure," Ian laughed. "Some days are quite warm already. Of course, it helps that Easter is a bit later this year than normal."

"Are the golfers out already?" asked his father-in-law, noticing that the house backed up to a golf course."

"I really can't say," replied Ian. "I've been too busy to notice; and besides, I am not a golfer like my Dad."

"Michael, did you collect many lost balls last year? I imagine that a lot of them land in your backyard, unless this course only attracts pros."

"Not too many, Grandpa," said Michael, "but Bob, our neighbor, says he's never had to buy any golf balls, 'cause of all the balls that land in their yard."

"Someone has been really thoughtful," said Mrs. Calhoun. "Hal, look at the beautiful bowl of fruit in our bedroom, and I love the pot of daffodils! They smell so fresh…like sunshine indoors!"

"Give Mrs. Harding credit for those touches. She's really been a gem. I'd never have thought to put them in your room," confessed Ian.

"I hope we can meet her," commented his father-in-law. "I know we're indebted to her for stepping in when Helen broke her leg. Sadly, there's been no way to get here sooner than this."

"I'm sure you'll meet her at church on Sunday. Her sisters are coming for the week-end, so she's sure to be there." Ian assured them, then added, "You can also meet their 'substitute nanny' as the kids call her. I told you about Margaret – Peggy – Gerber. She's their Montessori Directress who stepped in to take care of the kids when Ida was called to Denver to deal with her daughter's emergency. It was actually Michael and Mia's idea to ask her to fill in here at the house. We're all indebted to her for helping us out."

"How kind and generous of her to leave her own family to come in to assist yours," observed Helen.

"No, Nana," corrected Mia. "Miss Peggy lives alone. Her family lives on a farm someplace else."

"Yeah," added Michael, "we think she liked being here with us, so she wouldn't be all by herself. Besides…she likes us!"

"Of course she does," laughed Nana, "who wouldn't fall in love with the two of you?"

Ian and the kids were delighted to play tour guides, as they drove Grandpa and Nana around the MSU campus and pointed out the famous bell tower, Spartan Stadium and the Breslin Center where they had attended a women's basketball game. Of particular interest to the Calhouns were the new Broad Art Museum and the Wharton Center theatre complex. They stopped by the children's school to show their grandparents the school grounds but were surprised to find Miss Grace, the school administrator there. So they were able to give their visitors a tour of the Ojibwa Montessori School…and their classroom.

"I love your school, kids. And I must say, living adjacent to a university campus certainly has many benefits," noted Helen. "We've always appreciated living fairly near A & M. It's been wonderful to have access to so many outstanding speakers, sports and cultural events all these years. And, of course, it's great to have so many young people around."

As always, the twins insisted that no trip to campus would be complete without a stop at the Dairy Store. So, of course, the group had to stop for cones.

"We've certainly given the Dairy Store our share of business since arriving in town," remarked Ian. "We also buy a lot of the Spartan cheese they make here."

"And we know how good that is," Hal said. "We loved the box of Spartan cheese you sent us for Christmas. It was a huge hit at the open house we hosted over the holidays."

The next day, the plan was to attend church a bit early, so Helen and Hal could meet some of the Mahoneys' friends before the service began. The children tumbled out of bed at the crack of dawn anxious to see if the Easter Bunny had come.

"Grandpa, Nana, Daddy!!!" shrieked the children as they discovered two baskets outside their bedroom door. "The Easter Bunny came!!!" They couldn't wait to paw through the contents of their brightly colored baskets filled with Easter surprises, plastic grass, jelly beans, chocolate eggs and bunnies.

"I guess a few sweets on Easter morning won't hurt anyone," laughed their dad. "Now you can each have two small pieces...then we have to have our breakfast before Sunday School."

After breakfast the children dressed for church. Michael looked so grown up in his new khaki pants and navy blazer. Mia loved her new yellow dress with its matching purse and tam. Helen was glad she'd gotten the children's sizes and brought the new Easter outfits for them as a special surprise.

As they went outside, they were even more surprised to discover two more small baskets on the front porch. Each was topped with a funny bunny hand puppet. Now how did the Easter Bunny know that they loved playing with puppets?

And how lucky were they to each get another surprise basket before church!

The parking lot was filling with cars when the family arrived. Pastor Becky was in the entry greeting folks as they came in and was delighted to meet Ian's in-laws from Texas. "We're so pleased that you made it and can worship with us this morning," Becky said sincerely, giving each of them a warm, welcoming hug. We've heard so much about you! Easter is always such a special time for families...and we're glad you can be part of our church family today, as well!"

"She seems very warm and friendly," Helen observed. "What a blessing to have a pastor as a next door neighbor. She's no doubt become a very special friend."

"Not only Becky," Ian replied quickly, "the whole family's been a Godsend to us. Rod, her husband, is the American history teacher at the High School. He's writing a biography about the Indian Chief for whom our town is named. Their two children are the greatest! Libby's in high school and sometimes babysits for us. Bob's an MSU student and an Eagle Scout. He often brings his guitar to neighborhood and church gatherings and leads us in singing camp songs."

"Hello there, Mahoneys," came a friendly greeting. "And these must be the famous Grandpa and Nana Calhoun. Welcome to Michigan! I'm Peggy Gerber, the twins Montessori teacher," said Peggy. "I feel as if I already know you, since Michael and Mia talk about you so often. They've been telling us about your visit at school for days."

"And we're delighted to meet you, Miss Peggy! How can we even begin to thank you for stepping in and looking after our grandchildren when Ian was in Mozambique! It was an emergency on top of an emergency...and you saved the day! I can't tell you how disappointed we were to have to cancel our visit...but we knew Ida Harding was there for the kids, so we were fine. Then, to find out she was called away! I guess it's a good thing we didn't know about that until afterward. You're really something, my dear. We were so sorry to miss being here with the kids, but we're grateful that you were here for them!" Nana unexpectedly hugged Peggy, and whispered in her ear, "You are, indeed, an angel, Peggy Gerber!"

The Easter service was truly uplifting, especially the rousing anthems sung by the choir. Pastor Becky's message was straight to the point. "Christ died for all of us, and in so doing forgave our sins. Praise the Lord! He has risen! We, too, can rise to be the persons God intended us to be!"

The Calhouns thought it would be great to join the other church-goers, who normally had brunch together after church. The baked ham, hard boiled eggs and Easter cut-out cookies that Mrs. Harding and the children baked would be just fine as an early-evening Easter feast. The gathering allowed the Calhouns to meet the rest of the Lane family as well as Mrs. Harding and her sisters. They also had an opportunity to chat a bit with Peggy about her family and the children's progress in school.

The group who gathered for brunch wanted to hear more about Ian's trip to Africa. He spoke briefly about the project and the country, but focused mainly on the villagers and many kindnesses they had extended to his group. He concluded by thanking them for agreeing to partner with the small out-back church in Mozambique.

Before they left, Ian managed to catch Peggy's eye, and mouthed a quick, "Thank you for the Easter baskets." Her smile and wink confirmed what he had expected. She was, indeed, the Bunny who had dropped surprise baskets on his porch that morning on her way to church.

The Calhouns seemed to be enjoying their visit to Michigan and were eager to take in as many sights as possible. It was almost as if they didn't plan to return. To Ian, his in-laws seemed a lot older and less energetic than he remembered. The loss of their only daughter had no doubt taken its toll on them. That evening, after the children were in bed, the three adults sat down to chat and relax.

After settling in, Mr. Calhoun leaned forward and looked earnestly at his son-in-law, "Ian, we have something we want to tell you. We've made a big decision, and we want you to know about it."

"Oh, my," Ian replied, "that sound's ominous."

"Not at all," Hal chuckled. "Actually, it's a decision we've been considering for a while now. The ranch is getting to be a bit overwhelming...even with extra help. So, we've decided to sell the ranch and move to California where we have relatives. We were thinking about it before, but since Helen was thrown, she no longer cares to ride, and riding alone is no fun for me. We've decided we're ready to seek some new adventures...and now seems like a good time."

"Whoa," Ian replied. "That is a change! I can certainly understand about the riding...and the ranch is a heck of a lot of work. But you two are so active. It's hard to imagine you just sitting around...even if it is in California."

"My first cousin and his son own a small vineyard near San Louis Obispo." Hal continued. "They're in the process of opening a cafe and tasting room on the property, and they need some extra help. They've invited us to be part of their operation. You know that Helen's always wanted to open a bed and breakfast. So she now she'll be able to show off her culinary skills without having to do the daily beds/laundry/ cleaning chores of a B & B. We hope this will be both a challenge and a blessing for us both."

"Yes, Ian," Helen added. "We think the change of scene will be good for both of us. The folks in California are our only living relatives, besides you and the twins; so being near them will mean a lot to us. We should also tell you that we've finally come to grips with Laurie's death. It's been a hard journey, but we've finally forgiven the young man who ran that stoplight and ended her life. Forgiving him was the hardest thing we've ever done...but it helped us find peace. Our hope is that you, too, are able to forgive. We pray for you each night, dear Ian, for we now know that without forgiveness, your pain and suffering will never end."

Ian looked down at his hands. It was still hard for him to talk about Laurie's death...especially with her beloved parents. Slowly he lifted his eyes to theirs and said, softly, "Yes, Helen...and Hal...I think I understand. I, too, have been struggling to forgive him. I'm almost there, I think. God has touched our lives in so many ways this past year. I can only think that Laurie, our guardian angel, is working with Him to heal us."

Ian pulled his in-laws close and hugged them both. "We'll have to plan a trip to see you as soon as you're settled. California would be a great place to visit...and, after all, it's only a plane-ride away...just like Texas! We'll have to make a point to get together both here and in sunny California more often. I know the twins have missed spending time with the two of you...and so have I."

"You know you're always welcome and remain our favorite son, Ian dear," Helen continued. "Now forgive me for being an old busybody, but Hal and I have talked about this a lot. We – and we know our Laurie also – hope that you are moving on with your life. You're a wonderful man with much to offer. We know what a great husband and father you are... we've seen it firsthand. You're much too young to spend the rest of your life by yourself...and our grandchildren will need a mother more and more as they grow older. I guess what we're saying is: allow yourself to live…to love…to take a chance again. Let love happen again."

There were tears in the eyes of all three as Hal continued where his wife left off. "We also want you to know that we've cashed in the insurance policy that we took out on Laurie when she was a child. We decided to establish a small endowment in her name at the university. Each year, a promising young journalism student will receive a Laurie Calhoun Mahoney scholarship to assist him or her financially. It's just one small way that we can honor our daughter and at the same time… make a difference."

Ian was without words for a moment. Then he choked, "Laurie would be so pleased! You know how she loved working with young people. That's truly a wonderful and fitting memorial. As the children grow up…it will mean a lot to them, as well. Thank you both for this amazing gift…for Laurie, for me, and for our little ones, too!"

"And there's one more thing," added Helen. "You know how much she loved that old horse of hers, Stubby Tail?"

"Yes, of course," laughed Ian. "Who could forget Stubby Tail?"

"Well, he's not quite ready for the glue factory yet, and he's about the gentlest horse alive," Helen continued. "So we decided to donate him to the special needs program in our county that offers horseback riding to children with disabilities. Do you remember that Laurie worked with that program for several summers when she was in high school? She even took old Stubby with her on a number of occasions. They're always thankful for an additional horse that can be trusted with children."

"You two are so thoughtful!" Ian said, as he shook his head. "Let's hope that old Stubby has many more years ahead of him!"

Having this conversation was not easy for any of the adults, but they all knew that it was part of bringing closure to the sadness of the past few years. Yes, each was healing in his or her own way. They all knew the future would not be without sad moments, but with God's help – and with forgiveness – grieving would slowly turn to hope – and perhaps, even optimism.

After the Calhouns had gone back to Texas, Ian thought about setting a time to talk with Pastor Becky. He really wanted to share what the Calhouns had told him…how they had found peace…and what he was beginning to feel himself. During the past months he and Becky had talked several times about blame, forgiveness, healing and moving beyond grief. Becky's counsel had lifted him up and was helping him work through his feelings. She – like the Calhouns – spoke of the future and his need to look ahead.

Becky had watched as Ian and Peggy had become friends. She couldn't help but notice that the friendship seemed to becoming something more. As she prayed for the Mahoneys – for Ian and the twins – her prayers always included a special word for Peggy Gerber. Peggy Gerber, the young woman she admired and loved as a second daughter…the young woman who just might be falling in love with this very special man.

CHAPTER THIRTY-THREE

After the twins were asleep, their Dad decided to relax a bit on the patio and enjoy thinking about all that had happened since they came to Michigan last August. What a blessing the move had been! The twins were thriving, really enjoying their time at the Montessori school; and they had made many friends in the neighborhood, too.

Ian's work was progressing on schedule with excellent inputs from colleagues and his graduate student team. He had made some new friends at church and thoroughly appreciated his partnership and growing friendship with Peggy Gerber while over-seeing the church's youth group. She had come to be a very special part of his life as well as being loved by the twins. Ian thought about Peggy. Yes, she was his friend, but he had to be honest with himself...Peggy was really becoming much more than a "friend," and he was thankful she had stepped into his life.

The recent visit by Laurie's parents had helped him bring closure to the grief of his wife's death that had been so difficult to overcome. Like them, he truly wanted to forgive the fellow who had caused Laurie's death. He was coming to accept that people sometimes make poor choices that can have serious lifelong consequences for others...even when the intent to harm is not there. If Jesus Christ could forgive those who wronged him and even Laurie's parents were able to offer forgiveness...surely Ian could forgive as well. As Pastor Becky had promised, with forgiveness would come peace – something he was beginning to experience for the first time since he'd lost his Laurie.

Living next to the Lane family was another blessing for him and the children. Rod was a great guy…always ready to assist with home maintenance projects and inquire about how his research project was going. Libby and Bob were fine role models for the twins and never too busy to answer the "bazillion" questions the curious youngsters posed. Becky, of course, had become a special friend and spiritual counselor. He certainly had much to be thankful for.

As he was preparing to have his nightly chat with God, he noticed Becky had wandered into her backyard. Becky, who had just returned from a church meeting and like Ian, was eager to take in the night sounds and enjoy the fragrance of the spring blossoms, noticed Ian and sang out a cheerful, "Hi there, Neighbor! I hope I'm not disturbing your reverie."

"Not at all, Becky," he waved to her and motioned for her to approach. "Come on over and join me. It's such a lovely spring evening. I didn't want to waste it by staying inside."

"I'm eager to share some good news with you," Becky said enthusiastically as she walked onto the patio.

"Please do! I am all ears."

"Well, I – or should I say we – just received a long letter from Pastor John. He and his congregation in Mozambique are most appreciative of the funds and educational materials we sent them."

"I'm so glad they arrived safely" Ian said. "One is always wary when sending things to such a remote site."

"But there's even better news!" Becky continued.

"Yes?"

"When John told his bishop of our plans to partner with his congregation, the bishop was over-joyed. He immediately began to brainstorm ways to expand the partnership idea to involve other congregations both there and here. Because he's a real go-getter, he offered John a sabbatical to come here to refine the details of our arrangement and to explore the possibility of identifying other Michigan congregations that might have a similar interest in partnering with an African congregation."

"What a wonderful idea!" Ian responded.

Becky continued, "For many years Michigan towns and cities have had partnerships with towns and cities in Japan in a program called, 'The Sister Cities Program.' In fact…as we both know…many American churches have special outreach programs with other churches all over the globe."

"Actually," Ian added, "since MSU has a long history of working with various African nations, this would be a fine complement to those efforts…and I imagine that our grad-student, Christian, could be a big help in making the bishop's dream come true."

"I think you're right," Becky agreed. "How much longer will he be in Michigan?"

"At least one or two more years, depending on his decision about pursuing his doctorate," Ian said. "When will Pastor John be making the trip to the U.S.?"

"I'm not sure, but it could be as early as this fall. Will you serve on the committee that works with him?" she asked.

"Yes, of course!" Ian answered enthusiastically, "and I think that Peggy'd be interested in the project, too. I know she and her family are well connected with churches in the Saginaw area…giving us another community that might want to participate."

"You and Peg make such a good team, Ian!" Becky pursued the topic of Peggy. "While on the youth group mission trip, Rod was amazed at the positive things he heard that the two of you have done to facilitate the young people's social and spiritual growth this year."

"Thanks, Becky. It's been an unexpectedly satisfying experience for me too," Ian admitted. "I think that's because of the candor and spiritual insights of our Miss Peggy. In my book, she's one in a million."

"She is one in a million, Ian. And I don't say that because of my special relationship with her, either. It's because she cares about people. She's fun and smart and committed. Just like with her teaching, she's going to make a wonderful wife and mother someday," Becky said...throwing the not-too-subtle hint out there for Ian.

"Yes, that's for sure. In fact, I have to admit, Becky," Ian said gingerly. "I think she and I are becoming closer than just friends. She's amazing with the children, and they love her dearly. She's been pretty amazing with me, too. In fact, sometimes I wonder what I ever would have done without her." Ian was stunned that he had openly expressed so much of what had been in his heart. "I find that I just want to be with her more and more."

"You know, Ian," Becky offered. "You and Peggy are both special people. You both care about others...and it's natural for people with so much in common to be drawn to one another. Don't fight it...just let this relationship become what it will become. You have Someone looking down on you from above...trust that He will guide you."

"Thank you, Becky, it's really a relief to finally admit what has been on mind for some time now," Ian said, "and I think you're right. I'll just let the Good Lord help me find my way...perhaps I'll stop denying what's in my heart. Let love happen."

Becky nodded and changed the subject, "Hey, I haven't asked recently how your work's going? Will you be making another trip to Africa soon?"

"The seed research is steady, but it takes time, Becky," Ian explained. "I feel confident that we're on the right track. In response to my quarterly reports, our funders have been quite pleased."

"That's good news," Becky said, "and it bodes well for future funding, I would think."

"Yes, but wait just a minute. There is both bad news and possibly good news about what's actually happening on the ground in Mozambique," Ian added.

"What do you mean?" Becky asked, sitting forward in the lawn chair.

"Well, since our return from Africa, I've had an opportunity to talk with another MSU ag professor, who spent time in Mozambique working on economic issues," Ian explained. "His assessment was that it was unlikely that Jatropha would be a viable export crop in the foreseeable future – mostly because of the lack of local infra-structure. This only confirmed what we noticed when we were there. However, on a more optimistic note, this professor recalled hearing about one area that we didn't visit where farmers banded together and had access to a small processing plant within a reasonable distance of the production area. Those farmers were successful in making enough biodiesel to meet their local needs for buses, trucks and other vehicles. Of course, we'll have to follow-up on this information, but it does hold promise. Perhaps it could be a way to expand on the contract-farming initiatives we saw in operation already. There might be local or governmental funds to help build small processing facilities. That would certainly enhance the income for the growers."

"Starting on a smaller scale might prove helpful in raising modest financial investments, as well," Becky said grasping Ian's point immediately.

A recent report indicated that there are about 4.3 million farms in Mozambique, but the vast majority – 99 percent

– are small household farms. The President maintains that agriculture remains at the top of the national development agenda.

"Another positive is that because of feedback from the USAID representative who was with us in Mozambique, apparently USAID is prepared to fund a grant for an educational initiative for farmers there. USAID sponsors such programs all around the world."

"What would be the goal of that grant…more research dollars?" Becky asked.

"No," Ian shook his head. "Actually, it would be a training grant to help teach rural farmers about some basic agricultural practices that they could adopt without big financial investments. Obviously, they have little money. During our visit there, it became clear that farmers lack the understanding of how to grow crops profitably. However, they were very eager to learn ways to improve their production."

"Would you be part of the training team?" she probed.

Ian chuckled. "No, my plate's pretty full, and that's not really my area of expertise. However, I hope that once we have more information about the grant…two of my colleagues will take the lead in developing suitable teaching plans that could be delivered without a lot of stress on the learners. I would expect Christian Rosario and another of my grad assistants, Dana Walters, to be part of that team. Dana has a strong farm background as well as political skills that will come in handy. Both of these young people are excellent teachers, and this experience will certainly add to their portfolios. This assistance fits right into President Nyusi's urging managers in public administration to monitor the transfer of knowledge to the agricultural producers."

"Ian, that's one more project to add to my prayer list," Becky responded. "I've always had high regard for the

Biblical story that tells us it's better to teach a man to fish than to give him a fish."

"I say 'Amen' to that!"

"Look at that full moon, would you," Becky said gazing up at the sky. "I hate to break up this conversation, but I guess it's time for me to head next door. Rod will be wondering if I've been kidnapped."

"Well, I guess he'd be right...I did kidnap you!" Ian laughed. "It's your own fault for asking about my work and for being such a good listener! Thanks so much for coming over and sharing the great news about Pastor John, Becky. And thanks for letting me bare my soul about Peggy. It means the world to have such a special person living right next door. Please give my apologies to Rod...and thanks again, Becky. Good night!"

"Good night to you, Ian. I guess there was a reason God put you and those darling children next door to me..." she said smiling. "It's a blessing for us all!"

As the two parted, the pastor gave a quick prayer of thanks for the fine young man her family had come to know and love. With her whole heart she prayed that if it was God's will, the relationship between him and Peggy Gerber would continue to grow and bless them with a meaningful future together.

CHAPTER THIRTY-FOUR

May marked another milestone for Ian's grant. It was time for him to make a quick trip to Washington D.C. to give his annual report to the funders. The funding review committee and all those in the Department of Energy who attended his Project Review Seminar and read his annual report were very pleased with all that had transpired over the past year. Learning that a number of other scientists in his department at Michigan State were volunteering their time to bring added expertise to the project was quite unusual, and the review committee was thoroughly impressed – not only with Ian's progress on his original proposal, but with the expansion possibilities that had emerged.

They were also pleased to hear about the investment USAID was prepared to make in the area to help local farmers. In fact, the committee actually suggested that Ian, the principal investigator, file a request for supplementary funds to help with operations and begin formulating a proposal for ongoing long-term funding. Ian was surprised and flattered by the review committee's feedback. He would certainly oblige! Getting another $100,000 for the department would be a way to give back to his colleagues who had joined his Jatropha research team. And the prospect of long-term funding reassured and energized him even more.

Upon his return, Ian reported the good news to his Department Chair who at the very next faculty meeting publicly thanked Ian, his team and all other faculty members who had volunteered to assist with his research. He reported that the recognition Ian's project had received in Washington had been noted at the highest levels in the university. It was because of the interim results achieved by the combined efforts of so many in the department that the project was so well reviewed.

These efforts and the potential for further project expansion were good not only for the department...but for the entire university. As all eyes in the room moved to Ian, a warm feeling of pride and appreciation crept up his spine. He was, once again, thankful...truly thankful for his decision to move to this university...and for the blessing of the people who had become his professional colleagues...and friends.

A few days later, Ian received an interesting email directed to all faculty and staff members who had young children. The message was a reminder that the traditional "Small Animals' Day" was scheduled for the following Saturday.

"What fun! I remember attending that event several times when I was a child," Ian said to no one in particular. "Maybe I could invite Miss Peggy to be our guest," he mused. "She would be a big help in explaining the myriad of questions the twins are sure to ask about farming and raising animals."

"Besides," he continued confiding to himself, "I've been looking for ways to repay her for her help while I was gone." He had, of course, sent her a big arrangement of spring flowers upon his return and taken her to dinner, but she had emphatically refused to accept any financial compensation for time she spent with the twins.

He forwarded Peggy the email about "Small Animals' Day" and asked her to pass it along to other Montessori families who might not be aware of this educational opportunity for their children. He also asked her if she was free next Saturday and might be able to join him and the children to visit the university farms. He said he would be calling to see if she would like to come.

Of course Peggy said "yes."

"Small Animals' Day began back in 1983," the professor told his guests as they headed for the campus. "I understand that the format has changed through the years, but the purpose of the day has always been the same – to provide an opportunity for kids and curious grown-ups to get up close to animals both domestic and wild."

"I expected that this would be an out-door event with a drive around the university farms to see the young animals each spring," remarked Peg.

"That used to be all there was to it; and we'll make sure to take that drive around after we take in the first part of what is planned. Recently, a part of the experience is held here in the MSU Pavilion."

"Oh, Daddy! See all the cars. I wonder if some of our friends will be here?" asked the twins.

"I've always wanted to see the inside of the Pavilion. They seem to have a lot of horse events here every year. At least I've often seen the parking lots filled with big horse trailers," observed Miss Gerber.

"Yes, the Pavilion is used for numerous agricultural and other events. Today there will be booths with live animals staffed by I am told 25 different student clubs."

"Will there be cows and sheep?" wondered Michael.

"Of course, son. And I'm told the Avian Science Club will have chicks you can hold if you'd like to do that."

"I hope there's a petting zoo with all kinds of animals like baby pigs, sheep and ponies," remarked Mia as they walked into the building.

"It'll be a great chance for visitors to explore different aspects of agriculture," observed the teacher who had grown up on a farm. "Learning to connect to the food we eat is something my Dad has always stressed."

After spending more than an hour going from exhibit to exhibit and even spotting some snakes and lizards that were on display, the twins had enough "hands on" experiences and were ready to drive around the campus and look at the many new babies that had arrived recently. It was fun to be outside on such a lovely spring morning.

Driving around the university farms was a pleasant experience – even without a special guest. But having Miss Peggy along on a Saturday was truly a delight. The first stop was to look at the new lambs. There were dozens of them, and they looked so cute and cuddly romping around butting into one another or cuddled together in sleep.

"Why are some of them black and others white or brown?" Michael wanted to know. Peggy was left to handle that question.

"Animals, like people, come in many different colors depending upon their parents and where the animals came from originally. These breeds actually came from all over the world. I think that it makes the animals more interesting, don't you? Think how boring it would be if they were all only white. You know…it really is the same with people. When communities have folks who come from different places and have different backgrounds and interests…it makes life much more interesting. And communities are stronger when people bring their own ideas, customs and cultures together."

"Yeah," Mia said, "at Ojibway we have kids whose families come from lots of different places…and we all look sort of different, but sort of the same."

"Yup," laughed Ian. "That's true. We're pretty lucky!" He gave Peggy an appreciative wink.

"Does it hurt when the lambs get a haircut?" was Mike's next question.

"It's called shearing," replied their dad. "Lambs don't get sheared, only the mothers and dads who are called ewes and rams. I expect that sometimes their skin can get scratched a little, but if it's done properly, it doesn't hurt. In fact, it feels good to be rid of such a heavy wool coat when the weather turns warm like it is today. Turning that wool into yarn and thread that can be used to knit mittens and make coats is an interesting process, too. Someday we can go to the museum on campus and see how it's actually done."

Next, the little group moved on to the cow barn. The noisy little calves were cute, and their color differences and sizes and breeds were again noted...but they lacked the appeal of the wooly little lambs. Ian remembered when he had visited Small Animals' Day as a child. Back then, they had a demonstration area, where children could try their hand at milking. He told the children about his childhood visit. "For the record," he said, "that was the only time I ever milked a cow!"

Peggy laughed. "It's clear that you've never lived on a farm. All of us had to help milk when we kept cows. Because we weren't big dairy farmers, the milking had to be done by hand – no fancy milking equipment to make the job easier. I know that my brothers and I were glad to see Dad get rid of the cows."

"You got to milk cows?" Mia gasped. "Wow! That's so cool. I would love to milk cows every day."

"Well, it was fun sometimes, but it was cold in the winter," Peggy explained, "and my brothers and I had lots of other chores to do, also. But the milking had be done twice a day... every day...and that could sometimes get in the way of doing fun things."

"Yeah," nodded Mia. "How did you do it, if you had to go to school?"

"Well, that's the other thing," Peggy went on, "My younger brother, Jake and I only had to milk two cows each, but my older brothers had to do more than that. We had to get up really early to milk the cows and still shower, get dressed, eat breakfast and get on the bus. You can see why we were happy when Dad sold those heifers."

"You are sooo lucky!" Michael said with unbridled admiration. "I would love to live on a farm!"

"Well, perhaps someday you could come and visit the farm where I grew up," offered Peggy. "I think you'd love seeing all the animals."

Both children stopped in their tracks and gazed at Peggy. "Really? Wow! When can we go? Daddy, can we, can we, please, please?" both children exclaimed at once.

Peggy and Ian laughed and looked at one another… reddening a bit.

"Well, we'll just have to see…maybe sometime that would be fun, if Miss Peggy's family doesn't mind a couple of hooligans like you running around the farm." Ian replied, "but let's see what other animals we can visit today," he said changing the subject.

"I want to go see the horses," chirped Mia.

"I'm with you, honey," agreed Peggy. "My mom called me yesterday to report that we have a new colt on our farm already. I want to go meet him soon and help give him a name."

"A new baby horse? Really?? Oh, how I wish I could name a baby horse!" sighed Mia.

"Me too!" added Michael, "I've never named any animal before."

"Hmmm, well, maybe we can arrange something like that for both of them," Peggy thought to herself as she remembered her visit home the next weekend.

When they arrived, there were eight new colts scampering around the field outside the horse barn. Some stayed close to their mothers, while others frisked around without regard for their parents.

"The mother horses are called mares," instructed their teacher. "The little guys are called colts or foals, and they stay close to their moms so they can drink her milk...just like the calves we saw earlier...until they are able to find food on their own."

"All babies need their mommies to feed them," said Michael, "but in school we learned that sometimes daddy birds help take care of babies, too. Remember when we watched a daddy cardinal...that's the red one...scare away a big bird from his nest of babies?"

"I remember that... I wish we had both a mommy and a daddy," Mia said matter-of-factly, "but our mommy's in heaven with God."

"Yes, that's true," Peggy intervened, "but you have a wonderful daddy and grandparents who love you very much!"

"Hey," said Dad changing the subject, "is anybody ready for lunch?"

The little troop headed back to campus to get a sandwich at the Dairy Store Cafe; yes, and ice cream, of course. Ian hated to see the outing end, but he couldn't think of a legitimate way to extend it.

"Thanks for inviting me to share your morning," Peggy said as they drove toward her apartment. "It was great fun, and you know how much I like Spartan ice cream." She paused a moment, then went on, "I have an idea. How would you like to join me on my trip to our family farm next weekend? It's my brother Jake's birthday, and he's requested one of my mom's chicken dinners that day. By then, there might even be a second colt. I know one is expected. At our place, my dad would even let you pet them."

"That would be a big treat, wouldn't it, kids?" Ian said pulling into a space in Peggy's parking lot and taking out his phone. "Looking at my calendar here, it seems to be another free week-end for us. What do you think, kids?"

"Really? Really?" Mia sputtered. "Are we really going to get to go to your farm? Thank you! Thank you, Miss Peggy."

"Yippee! Yippee!" exclaimed Michael.

"Well, it's decided then. Thanks so much for the offer, Peg. I'd be happy to drive, but you'll have to be the navigator," he added.

"Is your brother a kid?" Michael wanted to know.

"Well, you might say that," Peggy laughed. "He's turning 21 next week, but he loves to play games and run around the farm like a kid. Jake is my brother who hopes to become an animal doctor, a veterinarian. This summer he has a job at the Small Animal Clinic on campus. "

"That'll look good on his resume," Ian offered. "I hear that it's often harder to be admitted to vet school than it is to get into medical school."

"I think I'd like to be an animal doctor," contributed Mia. "Taking care of dogs and kittens sounds like fun."

"Not always," reminded her twin. "Somebody has to keep the cages clean. I don't think that would be fun…and some animals can be mean…especially if they're hurt or sick."

"Well, they wouldn't be mean to me, 'cause animals love me…and I don't mind cleaning cages," Mia replied emphatically. "I sure wish we had a pet so I could practice taking care of animals."

Ian cringed a little when he heard these words. He'd been thinking about getting the children a pet…but it had never seemed to be the right time. Peggy, once, again, saved the day.

"You know, Mia," Peggy calmly explained, "having a pet is a big responsibility. You have to feed it, train it, clean up after it and love it. I just know you and Michael would be good at that…but the time has to be right. I think your dad will know when it's the right time to add a pet to your family."

Peggy climbed out of the car. "Thank you for including me in your farming adventure today, Mahoneys! I'll double check with my mom about next weekend, but I'm sure it will be fine to have the three of you join my family."

Peggy headed up the walk to a chorus of good-byes and thank-yous and see-you-tomorrows. She waved back as the kids, and Ian honked and waved to her. As she unlocked her door and slipped inside, she could not hide the smile that crept across her face.

Peggy couldn't wait to tell her mom that there would be three more for the birthday lunch on the following Saturday.

On the phone, Rosemary assured her that there would be plenty of food and that Ian and the children would be more than welcome.

In fact, her mom couldn't wait to meet the mysterious professor and the adorable little ones she had heard so much about. Rosemary was somewhat surprised, however, that their daughter had actually gone ahead and extended an invitation to the Mahoneys. Peggy had been so careful to say he was just a "friend."

Peter Gerber noticed the look on his wife's face as she told him about the new plans for the following weekend. "Now don't you start to speculate on there being anything more than a casual friendship between Peggy and the professor," admonished her husband. "I know that we're both hoping she'll find someone she cares about, but it's really not our place to speculate or try to push her into a relationship that may not be right."

"I know, I know," replied his wife with a sly grin, "but I can hear the joy in her voice when she talks about this man and his children. He's different. I just know it…and you know it, too. I can't wait to meet them."

Peter laughed, "You're incorrigible, Dear. But I have to admit…there is something special about this one. I'm anxious to meet them, too. Next weekend will be special, indeed…for many reasons."

CHAPTER THIRTY-FIVE

The car ride to the Gerber farm was a lot of fun, and the time passed quickly. The twins from their perches in the back seat kept up a steady conversation as they commented on everything they passed, played Eye-Spy with the adults and sang songs. They had brought Jake a gift card from the campus book store, something that worked for most college students.

"I wonder if they'll have balloons," Mia said. "You're always supposed to have balloons at birthday parties."

"Not at parties for big people." said her twin knowingly.

"At our place everybody has balloons," laughed Peggy.

"See, Mikey! I told you there had to be balloons!" bragged Mia.

The farms in the Saginaw Valley were well tended and suggested that this was a very prosperous agricultural area. Peggy made a point of describing the nature of her family's farm. The main business was raising corn and soybeans, but many of their neighbors were concentrating on sugar beets, another popular crop in the area. Her family had kept horses for as long as she could remember, because the four children had been eager to ride. Through the years the kids had been the ones to care for the horses…their parents had said it was a good way to learn responsibility. Now, however, the responsibility was mostly on Rosemary and Pete.

Ian noted what a close relationship Peg had with her parents and brothers. As they emerged from the car, Sam and J. R. grabbed Peggy in turn and twirled her around in big bear hugs. Peggy's mom shook hands with Michael and Mia and introduced them to Trixie, the barking, wagging, wiggling collie that had raced to the car to see Peggy and welcome the guests. Peggy's dad shook hands with Ian and laughingly said, "Welcome to the Gerber Farm…or should I say the Gerber Zoo!" Ian felt at home immediately. What an amazingly warm and welcoming crew.

"Do come and relax on the porch," suggested Mrs. Gerber. I just made a pitcher of lemonade…let me get some while you get acquainted."

"That'd be perfect, Mom. I'll help you get it and leave the boys to fend for themselves," offered Peggy.

"The adults settled in the big wooden rockers and old-fashioned swing that graced the porch while the twins dashed into the yard to play with Trixie, who could not believe her good fortune to actually have kids to play with. They began to roll in the grass trying to avoid the sloppy kisses Trixie was trying to bestow on them both. Their laughter echoed across the lawn.

Ian turned to Peggy's oldest brother. "I hear you're in the farm management business in this area. Do you have many absentee landowners, J. R.?"

"Actually, most of my clients are big producers, but I also have some absentees. It keeps me pretty busy, but I like being close and able to help Dad on the farm. It's really too much for one person," J. R. explained.

"Besides, farming's in my blood," he chuckled. "You know what they say…'you can take the farmer off the farm, but you can't take the farm out of a farmer.'"

"Well, I was able to leave the farm…no problem," Sam piped up. "I'd have to say I don't miss those early days of 5 a.m. milkings."

"Oh, Sam," Peggy chided. "We got rid of those cows years ago…you haven't milked in more than 15 years and was fun!"

"Really?" Sam asked innocently, "you only had to do TWO cows, so it was easy for YOU, maybe. Boy, has it really been 15 years? That hardly seems possible."

"So where do you practice law, Sam?" asked Ian. "And do you have a specialty?"

"Thanks for asking, Ian," Sam replied. I'm an associate at a firm in Midland…not too far from here. It's a corporate practice, so we represent many businesses in Midland and consult with in-house attorneys at Dow Corning."

"Do you like it?" Ian continued.

"It's long hours, but every day is a new challenge… contracts, personnel issues, mergers and much more. It's a steep learning curve, but I'm learning a lot, that's for sure."

"Well, loving what you do is more than half the battle," Ian agreed.

When asked, the senior Gerbers told the gathering about how they had met while students at Michigan State. They were proud that all of their children had decided to go there, too. "I guess you could say the entire Gerber clan bleeds green," quipped Pete.

Pete Gerber was continuing his relationship with the university by serving on one of its agricultural advisory boards. Big Mike Mahoney would certainly have welcomed a conversation with Pete, since he had always kept in close touch with alumni and agricultural stakeholders. Pete also served on the County Commission. He and Ian immediately launched into a conversation about environmental issues, infrastructure shortcomings in some of the rural areas and the newest advances in crop management. J. R. had a lot to say about that, as well.

Peggy was pleased to see how easily Ian fit in with the Gerber men. Never, she recalled, had her dad and Donn Bahler been that congenial. Donn never seemed to respect the older man's view about anything...in fact, he was seldom interested in anything others had to say...and he rarely asked questions. That was clearly not true with Ian. Peggy hugged her arms around herself and smiled as she rocked and watched "her men" interact.

Jake arrived to another flurry of hugs, barks and handshakes. He was eager to get acquainted with Ian and the kids. He immediately invited the twins to go take a look at the big tractor they had in the shed and promised that after lunch he and his dad would take them for a ride...and to see the two little colts that had arrived in the last couple of weeks.

And, yes, there were balloons greeting them as they all crowded around the huge dining room table for lunch.

"See, didn't I tell you we celebrated with balloons at this house?" asked Miss Peggy.

Rosemary said the blessing before they all dived into the fried chicken, mashed potatoes and gravy, green bean casserole, Waldorf salad and hot rolls she had prepared.

"Thanks, Mom," said Jake appreciatively, as he smacked his lips together. "This is my always-requested birthday meal...and nobody makes chicken like Mom!"

"Mmmm, this is SO GOOD," cooed Michael digging into a second helping of potatoes. "This chicken tastes just like what our Mimi fixed when she came to visit at Christmastime."

"It's probably a grandmother kind of thing," laughed Peggy. "This is how my mom fixed fried chicken...so this is how I do it. I used to think that my grandma made the best chicken, too!"

"You can say that again," added Sam. "With three hungry sons plus a daughter who was never a slouch when it came to eating, Mom has had plenty of practice. Thanks, Mom for preparing our favorite meal. You're the best!"

"Here, here!" agreed J. R. "I'm lucky to be close by, so I get this yummy chicken often.

"I'm thinking I have to get over here more often, too," added Sam. "Midland's not too far to come for THIS!"

Rosemary smiled, "Oh, you boys…always the flatterers. Well, I guess it works…'cause here we are…feasting again for our Jakie."

Jake went around the table to give his mom a big kiss. "Thanks, Mom, and thanks, to you, too, Mahoneys, for the gift card! That was so thoughtful…and I can really use it with the cost of books! And Sis, I love the Spartan vest you made for me. I've been hoping to improve my Spartan wardrobe. It fits perfectly! Sam and J. R….you know I appreciate your gift certificate to Crunchy's. Sometimes you just have to have a break from dorm food."

The eyes of the twins grew big when they saw the lighted birthday cake brought in from the kitchen. It was huge and had lots of fluffy frosting hiding the layers of chocolate cake.

"Here's some homemade ice cream to go with it," said the man of the house. "I helped Rosemary make it this morning. I hope you like strawberry since the berries are from our garden."

"You should know…our weakness is ice cream," replied Ian. "We are among the Spartan Dairy Store's best customers. The twins think that no trip to the campus is complete without ice cream cones. But we've never had homemade ice cream, so this will be a new experience and special treat."

After lunch, the men took the twins to meet the colts and their mothers. The four animals were in a small corral surrounded by a white fence. Pete had brought along several apples so he and Sam could distract the mares while Jake and

J. R. went to bring the colts to the fence where the youngsters could pet them.

"They are so soft," observed Mia, "and they seem a little wobbly, especially the smaller one."

"I like the way they swish their tails," added Michael. "It's like they can use their tails for a fly swatter. What are their names?"

Peggy and her mother looked at one another and the older woman winked. "Actually," said Mr. Gerber, "when Peggy said you were coming, we thought it would be fun to have you help us pick out their names. That was something our children used to have fun doing. What do you say? Do you have any ideas?"

Mike and Mia were speechless…but not for long.

"Really? Really? We get to help NAME the colts?!" exclaimed Mia.

"I can't BELIEVE IT!" giggled Michael jumping up and down.

Mike and Mia looked at each other, not knowing where to start. This was serious business. What could they name the colts? The older, bigger one was a boy they remembered. They didn't know about the newer smaller one.

Mike and Mia whispered to each other for a few minutes, then Mike announced, "We think that one should be called Tornado, since that mark on its forehead looks kind of like a tornado."

"What a great name!" Sam said. "That white marking does resemble the funnel of a tornado!" The other adults readily agreed.

"Now what should we call this little mare?" Pete asked.

"Does that mean that we need a girl's name?" asked Mia.

"Yes, female horses are called mares," Jake explained.

This was a much harder decision since there were no

special markings on this little colt. After looking at the animal for some time, Mia pointed to the young horse's very long legs and whispered to Mike. The others noticed where she was pointing. Mike nodded vigorously.

"We've got it!" said Mia gleefully. "We think we should call her Lady Long Legs – Lady for short."

Everyone agreed. The names the twins selected were perfect. A camera and several cell phones appeared and photos were clicked…shots of the kids with the horses, kids with the brothers, Ian and the twins with the newly-named colts and many others.

What a memorable experience for both of them. They could hardly wait to tell their grandparents, especially the Calhouns, who were also horse people.

"You'll have to come back again and help us teach them their names so they'll come when they're called," Rosemary suggested when they returned to the house.

"We'd love that! Thank you so much!" exclaimed the twins looking at their father for confirmation of the plan. Ian smiled and nodded.

Jake said, "Hey, Dad…how about taking these two farmers on a tractor ride?"

"What do you say, Ian?" Pete asked. "Our kids grew up on tractors, so we know how to keep them safe, while bumping over some of our property out back.

"Well, what's a trip to the farm without a ride on a tractor?" he asked. "Perhaps I can take a little spin myself."

The kids and men headed off to the shed.

While the others headed for the tractor, Peggy and Rosemary had a chance for some mother-daughter talk. Peggy indicated that she would not be teaching summer school this year. After five years on the job and with all her volunteer activities, she was feeling a bit burned out and thought taking the summer off would be a good decision.

Her mom agreed that was a good idea but wondered how she intended to spend the summer and where. "Have you thought what you want to do? You have plenty of out-of-state friends who would welcome a visit. You know you're always welcome to come back home…I can always use an extra hand with gardening and canning."

"Well," confessed her daughter, "I've been thinking about both of those options. I can probably work both of them in during the summer break. But I've been thinking about maybe going back to Europe. There's a special week-end event at the Montessori Academy in Italy, and there're a couple of other places on the edge of the Alps that I've always wanted to see. Is there any chance that you might come with me for a sort of 'Girls Only' adventure?"

"Now, that's a thought!" her mom said hesitantly at first… then with enthusiasm. "When are you thinking? I know your dad would think it's a great idea, since he doesn't much care for foreign travel, and he knows how I've longed to get back to Europe. I'll bet we could make it work!"

She grabbed her daughter and gave her a huge hug, "You are such a dear…I'm so lucky to have you for my daughter. This will be a trip to remember for a lifetime. It's so sweet of you to think of me!"

"Oh, Mom, of course, I'd think of you! We'll have a fabulous time," she said returning her mother's hug. "I was thinking about going early in August. It could be a sort of 30th birthday celebration for me. I've been thinking about perhaps spending a few days in both Innsbruck and Salzburg."

"As you know, I've never been to either…and I'd love to go. Those places as well as Bergamo, where you attended school, would be fantastic!" Then she added, "Did you know that some of our ancestors came from that part of Austria as well as from Germany, so we could even do a bit of genealogy tracking while we're there."

Neither woman mentioned much about today's visit except to acknowledge that everyone seemed to enjoy each other's company. Rosemary commented on how absolutely darling the twins were and what a good job Ian must be doing as a single parent.

Before the guests left, Mr. Gerber brought out an old cigar box filled with arrowheads. "These arrowheads have been found on this land during ploughing over many years. "I've been saving them for someone who might really appreciate them. Would each of you like to choose one to take home with you?" he asked the twins.

Once, again, the twins were speechless. Arrowheads! They couldn't believe their eyes.

"Oh, Mr. Gerber, thank you so much!" said Mia in a whisper, pawing carefully through the box.

"I can't wait to show our neighbor, Mr. Lane!" exclaimed Michael. "He's writing a book about Indians...so he will be really excited to see this!!!" Michael grabbed one and held it up for all to see. "Thank you so much!"

Always the teacher, Peggy said, "Hey, Mike and Mia, did you know that the same Ojibwa people we learned about at the Cultural Center actually lived in this area, too? Wouldn't it be interesting if our own Chief Okemos or his family actually camped here on this farm and these arrowheads were his?"

Peggy went on to tell them that while the bow and arrow was used to hunt animals for food, to defend their camp, and sometimes for competition, perhaps the most surprising use of the arrow was that it was sometimes used as a spear to catch fish – even at night.

Before they left, Jake promised that he'd look into arranging for them to tour the Small Animal Clinic after he started work there during the summer. Jake couldn't believe how curious and well-behaved the two of them were. No wonder his sister loved working with little people like these two!

Before piling into the car, there were hugs all around once again. There were thanks and promises to return. Ian invited them all to come to campus and promised an "inside" tour that he and Jake would personally arrange.

The trip home seemed faster than the journey to the farm. Perhaps because both kids immediately fell into comatose sleep as the car sped down the highway. "Well," Ian reflected, "I know what those two are dreaming of. What a day for them to remember. Naming colts? That was a dream-come-true for those little munchkins. How can I begin to thank you for creating such special memories for all of us?" Inside, Ian hoped that they wouldn't be too disappointed if this turned out to be their only visit to the farm. He had to admit silently to himself that he, too, would be disappointed if this was his only visit.

"Your brothers are great, Peg...and your parents are very special, indeed," Ian said. "I was very pleased to meet them all."

For her part, Peg was happy that everyone had gotten along so well. And she was so proud of the kids. She really had expected no less from them, but one can never predict what five-year-olds might say or do in a new circumstance. Peggy had sort of been hoping for some little sign from Ian that she, Miss Peggy, was someone special in their lives. She knew, however, that he was quite reserved and probably telling her parents how much he appreciated her playing substitute nanny during his absence was all that she should have expected. It was a great day, though, and Ian seemed to have a good time.

In fact, Ian had a barrage of pleasant thoughts about the visit. He had really enjoyed talking with Peg's dad and hearing about all that was going on in rural Michigan. Jake, J. R. and Sam seemed like such great guys. How kind of them to take such an interest in the twins. Peggy's Mom was so warm and such a gracious hostess...a lot like her daughter, he mused. He couldn't help but think that Rosemary and his mother would really hit it off together. The whole family had greeted him and the twins so warmly, almost as if they were part of the family. He had been missing that kind of relationship. He found himself hoping that they could make another trip to the Saginaw area to visit the farm and these very special people. Peggy was certainly full of pleasant surprises. He couldn't help but wonder...what would be next?

CHAPTER THIRTY-SIX

A pair of animated twins dominated the dinner conversation on Monday night. "Oh,

Daddy," Mia said "we had great fun at school today! Our class is going to be Africa for International Night in a couple of weeks."

"Yeah," added Mike. "Today we learned some neat things about Africa, and we started to work on a mural thing that will be part of the background for our stuff," interrupted his twin.

"I see," said their father, nodding…then lifting his hands in confusion, he said, "No, I really don't see. What's this all about?"

"It's a special Friday night program for families and friends," Michael explained. "Our school has one every May. We don't have afternoon class that day so the teachers can get ready. Every class gets to be a different part of the world. Our room will be Africa this year…the same place you went… isn't that funny?"

"It sure is. Besides decorating the room, what else happens?" Dad asked.

"Everybody gets a pretend passport," Mia explained. "You know what that is, don't you, Daddy?"

"Of course he does, silly," lectured Mike. "He had to have one when he went to Africa!"

"I'm sorry I never showed it to you," Dad said. "So guests take their passports and go from place to place like a trip around the world? Is that the idea?"

The twins nodded both "yes" and "no" before Mia continued the explanation. "We get to learn how to play games from other countries and do lots of other things that kids around the world like to do. It'll be loads of fun!"

"We brought a paper that tells all about it," Michael added as he reached into his backpack and handed his father a colorful flier. "Every family has to bring some food, too… ours has to be food from Africa. What can we take, Dad?"

Ian thought for a moment, "Hmmm…that's a good question. Since it's May we probably should take something that won't need to be heated or kept cold. I suppose the food tables will be in the gym where there's no air conditioning. Maybe I can ask Christian for some ideas…and we can talk to Mrs. Harding about it, too." After a pause, he added, "Actually, do you think there might be things that Christian and I can do to help with your classroom exhibit? "

"Miss Peggy asked if any of our parents would be willing to help," Mia said. "I know she'd like YOU to help, Daddy."

Ian laughed, "You're right…she can always use help from parents. I think I'll call her right now." Ian reached for his phone.

"Hi, Peggy, this is Ian," he began. "The twins have been telling me about International Night. I hear your class is going to be Africa. Could you use a couple of fellows who have been there recently to add a bit local color to your exhibit? I think Christian might be willing to help…although I haven't asked him yet."

"Ian, of course! When we were assigned Africa, I thought of you immediately. I was hoping you'd be able to help!" Peggy said enthusiastically. "Do you have anything specific in mind? We could use some live entertainment to go along with the African art, maps, trinkets and artifacts we've started to make and collect. Are you men a song and dance team, by any chance?"

Ian laughed out loud, "That would be a stretch, Peggy, but both Christian and I took lots of interesting pictures. Perhaps I could combine them into a continuous-play, PowerPoint slide show that could be running on a computer or a screen in your room. We could even dub some African music in the background. I don't know if Chris has any African garb with him, but he might be willing to dress up and sit in your room to answer questions about life in his country. Is it okay if the pictures and Chris's answers are about two different countries?"

"Of course!" Peggy answered. "We represent the entire continent of Africa, although we seem to be focusing on mostly sub-Saharan areas. So, the more countries that are represented, the better."

"I see that International Night's in about two weeks. How about if I put together a sort of pilot slide show and get your reaction to it? I'll talk with Christian tomorrow and see if he's willing to get on board. If so, I'll get him to send me his photos and I'll try to have a preliminary slide show ready for your critique after our next youth group meeting at church."

"Oh, Ian, thank you so much! That sounds fabulous!" Peggy gushed. "I just knew you would jump at a chance to combine your work and your travel with the education of your children. You and Christian are going to help make our event a very meaningful experience for the kids...and families, too. Please thank Christian for me and tell him I'm looking forward to seeing him. No pressure, of course!" She laughed.

When asked to help...Christian said he would be delighted to be part of the event. Deciding on which photos to use was no problem for Ian, since there were so many from which to choose. To make things even better, Christian had a number of pictures of children at play and in school that he had brought with him when he came to the U.S. in the fall. Photos of kids would make the slide show even more appealing to the students. Christian confirmed that he had, indeed, brought traditional African robes with him from home, and he said he would be flattered to wear them that night and answer questions about his homeland.

"We're on a roll!" Ian bragged to his children.

"Daddy, that's so neat that Mr. Christian will come to our school….and even wear his African outfit!" Mike exclaimed and clapped his hands excitedly.

"But, Dad," Mia said, pulling on her father's sleeve, "what kind of food are we going to take? Do you still have some of those good nuts you brought home from Mozambique? Could we make cookies with them instead of using regular nuts?"

"What a great idea!" her father agreed. "What would I ever do without you creative Montessori kids?" So it was decided that they would make a double or triple batch of cookies for the dozens of guests who would be in attendance. Perhaps Mrs. H could help with that endeavor.

Ian was pleased with the way the short PowerPoint turned out. When Peggy saw it, she offered a few minor suggestions about the order of the photos. Then, on impulse, she gave the producer a little hug to acknowledge his effort. "Thank you so much, Ian! I know how much time it takes to put together a slide show like that…and with music, too! It's just wonderful, and it'll enhance our class exhibit so much! You're a great dad, you know that? You're always willing to take time to do something meaningful for your kids. I know they're excited about it…they've been chattering about your 'show' all week!"

When the big night came, the children were asked to attend with the Lane family, who look forward to International Night each year. Ian wanted to get there early to make sure his computer, projector and speakers were operating perfectly... even though they were fine when he'd set them up at school that afternoon. He'd also helped Peggy hang the mural and put the finishing touches on the classroom.

The parking lot was filled to over-flowing, as enthusiastic parents, children and other guests arrived at the school. What a colorful sight they were, since some of the children and parents who had an international heritage came dressed in tradtional clothing from those countries! The Asian and South American outfits were especially colorful. Some of the staff members were also in international dress.

The buffet tables set up in the gym were heaped with foods from all over the world. It was truly a sight to behold.

The twins escorted Libby and joined their dad to move from continent to continent around the school, making sure that they got their passport stamped in each place. They were so excited to see that Mrs. H had come, along with several women from church. They ran up to her and threw their arms around her. "Welcome, Mrs. H! It's so good to see you here... at our school!" they chorused. Of course, she was touched by their excitement to see her...and she proudly introduced them to her friends.

The "world travelers" appreciated the African slide show that Ian had put together, but it was Christian who was the real hit in their classroom. He was surrounded by visitors of all ages and was peppered with dozens of questions. He was especially good at making eye contact and talking honestly and earnestly with even the youngest children. He allowed them to touch his robes and try the drums he'd brought.

By the time the evening ended, there was surprisingly little food left in the gym. And the cashew cookies? All gone!

What a wonderful evening! No wonder the staff at Ojibwa considered International Night the highlight of the school year. It not only spotlighted the creativity of the children, but involving so many families in so many different ways showed that Ojibwa was, indeed, a very special learning community. It was a community that valued diversity and celebrated people and cultures from all around the world.

Ian returned to the school the next morning to reclaim his equipment. Peggy was already there in tee shirt and jeans, busily trying to disassemble Africa. "Why not stay and help?" the man wondered. The children were enjoying a play morning with friends, so his time was his own. Four hands made shorter work of taking down the paper mural, packing up the loaned items for pick up or delivery and returning the classroom to its normal condition. "Whew," Ian said, "That was a lot of work, wasn't it?"

"Yes it was, but not as much work as yesterday…setting it all up after the children went home. I appreciated your help then…and I appreciate your help today!" Peggy said, her face flushed and glistening from the effort of moving furniture around. She tucked an errant strand of blond curling hair behind her ear and looked Ian in the eye. "Your hands and strong back made it go a lot faster, that's for sure."

"Hey, Peg," Ian said demurring from the compliments, "I'm heading to the Farmers' Market to pick up a few things, do you want to join me? I think the Purple Carrot food truck will be there today, so we can also grab a bite of lunch. The twins and I love the food, and there are tables in the historic village where we can sit and eat."

"I'm not really dressed to go out for lunch," Peggy said, indicating her stained jeans and disheveled pony tail, "but this sounds like a pretty casual operation so I guess I won't embarrass you too much."

"No chance of that" Ian said, surprised. "You look…beautiful…to me…"

"Why…thanks," stammered Peggy, as she blushed at the unexpected compliment.

They both picked up several items at the market and then strolled over to the Purple Carrot. This was one of the first food trucks to tempt local diners in the area. The owners focused on serving locally-grown products and kept a regular schedule at a location near the market and at several other area venues.

Today's feature was a turkey wrap with fruit salsa. Ian recalled hearing that the young couple who owned the Purple Carrot had also recently opened a small tapas restaurant in Okemos. It would be fun to take Peggy there before she left for summer break.

They grabbed their sandwiches and bottles of water and headed over to a picnic table in the shade of a giant oak. They rehashed the success of International Night, laughed about the kids' reaction to the colts and tractor rides on the farm and chatted about the times they had shared with their church youth group. Conversation moved easily from topic to topic. It was amazing to both of them how much they had shared in such a short time. And here they were…enjoying each other's company on yet another unanticipated "date."

Returning home after dropping off the loaned exhibit items, Peggy smiled to herself. She was remembering Ian rolling up his sleeves and hoisting boxes of African items on his shoulder and moving them to the front office for pick up or to Peggy's car for her to drop off. He was just such a great guy…willing to pitch in on whatever project or nasty job that needed to be done. She was reminded, again, how lucky she was to have met this one-of-a-kind man. If only…..

For his part, Ian could not stop thinking about Peggy… her face shining with a glow of perspiration as she moved desks back into place in her classroom…that blond strand escaping from her pony tail and curling around her lovely face. "I would hate to embarrass you," she had said glancing at her dirty jeans with a smile in her eye. He shook his head in disbelief. "Are you kidding me?" he thought. "How could I be so lucky to have such a beautiful woman beside me…whether at church, cleaning a classroom, or grabbing a sandwich at the food truck. She's really something. If only….."

CHAPTER THIRTY-SEVEN

One evening a few weeks later, Mia asked, "Daddy can we have Miss Peggy over for dinner the last day of school? We won't be in her class next year."

"Our new teacher, Mrs. Nancy, is nice," added Michael, "but she's not as pretty as Miss Peggy."

"Hey, Guys, that's a wonderful idea! You've been seeing Miss Peggy almost every day...and I know you will miss seeing her so often. Besides, she's done so much for our family this year. Having her over for dinner would be a great way to thank her for all she's done for us."

"Can we make her a special invitation, Daddy? Mike and I can draw and color different parts of it...and you can help us spell the words," Mia suggested.

"Yeah," said Mike. "Then we can take it to her tomorrow at school."

"You two are so thoughtful...I know she'll love it," their dad responded. So off they went to prepare their invitation.

"You two are so sweet!" Miss Peggy said when she opened their invitation the next day. "Of course, I'd love to come to your house Friday night for dinner. I will look forward to it all week! Thank you so much...and thank your dad, too!"

On Wednesday as Ian was getting ready to tuck the children into bed, Mike surprised him by saying, "Daddy, we really love Miss Peggy. It was so nice having her stay with us when you were in Africa."

"It almost seemed like she was a mommy...our mommy," added his sister.

"I wish Miss Peggy could be our REAL mommy," Mike went on. "I love her like a mommy."

"Yeah, me, too!" agreed Mia. "I think she would LOVE to be our mommy. Don't you, Daddy?"

"Well…" Ian stammered. "I know Miss Peggy will be a wonderful mommy someday…you're right about that!"

"Yes," persisted Mia, "but we don't want her to be someone else's mommy…we want her to be our mommy! Don't you love her, too, Daddy?"

"Leave it to children to cut straight to the point," Ian thought…not knowing how to answer his children.

"Are you still too sad about our Mommy who is in heaven, Daddy? Is that why you won't let us have a new mommy?" continued Mia as both she and Mike looked up at their dad with sadness in their eyes.

Ian gathered his two children into his arms and hugged them tightly. "The truth is…I'll always love your mother, the woman who gave birth to you two. She will always be special to me and will always be in my heart. That will never change." He paused. "But, do I love Miss Peggy? Hmmm…do I love Miss Peggy?" He paused again, and looked into their trusting eyes. This was a time to be honest with these two precious ones…and to be honest with himself. "You know what? I do love Miss Peggy…or I guess I should say, Peg. She has become a very special part of my life, too." With a huge sigh, he hugged them again. It felt good to admit what he had known in his heart for months.

"Thank you, My Dear Ones, for finally helping me see what's been right in front of me for months." Laughing, he tossed the twins onto the bed. "You two are incorrigible!"

"Then there's no problem!" Mia announced. "We can ask her to marry us when she comes to dinner on Friday!"

"Yes, Daddy....let's ask her then!" Mike agreed.

Ian laughed out loud and said, "Whoa, Partners!" A few seconds later, he added with resignation, "Well, I guess Friday is as good a time as any..."

"Good night, You Two," Dad said, tucking them into their beds. "Now get to sleep...you have school tomorrow and we have a dinner to plan!" Ian left the children shaking his head, wondering about what he had just done at the urging...no insistence of his children. It was crazy, for sure. But somehow, it felt right...and he felt at peace...at last.

Later, when Dad was gone, the twins crept out of bed and congratulated each other quietly, giving each other a "high five." "We did it! We did it! Michael and Mia Mahoney are going to have a Mommy!" they whispered as they danced around the room, much too happy to fall asleep immediately.

On Friday evening, promptly at six, Peggy arrived. She wore a cornflower blue sundress that matched her eyes and set off the smooth tan of her shoulders. She had taken special care with her hair, pulling it up and tucking a flower into the curls that cascaded from the clip.

Ian almost gasped when he saw her. "You...you look.... lovely, Peg," was her host's hesitant greeting. "Welcome. Come on in...there are two others here who are as anxious as I am to have you join us tonight."

"Thank you, it's kind of you to invite me, and I'm really looking forward to the gourmet dinner, I'm sure you've prepared," she laughed.

"We thought it might be fun to eat out in the four-season room where there's a great view of the garden with it's spring flowers. How lucky we are that the former owners planted all these perennials...they make the backyard so colorful. My helpers have already set the table there. They also thought we ought to have a toast to celebrate the end of the school year.

"Waiters, please bring us the tray of glasses," he pronounced. Ian poured a glass of Asti for each of the adults and sparkling grape juice for the twins.

"Here's to the end of the school year!" They all toasted their teacher and each other. "There will never be another year like this one." They all sat down, and Ian asked that they all hold hands while he said the blessing.

The dinner was indeed gourmet – grilled salmon, roasted asparagus, crusty French bread and a green salad that Mrs. H had prepared. Conversation was easy as topics jumped from stories of things that happened in the classroom, to the time Peggy stayed with them while Ian was away, to their visit to the farm, to what they all planned to do during the summer.

"We're going to see Mimi and Papa," reported the twins. "Mimi says there's a big swimming pool and even water slides down the block from where they live. And they're not far from the ocean, either, so we're going to the beach, too!"

"Now that Mike and Mia are such good swimmers, they've become real water dogs. I'm looking forward to a lot of good seafood. What are your plans, Peg? I know you said you won't be teaching summer school this year."

"It's true," Peggy nodded. "I've always done that before, but after five years I felt a change was in order. I'm going to visit a couple of out-of-state friends and get some R & R back on the farm."

"My schedule is somewhat lighter during the summer, too," Ian said, "but I'll still continue with the lab work, and there will be students on campus, of course. Maybe after we get back from South Carolina, we can try our hand at camping. As I recall, that's something you've often done with your brother; maybe you might even spend a few days camping with three greenhorns."

"For sure," Peggy said animatedly. "J.R. and I have always been the campers in the family. In fact, last year we spent about a week in the UP back-packing and tent camping. We avoided the black flies, explored the falls and camped on Lake Superior. So, yes, I think a camping trip with all of you would be a blast!" She leaned closer to the children winking, "You can rely on me, You Guys, I'm an expert camper…and I think I can even teach your dad a thing of two. But I haven't told you about my big summer news. My mom and I are planning a trip to Europe!" she added excitedly.

"Really? When are you going?" asked Mike.

"Where will you go?" asked Mia.

"How long will you be gone?" Dad chimed in.

The three Mahoneys had strange looks on their faces… almost disappointment. Peggy thought it was because they feared she might not be able to join them for the camping trip.

"Oh, don't worry," she said. "I think we could still fit in a camping excursion. The exact dates for my trip haven't been set yet. There's a Montessori reunion in Bergamo I'd like to attend, so I'm planning around that. But for the specific dates, we're waiting to hear from my Aunt Maggie, Dad's sister from Pennsylvania, who'll come to visit him while we're gone. Mom and I are thinking early August, so there'll be plenty of time for me to get ready for school when I get back. I'll have quite a few new children in my class, since many are graduating…like these two." Peggy smiled at her favorite students.

As the meal progressed Peggy noticed that her host was becoming increasingly quiet, and the two young ones were fidgeting and repeatedly looking at each other with quizzical expressions. "What," she wondered "was going on here? Were they all that worried about camping? Or were they concerned about the dessert? Surely, that couldn't be causing this strange behavior."

When dessert was served, it turned out to be simple watermelon and cookies, like those brought to International Night. Finally, the children could contain themselves no longer.

"Daddy! Just do it! Do it NOW," they demanded. "If you don't ask her now, we will!"

"Do what?" Peggy wondered. "Ask me what?"

Still Ian hesitated. "Just hold your horses, You Two," he advised.

But the usually obedient children had other ideas.

"Miss Peggy," they said in unison, "Will you PLEASE marry us?"

"Will I what?" she said, stunned.

"Marry us! Don't you understand?" Michael demanded.

"We ALL love you and want you to be part of our family," Mia added, pleadingly.

With that, Ian rose and walked over to stand next to Peggy. Taking her hand and pulling her to her feet, he looked deeply into her eyes and quietly and earnestly asked, "Margaret Ann Gerber, will you be my wife? I care deeply – no, let me say this right. I, as well as Mike and Mia, love you with all my heart. Nothing would make us happier than if you would agree to become my wife and their mother." Ian's eyes filled with tears as he leaned down and kissed Peggy softly on the lips.

Peggy could not believe her ears. Tears of joy sprang into her eyes and overflowed down her cheeks. She pulled Mr. Mahoney to her and kissed him hard on the lips. Smiling, she gathered them all in her arms, "There is nothing in this world that would make me happier," she said, her voice shaking. "I've loved the three of you for a very long time, but was not willing to admit it." She grabbed Ian's hands in both of hers,

"Yes, of course, I will marry you!"

Turning to the children, she said, "Becoming your mother would be the greatest gift of my life." She hugged them and kissed them both.

"Kiss her, again, Daddy! Kiss her, again!" the twins shouted, jumping up and down.

But Daddy didn't need their instructions. He and his future wife were already lost in the long, deep kiss that had been on hold for many months. As they drew back, both quite breathless…they joined the children laughing, holding hands and dancing around in a circle.

"We're going to be a family….we're going to be a family!" they sang as they danced.

"Won't Mimi and Papa be excited?" Mike said.

"Mimi'll probably cry," Mia added. "She's been worried that we didn't have a mommy. We heard her say that to Papa when they were here."

"I know that's true," Ian agreed. "The Calhouns also encouraged me to consider remarrying – not only for the children's sake, but also for mine. How about your folks, Peggy? How will they react to our news?"

Peggy laughed. "Rest assured. They, too, will be delighted. All they've ever wanted was for me to be happy. They've always hoped that I would find a man who loved me without question, who had the same deep Christian values I do, who would be a good parent, and who would respect them for who they are. I guess that describes you, Dr. Mahoney, in a nutshell. Yes, saying they'll be pleased…is really an understatement."

"When's the wedding?" the twins asked together.

"Can we be in it?" asked Mia.

"Do we get to go on the honeymoon with you?" added Michael.

The adults laughed. "That is a lot of questions with different answers," their dad answered, looking at Peggy with a wink. "We don't know yet when we'll have the wedding…of course you can be in it…and NO you won't be going with us on our honeymoon."

"Let's call my parents and share the good news," suggested Peggy.

"Right, but I need to speak with your dad first. I should have asked for his blessing before I asked you…but this was all pretty sudden."

So the call was made. "Mr. Gerber, this is Ian Mahoney," began Ian.

"Hi, Ian," responded Pete. "How's everything in Okemos?"

"Actually, Peggy's here with me," Ian continued. "There's an important question I'd like to ask you, but I'm going to put you on speaker phone so Peggy and the children can hear, also."

"Well, okay, I guess," said Pete, confused.

"Call me old-fashioned, but I do want to ask – Sir, do I have your permission to marry Margaret? The children and I have just asked her to marry us, and she's said yes! We love her dearly and promise to do our best to make her happy. I'm not a wealthy man, but I do have a steady income and no debts. The twins are good kids – most of the time – and really want her to be their mommy. Do we have your blessing and that of Peggy's mom to go ahead with plans for a wedding, perhaps even before the summer is over?"

"Oh my goodness!" sputtered Pete. "Honey, get on the other line, please. I want you to be in on this discussion. Ian, you have just made our day. Of course, you can marry our only daughter! Rosemary, isn't it wonderful? Ian and the children have asked Peggy to marry them! Son, we're delighted to be adding another male to the Gerber clan. No, I should say two more guys counting young Mike."

"Oh, Ian," interrupted Rosemary, "I'm so excited! It's what I've been praying for! And Mia, we NEED another female in this family...and you are the PERFECT one!!! Peggy and I have had a hard time managing all these fellows on our own, but I think the three of us can do it...even if we're still outnumbered. And Peggy, dear, I'm just so happy for you....I'm sending you the warmest, tightest hug and biggest possible kiss that will fit through this phone!!!"

Peggy laughed and cried at the same time, "Mom, Dad, thank you for adding your blessing to what has turned into a most blessed day. As you probably suspected for some time, I've loved these five-year-olds more than I dared admit. Also, knowing me as you both do, you've sensed my feelings for Ian, I'm sure. I suspect the brothers will be happy for all of us, as well. And I can't wait to tell Jodie!"

Peggy went on, "Mom, I don't think you heard Ian tell Dad that we might even get married this summer. Do you think we can pull that off, if we just plan a small, intimate wedding?"

"Of course we can, Dear, if that's what you two want. I guess our 'Girls' Only' trip will have to wait for some future date," she laughed. "I'm more than happy to postpone my trip to the continent, that's for sure."

Pete added, "I expect that you and Ian's mother will need to confer soon about what we parents can do to make all this happen smoothly."

"Of course, but it will depend on what Ian and Peggy want. I'll give her a call tomorrow, once Ian and Peggy have had a chance to talk with them. I'm really looking forward to meeting your folks, Ian."

"And I know they'll be excited to meet both of you, as well," Ian said. "They really enjoyed hearing about our trip to the farm, the horses and all the things both of you do."

"Well, let's get off the phone, Dear," Rosemary instructed. "These young people have other calls to make. Congratulations, You Two, we are so happy for both of you…we love you very much."

"We couldn't be happier to have you in our family Ian, Mia and Michael!" added Pete. "Til later, then…bye!"

After hanging up, the group on Ottawa Drive prepared to place the call to South Carolina. Ian, again, asked to be placed on speaker phone, "Mom, Dad, Mimi, Papa," three voices shouted. "We're getting married! We're going to have a wedding this summer! You have to come!"

Ian's parents paused…then laughed out loud, "Three cheers for all of you!" Ian's dad shouted, punching his hand in the air.

Ian's mom continued, "So you finally got around to inviting Peggy Gerber to become a Mahoney? We knew that although you're sometimes a slow learner, Ian, you would eventually come to your senses and ask that lovely young woman to become your wife. We couldn't be happier. Welcome to the family, Peggy!"

Quick but excited calls to Jodie, Peggy's brothers and the Lanes followed. All were delighted about the news and added their best wishes and overall elation to the evening.

It was hard for the children to calm down and get ready for bed that night, so the adults bent the rules a bit and extended the story hour. Then all four kneeled down by Mia's bed and offered both individual and joint prayers. God must really be smiling, since He clearly had His hand in the formation of this family.

After the little ones were asleep, Peggy and Ian settled on the couch. Ian put his arm around his beloved, and they just sat there…thinking of the joy of the day. They were giddy and giggled as they remembered aloud how the proposal had actually taken place. The children had asked her to marry them! It was almost too perfect! After a while, they began to make some preliminary plans.

Ian wanted to discuss the honeymoon. He knew Peggy wanted to go to the Montessori reunion in Bergamo…perhaps they could do the European trip Peggy had planned with her mother. Peggy immediately agreed. Ian was interested in learning about the celebration in Bergamo and said he would be honored to attend with her. While he had made several trips to Europe, he had never been to the places that Peggy and Rosemary had planned to visit. If they followed that basic plan and perhaps even extended it a bit to include some romantic surprise that Ian could plan…it would be perfect.

Peggy's "to do list" included the following: 1.Talk immediately with Pastor Becky about the date and availability of the little church in the historical village; 2. Ask both Ian's and her mom about possible wedding and reception plans (they wanted something simple, for sure)…perhaps they could do a conference call; 3. Once Ian was sure that the proposed dates were clear on his office calendar, reserve two spots for them in Bergamo both for the main event and for lodging at a lovely little guest house she remembered; 4. Start thinking about her dress; 5. Talk with her mom about making a guest list.

Ian's list began to form, as well: 1. Call Laurie's parents to tell them the news; 2. Check and clear his office calendar; 3. Make plane reservations and book accommodations in both Innsbruck and Salzburg; 4. Choose another surprise, romantic location where they could end their honeymoon; 5. Confer with his parents before starting to develop his guest list.

Yes, June and July were going to be busy months for the newly-engaged couple. Ian hadn't even listed an engagement ring for the future Mrs. Mahoney on his to-do list. He needed to talk with Peggy about what she might like. And, again, conferring with his mother might be helpful. There was, after all, his Grandmother Dolan's set of wedding and engagement rings. A resetting of those stones might just fill the bill. Since they came from her side of the family, they were Katie's to give. She had offered them when he became engaged to Laurie, but somehow those stones didn't seem to fit Laurie; so he had declined the offer and purchased a simple marquis diamond in a platinum setting for her. That ring would someday be Mia's.

That night, after his Peggy had left, Ian was exhausted. Although beyond tired, the man was unable to sleep for a very long time. He kept replaying the evening. He didn't know how it could have been more perfect. The children had saved the day…and had made the wedding proposal a family proposal… embraced by all. Once again, Ian smiled in delighted peace… his prayers had been answered. He was, at last, following his heart into the future.

For her part, Peggy drifted off to dreamland almost immediately – happy thoughts of fairy-tale weddings and happily-ever-after dancing in her head. Before drifting off, however, Peggy, too, had closed her eyes and thanked the One who had made her fondest dream finally come true.

A few days later, Ian made the call to Texas to share his good news with the Calhouns. He thanked them sincerely for helping him look to the future. He told them that it was their ability to finally forgive and move on that had inspired him to do so. As they had intuited, Peggy Gerber, the twin's teacher, did mean more to him than he'd been willing to admit.

"We thought she might be the one," Laurie's parents admitted, "knowing how much the children loved her. We found her bright, energetic and fun. She has a deep, personal bond with our grandchildren that convinced us she was special. We're so glad your family will soon be whole again. Do extend our best wishes to Peggy and the kids. We look forward to getting to know her better and including her as part of our family. Laurie would have wanted it to be this way."

"What a wonderful couple they are," thought Ian as he assured them that a trip to California, once they were settled would be high on the Mahoneys' agenda. He thought, again, how lucky he was to have been embraced by two such wonderful pairs of in-laws. He, once again, gave thanks for blessings he could not have imagined...even as recently as one year ago.

CHAPTER THIRTY-EIGHT

The weeks that followed were busy for everyone in the Mahoney and Gerber families. The children were having fun in summer school and especially enjoyed working in the school greenhouse…the place they had first met Miss Peggy, as they still called her. The bride-to-be had remained in Okemos except for a few hurried trips to Saginaw with her mother to select fabric for her wedding gown, bridesmaids' dresses and Mia's flower-girl frock. Peggy would stay in her apartment until after the wedding.

The groom completed his pre-wedding assignments in short order. He spent extra time planning the secret destination that would end their European honeymoon. At Mrs. Harding's suggestion, Ian encouraged Peggy to select new countertops for the kitchen and a new paint color for the master bedroom…a way to start making her new home her own. He contracted a carpenter who was able to complete the work by the end of June. He also scheduled carpet cleaners for the last week of July.

Peggy's lovely white rattan furniture would be moved to the four-season room. They planned for several other pieces of Peggy's furniture and décor to be integrated with the Mahoney furnishings. Some of Ian's well-worn pieces, as well as unwanted odds and ends from Peggy's apartment were ear-marked as contributions to several charities in need of household furniture and other items. The couple was surprised that combining the two households was going to be a lot easier than they had anticipated.

The two mothers kept the phone lines busy throughout the month of June. Kate and Rosemary bonded immediately. Kate and Mike flew to Michigan for a "planning" weekend with Peggy, Ian and the Gerbers. Since Ian and Peggy continued to insist on small and simple, it made the planning fun and much easier than it might otherwise have been. Since Ian and Peggy wanted to get married at the chapel in the township's historical village, Rosemary contacted them and was delighted to find that the reconstructed 19th century church was available for the proposed wedding date and could accommodate the anticipated 100 guests.

Over lunch with Kate and Peggy, Rosemary reminisced about Pete's and her own wedding…which took place right here on campus thirty five years earlier. She described their wedding ceremony which was held in the University Chapel and their reception at the MSU Gardens.

"What a lovely place for a reception," remarked Kate. "Did you have a tent?"

"My heavens no! We didn't even think of it," Rosemary laughed. "I suppose that's because nobody had the money for that kind of expense in those days! But I do remember we did a lot of praying that it wouldn't rain."

"Your prayers were answered, I presume…although they say rain on a wedding day is good luck. Too bad you couldn't have had a rainbow to bless you!" laughed her new friend.

"Why don't we have our reception in the gardens, Mom?" asked Peggy excitedly. I always loved the pictures of your reception…blooming flowers, rich foliage to offset your gown and the bridesmaids dresses. It was so lovely. I'm sure Ian would agree that the MSU gardens would be the perfect setting for our reception, too!"

Ian, as anticipated, loved the idea of an outdoor reception on campus. Both sets of parents agreed that they would have to rent a tent.

"Dodging raindrops for one Gerber wedding was fortunate but let's not take any chances this time," Rosemary insisted. "Then, if we do get rain and that illusive rainbow…we can view it all from a dry location."

Planning the rehearsal dinner was fun, as well. Again, Peggy and Ian insisted on small and informal…but when Kate and Mike suggested a buffet dinner in a small room at the Kellogg Center, everyone agreed. That was where all the out-of-town guests would be staying, so it was not problem making the arrangements.

When they discussed the ideas with Pastor Becky, she loved the entire plan. She had done weddings in the historic chapel before, so she was familiar with the protocols.

Pastor Becky couldn't wait for that very special day in August. She loved this young couple…and the children. She had prayed for these four to become a family so many times. It was the honor of her life to be the one to actually perform the ceremony and bless their union…to help make their (and her) dreams finally come true.

When Ian discussed an engagement ring with Peggy…she insisted that he surprise her. She had no interest in selecting her own ring…but said she would cherish whatever he chose to give her.

Ian had gratefully accepted his grandmother's rings from his mother and worked with a local designer to craft a beautiful and unique setting.

Early in July after Ian and Peggy had met with Pastor Becky for a meaningful premarital consultation, they went out for a lovely candlelight dinner alone. Ian was anxious to make the moment special. They enjoyed their meal, discussed the dozens of wedding details, and just held hands, gazing into each other's eyes. Unexpectedly, Ian stood up, went over to Peggy…in the middle of the restaurant…and got down on one knee. He pulled out a deep green velvet box…opened it and said, "My dearest Peggy, I am so honored that you have agreed to be my wife. May this ring always represent our love…"

Peggy gasped as she gazed at the radiant cluster of diamonds that sparkled and shimmered in the overhead light. Tears streamed down her cheeks, as Ian placed it on her finger. "It's…it's breathtaking," she whispered. "I will cherish it… and you, forever." She stood up slowly, pulled Ian up, into her arms and kissed him deeply. Just then, the entire restaurant erupted in happy applause and cheers.

Plans were coming together beautifully. Of course Jodie Allen, Peggy's best friend, would be her Matron of Honor. Five years earlier, Peggy had been Jodie's Maid of Honor, so, of course, Peggy would have no one else. Ben, Jodie's husband, and Ian had become good friends, so he was thrilled when Ian asked him to serve as an usher.

Because they had shared so much and become such good friends over the past year, Ian also asked Christian if he would like to stand up with him during the ceremony. Christian was overcome. He and Ian had shared more than overseas adventures and international bridge-building…they shared a deep faith in God and hope for the future.

Peggy asked Libby Lane, who was such a special part of both their lives, to be a bridesmaid. Libby was surprised and honored to be a part of this very special occasion.

After much thought, Ian asked his father, Big Mike, if he would stand with him as best man. Once again, surprise and delight…and even a tear expressed how touched Mike was to be so-honored by his only son.

Because this was going to be a family affair, Peggy asked Sam and Jake to be her attendants, also, and J.R. to stand with Ian. Peggy was very close to all her brothers. In fact, she thought of them as best friends as well as brothers. She could not imagine her wedding not including these three very special people.

Peggy and Ian laughed when they looked at their list of attendants. "We'll have more people in the wedding, than at the wedding," Ian said.

"That's true," Peggy agreed, "but we want those we love around us…and now they will be!" It was agreed.

Not surprising, a series of bridal showers were held honoring the young couple. The Montessori staff held a surprise luncheon and gave the couple a lavender lilac bush for their backyard…the same color Peggy had chosen for the wedding.

Ian's colleagues hosted an after-work engagement gathering…including spouses, so that Peggy could meet everyone. They presented the couple with a generous gift card for the University Club.

Ottawa Drive neighbors planned a post-nuptial surprise for the traditional Labor Day block party.

But perhaps the most meaningful event was a surprise party hosted by the church youth group during their last meeting of the year. They had decorated the church commons with balloons and each of the students had brought a snack or soft drinks. The kids presented Ian and Peggy with a lovely white family Bible.

"After all," Libby reminded them, "it was Christmas in October that really got you two together…so we feel like this wedding is all thanks to us!" Ian and Peggy could not have been more surprised and warmed by their thoughtfulness.

Peggy vetoed the idea of yet another shower that Jodie and Libby proposed. "This is supposed to be simple," she protested.

After talking about what they could do, instead, Libby and Jodie proposed an alternative. "Ok, then, Pegster," Jodie began, "Libby and I will host a 'girls luncheon' at my house the day before the wedding. It will include Rosemary, Kate, Aunt Maggie, Becky, Mrs. Harding, Mia, you, and the two of us…and any other family females who come from out-of-town. We will take a moment in the midst of pre-wedding craziness to relax and enjoy each other for a couple of hours."

"Okay," Peggy gave in, "it really sounds lovely…the perfect thing for my last day as a single gal. Thank you both so much!"

It was hard to say who was more excited about being in the wedding – Libby or the twins. All three did a lot of practicing. Libby bought her first pair of high-heeled sandals, and wore them each day, simulating the walk down the aisle. She certainly didn't want to stumble, much less totter all the way to the altar.

Since Michael, as ring bearer, would be leading the procession, he knew he had to set the pace and not allow the rings to topple off the pillow. "Wouldn't it be awful," he thought, "if they dropped on the floor and he had to crawl around to get them!"

As flower-girl, Mia knew she was going to have to go slowly, tossing petals as she made her way down the aisle. To make sure she did it just right, she filled her small Easter basket with petals she pulled from dying flowers in the front yard and had a daily practice walking slowly from room to room. Not skipping or even dashing down the aisle was going to be really hard for this little girl, who seldom walked anywhere.

Kate and Rosemary had an extended conversation about what they would wear. Neither wanted to buy a long dress or something too showy, and they didn't think that something dark like black or navy would be appropriate. So while Kate was in town, the two went to some stores in the mall and also stopped at several bridal shops to check out mother-of-the-bride dresses. They finally decided that cocktail suits would be the perfect compromise. Although different, the suits they chose blended – both with the lavender of the bridesmaids dresses and with each other. The men had no similar problem since they would simply wear dark suits...that would make it both easy and economical for all the men in the wedding. Young Michael, however, did require some shopping, since he had never had a real suit before.

For her wedding gown, Peggy selected a pattern for a softly flowing, strapless gown that crisscrossed at the bodice and fell into a chapel-length train in the back. Tiny seed pearls and sparking Swarovski crystals accented the bodice. Rosemary and Pete's sister, Maggie, busily basted and stitched and sewed Peggy's gown, as well as the lavender dresses for Jodie, Libby and Mia. Although Peggy offered to help, her assistance was declined.

Old-fashioned Peggy insisted on selecting something old (her grandmother's hanky), something new (her dress), something borrowed (Jodie's earrings), and something blue (her undies) to accompany her down the aisle. She even used the same lucky six-pence for her shoe that her mother had used 35 years earlier.

Planning a wedding really was quite fun, Peggy realized. Although getting married had not been an immediate priority for her, she had always hoped that someday she would meet Mr. Right and settle down to start a family. Little did she know one year ago, that it would all happen so soon.

And, although she hadn't spent a lot of time thinking about her wedding, clearly, she had stashed away thoughts about what her dream wedding might be. And this wedding was shaping up to be that dream wedding-come-true! She was so thankful that Ian was willing, eager even, to have a traditional wedding, even though he had been married before. From what Ian had told her, though, his first wedding had bordered on an elopement. This time would be different! It would, in fact, be a fairy-tale wedding for both of them…in fact, for all four of them!

CHAPTER THIRTY-NINE

The countdown had begun. The senior Mahoneys flew in from Hilton Head on Wednesday before the wedding. Aunt Marge, Uncle Patrick and Cousin Kathleen Dolan were arriving Friday. Peggy's Aunt Maggie had been in Michigan the entire week, finalizing fittings and last-minute fixes on the dresses. The rest of her family would come to East Lansing on Friday, as well.

Peggy and Ian had finished marking furnishings in both homes, and it was all ready to be given to charities by Rod Lane during their honeymoon absence. All of the improvements on the Ottawa Drive home had been completed, and the changes had really given the Mahoney home a fresh look for its new mistress. Peggy's passport was updated, and all arrangements for the honeymoon were in order. Peggy and Ian were excited about the upcoming nuptials, for sure, but the twins were near to bursting with excitement and joy. Thank goodness Mimi and Papa arrived to listen to their non-stop commentaries about the wedding, their upcoming visits to their grandparents' homes, and the fact that they would finally have a new mommy.

Jodie and Libby had been busily getting ready for the "girls' luncheon," and on Friday, they set up a big table on Jodie's patio and finished preparing the food. Shortly before noon, the guests arrived. The hostesses kept the menu simple but had planned some entertainment. Each guest was asked to share an anecdote or two about the bride and/or groom. When Mia told her story, there wasn't a dry eye in the group.

"When we met Miss Peggy at school..." Mia began, "Mike and I knew right away she was special. Mikey...no both of us…thought she was like a beautiful angel. When she stayed with us while Daddy was in Africa, she was just like a mommy to us. We love Miss Peggy…and we're so happy that when we asked God for a new mommy…he sent her to us."

Peggy pulled Mia to her. "Mia, my little one…no one could be prouder or luckier to be your mommy. I love you and Mikey with all my heart!"

Peggy wiped her eyes and stood up. She thanked everyone for her support…and for being a part of her life. Then she presented each guest with a small gift. She gave Jodie and Libby, her bridesmaids, simple silver necklaces with crystal heart pendants. Mia's gift was a delicate silver locket. She gave each of the mothers a jewel box engraved with the words, "MOM, Thank you for always giving so much!" Mrs. Harding got a beaded bracelet as a thank you for all she had done to help them get ready for the wedding. She gave Aunt Maggie a coffee mug emblazoned with a picture of the two of them and the words, Aunt Maggie, you're the best! Peggy had made a special white silk pastor's stole embroidered with beautiful gold crosses for Becky to wear for the ceremony… and in church thereafter.

The luncheon ended in time for those who wished to take short naps, before reassembling for the rehearsal and dinner.

The men were not without their special event that day, either. Since a traditional bachelor party didn't seem to fit this particular wedding, they decided to meet for a casual lunch by the MSU University Club pool. This provided Ian with an opportunity to present each of the guys with matching ties to wear to the wedding. After lunch, Ian and Peggy's brothers, Ben and Christian splashed around in the pool with Michael. Bob and Rod Lane, Big Mike, and Pete headed for the links to play a quick nine holes before going back to get ready for the evening festivities.

The 5:30 rehearsal went smoothly. The quaint church was the perfect setting for the wedding ceremony. Several church friends and campus colleagues arrived as the rehearsal was ending to begin decorating pews and rearranging the altar to accommodate the simple floral arrangement that would arrive the next day.

The rehearsal dinner at the Kellogg Center, was just what Ian and Peggy had wanted. The buffet was delicious; the setting was casual and fun. Pastor Becky gave a prayer of thanks, and there were many toasts, much laughter, and lots of shared stories. The twins felt comfortable darting from friends to grandparents, to Dad and their soon-to-be mommy. In addition to the wedding party and extended family from out of town, the Lanes and Mrs. Harding were included... since they were considered part of the family, as well.

An unexpected surprise was revealed at the dinner. The women of the church, under Ida's leadership, had asked to cater a post-wedding luncheon at the church. Students from the youth group would serve as the wait staff. Members of Ida's Bible Study Group would provide the food. Everyone in the church would be invited. It would all take place right after Sunday service the week Dr. and Mrs. Mahoney returned from Europe.

Ian and Peggy were overwhelmed. What a lovely surprise! They hugged Mrs. Harding and thanked her for being such a special part of their family.

After dinner, Patrick Dolan, Katie Mahoney's brother who was a Chicago television news producer, unveiled a video slide production highlighting Ian and Peggy's lives...separate and together. It was a wonderful collection of old and new photos – gathered by the two mothers and the Lane family. The twins loved seeing what their dad and Miss Peggy looked like as children, and the adults appreciated the clever artistry and humor that Uncle Pat had woven throughout the slide show.

The two extended families spent the evening getting to know one another...thus continuing the process of blending two families into one. Both sides valued the richness that the other was bringing to the union and looked forward to many other happy occasions they would share. All were confident that this marriage would certainly have the Lord's blessing!

The twins were in a quandary. They had been worrying all week about what they were going to call their new set of grandparents. They were sooo lucky to have THREE sets of grandparents...some kids didn't have any! Getting the names just right was important to them. They'd been talking about a number of different options, but they still needed more time to decide. After all, they couldn't go around saying "Mr. and Mrs. Gerber" or "Miss Peggy's mother and father" forever! Try as they might, they just couldn't decide.

Finally, they expressed their worry to Miss Peggy. She got down on their level, smiled kindly into their eyes, and said in a soft, reassuring tone, "Don't you worry, My Precious Ones. You will know when the right names pop into your heads. There is no hurry...sleep on it...just trust that the perfect names will come." Sighing with relief and smiling appreciatively... Mike and Mia ran off to beg Peggy's brothers to tell them some more stories about their soon-to-be-mommy when she was a little girl.

Since tomorrow was going to be a big day, the party broke up before nine o'clock. With fond farewells, hugs, and waves, people headed to their rooms or homes. Once tucked into bed...each person reflected on the happy couple and the delightful evening. Each took a moment to think happily about what the next day would bring.

The bridal pair parted with a tender kiss, a shared prayer

of thanks, and heartfelt, "I love you." As they set off to their homes…separated for the last time…they both shared the same thought, "I can hardly believe how lucky I am that love has found me here…right here in Okemos, Michigan!"

CHAPTER FORTY

"What a beautiful day for a wedding!" said the bride's parents as they arrived at Peggy's apartment bearing a bag of breakfast items.

"That it certainly is," responded their daughter smiling radiantly. "Just look at that blue sky – not a cloud in it! I just knew the day would be perfect for our wedding."

A bit later the three were joined by Libby, who planned to dress at the apartment and accompany this group to the wedding. It was a big day for her too. Having been chosen to serve as a bridesmaid was an unexpected privilege and a symbol of the friendship that existed between her and the woman who was her role model. Jodie, the matron-of-honor, would join them at the church.

Meanwhile, on Ottawa Drive, the normally active five-year-olds were very quiet and thoughtful, no doubt realizing that they had important roles to play in today's special event. Everyone knew they were ecstatic over the prospect of having a mommy before the day ended, but young as they were... they also seemed to sense the solemnity of the occasion.

The guests began arriving early, and the small church began filling well in advance of the posted time for the wedding. Lovely music, simple lavender and white bows and brightly-colored flower arrangements created the perfect setting for a memorable service. Soon a new family would be formed... and no one in attendance could imagine a more perfect union.

Two beautiful solos by Bob Lane preceded the ceremony.

His voice rang out as he sang the old-fashioned wedding number, "Oh Promise Me", a song that was part of the wedding ceremonies for both sets of parents. This was followed by a deeply moving rendition of "Ave Maria". Organ music then continued, as the mothers of the bridal couple were escorted down the aisle to their seats.

First, smiling Katherine Dolan Mahoney was escorted down the aisle to her seat by handsome Sam Gerber. Kate looked stunning. Her violet cocktail suit set off her auburn hair beautifully.

After a brief pause, a beaming mother-of-the-bride made her entrance. Rosemary Widder Gerber, on the arm of her oldest son, J.R., also looked lovely. Her silk suit was a soft mauve with silvery overtones. The two women looked across the aisle and smiled; some even suspected that a quick "thumbs up" was exchanged by the two who had become close friends.

The guests settled back for what was to come. The Reverend Rebecca Lane took her place in front of the altar. She was followed by the two tall Mahoney men and the other male members of the bridal party. Christian, Ben and J. R. stood next to Big Mike. Sam and Jake stood far to the right of Pastor Becky, leaving spaces for the women attendants to join them. Mike Mahoney gave his son's arm a warm squeeze of reassurance. He was so proud of his son and so pleased to standing with him on such a special day. Suddenly, strains of the wedding processional music filled the small church.

Leading the procession was young Michael. He was so solemn as he kept time to the music and held tightly to the satin pillow that displayed the wedding rings. He looked so grown up in his brand new suit and tie. He took his place in front of his grandfather at the front of the church and stood tall awaiting the arrival of the rest of the wedding party.

There were a lot of "Oos" and "Ahs" as Elizabeth Jean Lane made her way down the aisle. "My goodness," thought those who had known her since childhood, "what a stunning young woman she's become." No more braces, pig tails or casual pony tails…Libby's hair was pulled back and flowers were tucked into the cluster of curls that cascaded down her back. She was not only poised and elegant (no tottering in her first heels), but self-assured. She smiled brightly to the guests on either side of the aisle as she made her way to the front of the church. She joined Sam and Jake, then pivoted gracefully to watch Jodie, who was just starting down the aisle.

The maid-of-honor, a beautiful, tall brunette, complimented the coloring of her friend, the blond bride. Peggy and Jodie were closer than sisters, and Jodie could not be happier that her best friend had found her true soulmate. She would become a mother today and would immediately experience the challenges, joys and fulfillment of motherhood…just as Jodie had over the past two years. Her eyes glistened as she thought of her friend and how today would change her life forever. She proceeded to the altar and turned to stand next to Libby facing the congregation.

"Finally," thought the flower girl, "It's my turn! One, two, three – here I go." Slowly the little miss in her fluffy white dress with lavender satin sash and bow made her way toward the front of the church. She took her time to beam at guests on each side of the aisle as she carefully dropped rose petals from her basket. She took her place in front of Libby.

The music swelled, and the guests rose as one, peering back to catch a first glimpse of the bride. And there she was… clutching the arm of her proud father, who placed his hand on hers and gave it a pat. Peggy was simply breath-taking. You could actually hear gasps from the guests when they saw her for the first time. Ian, seeing his bride at the top of the aisle, felt tears spring to his eyes...how could he be so blessed?

Peggy's strapless gown fit her perfectly. The soft fabric with its sparkling pearls and crystals set off her long, beautiful neck and shoulders. Her blond curls were swept up and held in place with a ring of flowers, while escaping tendrils curled softly around her radiant face. She held a spray of calla lilies, and her flowing train followed Peggy and her father as they made their way down the aisle. She was truly a fairytale bride...and she smiled at her friends and family members who were staring at her in awe. Peter Gerber glanced lovingly at his wife as they both remembered their own wedding thirty-five years earlier. As Peggy approached the altar, she turned first to Mia, and gave her a fond pat and a smile...then she turned and winked at Michael, who was standing so straight and looking so serious.

When Peggy finally looked up and saw Ian, standing there, waiting for her with tears in his eyes, Peggy's eyes immediately misted, as well. She and her father stepped up and took their places before the pastor.

The Reverend welcomed the guests and began with joy in her voice, "Dearly Beloved, we are gathered here in the presence of God and these witnesses to join together this very special man and this equally special woman in Holy matrimony. We have come together today to celebrate the marriage of Mark Ian Mahoney and Margaret Gerber and to ask God to bless them and strengthen their union. Ian, will you have this woman to be your lawfully wedded wife? Will you love her, respect her and cherish her faithfully all the days of your life?"

"I will." Ian responded solemnly.

"And Peggy," Pastor Becky continued turning to the bride,

"will you have this man to be your lawfully wedded husband? Will you love him, respect him and cherish him faithfully all the days of your life?"

"I will." Peggy said, looking into Ian's eyes.

"Who gives this woman in marriage?" the Reverend asked.

"Her mother and I do," responded Peter as he placed his daughter's hand into the hand of her future husband. After giving Peggy a final hug, he turned and took his seat beside his wife.

Reverend Lane gave a brief scripture-based sermon blended with some practical words of advice, "Provide for each other's temporal needs, be slow to anger, listen and count to ten before you answer back, pray and encourage each other in the things that pertain to both God and your world of work, keep spaces in your togetherness, share both the joys and challenges of parenting and rejoice in the love that has brought you to this day."

The guests leaned forward to be sure to catch every word, their faces shining with approval.

"I, Mark Ian Mahoney," Ian vowed gazing into Peggy's eyes, "take you Margaret Ann Gerber to be my beloved wife. Before God and these witnesses, I promise to love you through good days and bad, and to honor and respect you and our children as we face together whatever life's journey brings our way. In sickness and health let our togetherness be steadfast."

"I, Margaret Ann Gerber," Peggy also promised, "take you Mark Ian Mahoney to be my beloved husband. Before God and these witnesses, I promise to love you through good days and bad, and to honor and respect you and our children as we face together whatever life's journey brings our way. In sickness and heath let our togetherness be steadfast."

When Ian turned to Michael, the little boy stepped to the center and held up the pillow as Ian removed Peggy's ring. He then gave Michael a wink and a smile.

"Peggy, this ring I give you as a pledge of our constant faith and abiding love."

Peggy leaned down and carefully removed the other ring from the pillow, and patted Michael gently on the arm, smiling.

"'Ian, this ring I give you as a pledge of our constant faith and abiding love."

As the couple held hands and gazed into each other's eyes, Bob began singing "The Lord's Prayer." His voice echoed in the chapel…and the congregants felt chills as his pure voice both beseeched and celebrated the Lord God above.

"Most gracious God," the minister then prayed, "look favorably on these two young people; help them as a couple to grow in fostering justice, peace and service to you. May their skills as parents be abundantly enriched so that Michael and Mia fully understand, accept and learn to follow the steadfast love their parents feel for you."

After a brief pause, she continued, "By the authority of the Lord Jesus Christ and the State of Michigan, I now pronounce you husband and wife. Whom therefore God has joined together, let no one put asunder."

Ian turned to Peggy, drew her to him, and the two touched lips in the long-awaited, marriage-confirming kiss. The guests were asked to join in singing the benediction hymn "Go Now in Peace".

Go now in peace, never be afraid,

God will go with you each hour of every day, Go now in faith, steadfast, strong and true, Know he will guide you in all you do.

Go now in love, and show you believe,

Reach out to others, so all the world can see, God will be

there, watching from above,

Go now in peace, in faith, and in love. Amen.

Suddenly, the organ peeled out chords of the recessional, and the church bells began to chime. Peggy turned to Mia and drew her into a hug, just as Ian did the same to Michael…then they switched children and hugged the other. All four joined hands, and to the clapping approval of those they loved, the new Dr. and Mrs. Mahoney along with their children proceeded back up the aisle, pausing to hug and kiss both sets of parents. They exited the tiny church and stood outside to greet all the guests that had joined in the celebration of their union. Then, as the family of four moved toward the waiting car and crowded in; clouds of bubbles cascaded down around them. Libby and Jodie had made sure their departure would be as magical as the wedding itself. In their honking car, festooned with balloons and streamers…the new family laughed with delight as they sped away to the gardens to enjoy a relaxing reception with their loved ones.

The reception was simple and delightful. Wedding guests made their way to the tables and chairs that had been set up under the tent in the middle of the MSU gardens. Beautiful flowers and shrubs of all kinds surrounded the gathering and graced the tables. Ian and Peggy welcomed their guests and thanked them and their parents for making this wedding day so special for the new Mahoney family. Pastor Becky gave a brief word of thanks and hors d'oeurves and refreshing cool drinks were served. People milled around chatting and laughing; greeting old friends and meeting new ones. A huge, tiered wedding cake awaited the couple…who stepped up, made the first cut together…and fed each other bites of the delicious confection. The children were the first in line for their slices, and greedily licked their lips and fingers as they ate their portions and affirmed it's excellence. Non-stop photos were snapped of the couple and innumerable groupings of guests.

The music Bob had prepared softly drifted over the crowd from speakers placed at all four corners of the tent. When a favorite song began….Peggy grabbed her father and moved to the center of the tent. They swayed together for several minutes before Ian bowed to his mother, took her hand and joined the first couple. Before long, Big Mike cut in on Ian and he and Kate moved off…while Ian cut in on Pete…who bowed and had Rosemary join him. Mia and Michael were up in a flash, dancing together next to their parents. Before long a few others joined in. Suddenly, Bob raised the volume and changed the music to a familiar, snappy, hand-clapping tune which brought even more guests out onto the grass to jump and bump and laugh and gyrate to the music. And so the afternoon went. Laughing, dancing, chatting, eating and enjoying one another's company.

Suddenly, Mia called Michael over and began whispering animatedly. Folks could see their two little heads bobbing and nodding as the two gestured and, finally, "high-fived" each other.

"Mommy, Daddy, come with us!" they squealed excitedly, as they pulled their parents over to the Gerbers, who had just collapsed into chairs after dancing to an old, favorite Motown song.

"We got it! We finally got it!!" Michael sputtered.

"Yes! Finally! We got it!" agreed Mia.

The two looked at each other…then at Mr. and Mrs. Gerber.

Mia turned to Rosemary, "Your new name," Mia announced, "is Gma!"

"And your new name," Michael added pointing at Pete, "is Papa G! What do you think?"

Rosemary gathered the children in her arms, "I love my new name," she said, "Why, how very smart of you to shortened Grandma…into Gma! I think I look like a Gma…thank you so much for honoring me with such a special name!"

Pete stood up proudly, "And I am Papa G!!! What a great name…how lucky I am to be called Papa G! And I'm luckier still to be your Papa G…thank you for making me so proud and happy." He hugged them both.

"Come on, Gma and Papa G…let's dance with Papa and Mimi…we're all family now!" Mia directed, as she and Michael pulled the older couple to their feet once again. Laughing, the four grandparents danced with their grandchildren, spinning them and all six joining hands to dance in a circle. Ian and Peggy could only stand there, holding hands, watching… feeling the warmth of pride spread through their hearts.

By late afternoon, it was time for the newlyweds to begin their new life adventure. Their bags were packed and had been placed in the car by Jodie and Ben. The bride and groom planned to stay at a fancy hotel not too far from the airport that night…and leave for Europe first thing in the morning.

The children were delighted to have their grandparents staying with them…and Gma and Papa G were coming tomorrow to spend some time with them, as well. In fact, Gma and Papa G had invited the twins, Mimi and Papa to come to the farm to meet the colts they had named. The children couldn't wait! They were so excited about the next couple of weeks, perhaps as much as their parents were…well, almost as much.

Ian and Peggy went around to all the tables in the tent and thanked each person, once again, for coming and for being a special part of their lives. They saved their most heartfelt thanks for their parents. All four had worked together to make this day…a day they would cherish forever. Hugs and kisses, tears of joy and thanks were passed among them.

And, finally, the children. Ian and Peggy called the children over. They knelt down and all four put their arms around each other. "At last we're a family," Peggy said. "I just want you to know how proud I am to be your mommy. I can't wait to get home, so you can teach me what to do."

Both Mia and Michael laughed, "Teach you?" Michael said, "You already know what to do…don't you remember… you did it while Daddy was in Africa!"

"Well, I guess that's true," said Peggy laughing, "but now when I make your dinner, or wash your clothes, or tuck you in at night, I will hear you call me 'Mommy' and my heart will burst with love and pride. I love you both…more than you know."

The four hugged again, then the kids ran to their grandparents, "Bye, Mommy and Daddy!" they shouted together.

To cheers and waves, Ian and Peggy climbed into their decorated car and headed off, waving and calling farewell to their loved ones.

"Today is, indeed, the first day of our new life together," Peggy said, "and I could not be happier."

"I am the luckiest man in the world," Ian said, grabbing her hand and bringing it to his lips as he drove. We are both truly blessed…and we have the Good Lord Above to thank for making us a true family. We indeed let love happen!"

And so, Ian, Peggy, Michael and Mia began their new life together. They were, indeed, truly blessed. Through a lifetime of challenges and joys…they never forgot Who it was that brought them together and made all their dreams come true.

ABOUT OKEMOS

Okemos is a real Michigan village settled in 1839 as a trading post with the surrounding Ojibway people, part of the Chippewa nation. The original name of Hamilton, was changed in 1859 to honor the warrior, John Okemos, who gained the title "chief" as a result of courage as a fighter rather than via hereditary claim. He was, however, the nephew of Pontiac, the powerful Chippewa chief, head of the "Five Indian Nations."

Along with his kinsman, Tecumseh, John joined the British and fought heroically with other Indian fighters in the Battle of Sandusky. Severely wounded and left for dead — according to legend — he was rescued and restored to health by a group of squaws, who had come to the battlefield to bury the dead. He returned to his favorite location along the Red Cedar River six miles east of Lansing to camp, hunt and fish.

Today many remnants of this Indian heritage remain in the village that bares the chief's name. Older sections of the town are identified by their Indian names: Tacoma Hills, Ottawa Hills, Chippewa Hills, Indian Hills; and numerous street names are also reminders of the past: Osage Drive, Tacoma Boulevard, Okemos Road, Ottawa Drive, Comanche Drive and Tomahawk Road to name a few.

Two of the middle schools, Chippewa and Kinawa, tout their Indian names as does Hiawatha Elementary. High school athletic teams are referred to as the "Chiefs." There is a restored historical village near the Township Hall, along with the Nokomis Cultural Learning Center, known for its historical displays and on-going workshops and programs focused on Indian crafts, culture and legacy.

The school system is among the best in the state, and 71% of the citizens have a bachelor's degree or higher. It is not surprising that the second Montessori School in the state was established here in 1968 by a group of interested parents. Today Montessori classes are also available in other private as well as the town's public school.

Once a small farming community, this unincorporated community has grown to a population nearing 25,000 and is now home to a number of small high tech firms.

The Okemos Interfaith Chapel and the Ojibwa Montessori School referenced in the book do not exist; they are both fictional, as are all characters in the book. Any resemblance to actual people is coincidental.

ABOUT THE AUTHOR

Maxine S. Ferris retired in 1996 as a professor in the Department of Agriculture and Natural Resources Education and Communication Systems and Director of Outreach Communications at Michigan State University. For 15 years she led a team of professional communicators whose mission was to help the public access the knowledge resources of the university in whatever format they preferred. Ferris is the author of more than 50 popular publications focusing on communication and management and has led more than 200 workshops on time management, team-building, leadership development and group process skills She is the published author of six non-fiction books. A graduate of the College of Wooster, Ferris earned a Master's Degree from the Ohio State University and a Phd from Michigan State University. A former high school teacher, she was also a faculty member at the College of Wooster and Bowling Green State University and headed her own consulting firm prior to joining the MSU faculty. She and her husband John (Jake) Ferris are the parents of two adult sons and two grandchildren. They currently reside in East Lansing, Michigan.